LIKE I NEEDED

HEATHER BAY BOOK THREE

CHARLIE NOVAK

For Louise, without whose valuable help and advice I would be lost.

Thank you for helping me bring Heather Bay to life.

CHAPTER ONE

Jamie

"CAN WE HAVE ANOTHER BOTTLE, please? In fact, make it two!" I called over the club's thumping bass line to the passing attendant who'd been looking after us all evening.

He was slim and pretty with soft lips and long eyelashes that he batted at me over the heads of my guests as he acknowledged my request. I didn't even need to tell him what bottles I wanted since we'd been drinking the same extravagantly priced champagne since we'd arrived several hours ago.

I wasn't even sure how much each bottle cost. I was sure I'd find out when I examined my bank balance in a few days or when my father's accountant rang up to berate me and threaten to cut me off from my trust fund yet again.

We were only three weeks into the new year, and he'd already called me seven times. It might be a new record.

Hedonism, thy name was Jamie Stone.

"Oh my God, Jamie, you are the best," Daisy said, hanging on my arm and giggling, her jewellery glittering in the low light. "You always know how to have fun."

"Of course," I said, giving her my most charming smile. "I don't want my life to be boring."

She laughed again and kissed my cheek before getting up and grabbing the hand of one of the other girls clustered on the low, plush seats around our table, dragging her across to the club's small but crowded dance floor.

I'd known Daisy for years because our fathers ran in the same circles, so we'd always met at the same parties, dinners, and later, clubs. Once upon a time, she'd tried to get me into bed and been utterly despondent when I'd told her she was very pretty, but I didn't swing that way.

Her boyfriend on the other hand…

He'd been giving me eyes all evening and had put his hand on my thigh at least twice. It was tempting, but I'd never cross that line. Instead, I'd tell Daisy tomorrow, when we were sober, and sit through the inevitable fallout. It wasn't the first time this had happened, and it wouldn't be the last. I didn't know where Daisy found these pricks, but she seemed to attract a never-ending stream of them.

Daisy could do better. But then again, I wasn't exactly one to talk since my little black book was a veritable who's who of London's queer men.

I watched Daisy for a moment as she was joined by more of the girls. I was pleased she was having fun. The club was packed like it always was on a Friday night, and the floor pulsed to the sound of drum and bass as the city's rich and famous partied in absolute exclusivity.

"Did I hear you order two?" I turned my head to see Kai, my on-and-off fuck buddy, sliding onto the seat next to me. He was a head taller than me with artfully styled dark hair and plush lips that looked so good stretched around a cock. He was dressed in a white t-shirt so tight it was almost see-through and dark trousers that clung to his thighs. I knew he wouldn't be wearing anything underneath them, and my dick throbbed in delight.

"You did," I said as Kai put his hand on my thigh and slowly dragged it upwards. "I thought we'd need it."

"You have the best ideas." He leant in close and brushed his lips against my neck, making me shiver. "What are your plans for the rest of the night?"

"I'm not sure. Do you have any ideas?"

Kai chuckled softly, and I grinned. "Always, darling. Always."

The attendant chose that moment to arrive with the two magnums of champagne, setting them down carefully in their ice buckets, the labels tilted outward so everyone could see what I'd ordered. There were fresh glasses too, although I doubted we'd need them. Kai and I would probably just drink from the bottle.

"Can I get you anything else?" the attendant asked, his eyes roaming over Kai and me. His beautiful smile had to be practised for better tips, or he really wanted to squeeze in between us. Either way it was working.

"That depends," Kai said, looking up and smirking. I knew that look well. It always ended in a good time, and a little shiver ran across my skin. "What are you offering?"

I'd expected the other man to blush or stammer, but

clearly there was more spark hiding under his twinky features. His practised smile melted into something infinitely more devious as he stepped closer and lowered his voice. "Do you want to see a menu? Or I can give you some *personal* recommendations?"

"Are you on the menu?" Kai asked, never one for subtlety. Not that he needed it. If there was something Kai wanted, he got it. Money was very rarely an issue, and if it wasn't about money, then Kai's charm got him the rest of the way.

We both played the same game. It was probably why we'd never work together long-term. The sex between us was off the charts, but I'd always gotten the feeling everything else between us would be a competition. One of decadence and grandeur and poor choices.

It was the story of my life.

And it was starting to get tedious.

"I might be," the man said. "But you'd have to wait until I finish my shift."

"And when will that be?"

"Another hour. Think you can wait that long?"

"Of course, darling. Come and find us when you're done," Kai said. "Jamie and I will show you a good time. Won't we, Jamie?"

"Absolutely," I said, not realising what I was agreeing to until after I'd said it. I didn't even realise I'd switched off and shook my head, trying to dislodge the strange feeling gnawing at the edge of my mind. Since when had I found any of this boring? This was my *life*.

It was one most people could only dream of.

4

And yet...

I shook my head again and watched the attendant walk away, letting my eyes rest on the curve of his ass. God, he was going to look pretty underneath me later. I reached for one of the bottles and two glasses, pouring one for Kai and another for myself. I'd save the rest of the bottle for later. We could take it home with us and spoil our toy for the night with it.

The rest of the people still around our table could have the other one. They were all partying on my money anyway, so they could take it and be grateful. I didn't even know who half of them were, although that was pretty par for the course. I invited friends, and they invited friends, and soon there were twenty or thirty of us.

All rich. All young. All beautiful.

All having the time of our lives. Supposedly at least.

I frowned and sipped my champagne. When had hedonism lost its lustre?

"What's wrong?" Kai asked, sliding closer until he was practically sitting in my lap. "Are you unhappy with my plans? Did you want someone else?"

"No, it's not that," I said, drawing him in for a kiss and hoping it would make me forget the strange feeling now accumulating in my chest. It felt like someone was slowly trying to squeeze all the air out of my lungs. "I was just thinking about later... how it might work... what I want to do to you and him..."

Kai moaned softly, swinging his leg across my thigh until he was straddling me. He plucked the champagne glass from my hand and set both down on the arm of the small sofa we'd been cuddled up on, smirking at me with wide, hungry eyes that glittered like gems. Nobody seemed to care that he sat on me, and if they did, I knew they wouldn't say anything. It wasn't like we were going to start fucking in public. This was just what Kai liked to do. He wanted to show everyone that he was mine, and I was his. At least for the night.

It was almost ridiculous, considering how little I knew he'd care about me tomorrow. But it was like he wanted to make someone, anyone, who might be watching jealous.

My hand slid up his thigh to grip his hip, and I suddenly wondered whether it would just be easier to walk away. To leave Kai and the beautiful attendant there to have their fun and go home to pour myself into bed. Or even into a deep bath where I could soak away my troubles surrounded by Elemis candles with my magnum of champagne.

God, that made me sound so fucking... boring.

What the hell was wrong with me?

"You look like you're thinking pretty hard," Kai said as he ran his finger across my jaw. "Do you need a distraction?"

I grinned. I knew what Kai meant by a distraction. "I thought you wanted to wait?"

"He's going to be an hour." Kai rolled his eyes. "And it'll be longer by the time we get him home. You look like you need something now." He leant down, his lips brushing my ear. "Don't worry, I know you'll be good for later too. And I'm so fucking desperate, darling, that if I don't get off soon, I'll be fucking you in this seat."

I chuckled, tightening my grip on his hip. "I don't think everyone wants to see that."

"They might."

"True," I said, looking up at Kai's wicked smile. "But I don't want them to. I only share when I want to, and I don't fancy sharing you with every man here."

"Mmm, I like it when you're possessive. It's really fucking hot." Kai groaned, grinding down on my lap. "Shall we find somewhere more private, then? You can fuck me now and get me all wet and sloppy for later. Then you can fuck me again at yours while I fuck our guest. Or maybe you can fuck both of us. Mmm, you should fuck me first while I'm inside him, then I want to watch you fill him up afterwards so I can taste you on him."

I groaned, all my earlier feelings swept away by a wave of lust. Kai's lips met mine in a deliciously deep kiss as he ground into my lap.

"Toilets," I growled out. "Now."

Kai hopped off my lap and held out his hand. "See, Jamie? You really do have the best ideas."

I woke surrounded by heat with a pounding head.

Opening my eyes, I squinted around and realised Kai and the twinky attendant, Reese, were cuddled up on either side of me, both deep in a blissed-out sleep. I couldn't remember how many times we'd fucked in the past few hours, but it had to have been at least three... maybe four. Everything was slightly hazy.

Sitting up slowly, I saw the reason for that littered on the floor alongside various articles of clothing: three empty magnums of champagne.

Evidently, I hadn't left the second one behind, and I'd gotten Reese to bring us a third too.

The vague memory of that swam back into my head, and I winced. It had been after Kai and I had come out of the club's plush bathroom. Reese had seen us and asked if we needed anything, and I hadn't been able to resist getting another bottle for the road. I knew I'd been showing off, but it was part and parcel of who I was.

What was the point of having money if I couldn't do anything with it?

Even if it technically wasn't my money.

But it wasn't like my father was going to cut me off. He'd just keep paying the bills and feeding my trust fund if it meant he and my mother didn't actually have to spend time with me more than a few times a year. They weren't exactly bad parents—they'd always made sure my life was a dream come true—but they weren't exactly what you'd call emotionally available.

I licked my lips and swallowed, suddenly realising how dry my mouth was. I desperately needed a drink—one that wasn't alcoholic.

It took me a minute to extract myself from the tangle of limbs wrapped around me. Both Kai and Reese seemed completely dead to the world, and neither stirred as I climbed over them, landing on the deep carpet under my bed. Grabbing my boxers off the floor, I pulled them on and slipped out onto the landing.

My flat was split over two floors, taking up the penthouse suite of a luxury high-rise overlooking the Thames. I'd debated between this or a house, but I hadn't needed an entire house to myself, and the flat had seemed so much more convenient.

Low-level lighting activated along the floor as I quietly padded down the stairs into the open-plan living space. The curtains that usually covered the floor-to-ceiling windows making up one wall were open, and I saw predawn light starting to set the city on fire. It was a beautiful sight, but one I was too tired to fully appreciate.

I turned and headed towards the beautiful kitchen tucked into one side of the space. I barely ever used it, preferring instead to eat the meals made for me by my private chef, Michael, who came in four days a week.

Michael would often prep me meals for other days when I requested them, but I enjoyed fine dining, so I didn't often need them. It was easy to eat well in London, and I never got bored. There were always new places to try and old favourites to revisit. The world's cuisine was my oyster, and I was happy to make the most of it.

All in all, I only ever used my kitchen for drinks, to fetch and reheat meals from Michael, and to make the occasional piece of toast.

"Siri," I said quietly, watching the small ball in the corner light up as I grabbed a glass out of the cupboard headed for the fridge. "What's the time?"

"The time in London is 7:37 a.m.," the soft voice replied.

"Fuck." I shook my head and poured myself some water from the fridge dispenser. I'd had even less sleep than I'd thought. We'd come back from the club around two-ish and had stayed awake for a long time after that.

I didn't even know why I was awake except for the fact the gnawing feeling in my chest was back. I wanted to put it down to a hangover, but I'd had enough of them in my life to know it wasn't one.

Taking my glass of water, I walked into my living room and settled on one of the sofas to watch the sun rise over the city.

This life should have given me everything I wanted, but it was starting to feel hollow. I didn't know why, only that it was. The parties had lost their glittering sheen, the bars their inviting lustre, and the restaurants their decadent allure. Even the endless carousel of beautiful men in my bed was starting to feel unappealing. The problem was, I had no idea what would make me feel better.

Ever since I'd left university, my life had been an endless stream of hedonism and debauchery that would make even Dionysus blush. And now... even if I wanted to change, I had no idea where to start.

I supposed I could get a job, but my lack of experience would mean I'd need help acquiring something suitable. And for once, that idea felt wrong.

Sipping my water, I traced the London skyline with my eyes, lost in thought.

Maybe the problem was staying here. It was hard to sit at home and think when I knew my friends expected me to be out most nights. Maybe I needed some time away, some-where secluded where none of my friends would decide to come with me and turn it into some shitty wellness retreat or winter party spot.

For once, I needed some time by myself, away from the maddening crowd. Maybe then I'd be able to work out what was actually bothering me.

Draining the last of my water, I grabbed my iPad off the coffee table and flicked the cover open.

It was time to find somewhere to escape to before I changed my mind.

CHAPTER TWO

Will

I DIDN'T KNOW why I bothered setting an alarm these days since I was always up before it. But at least today I wasn't waking up to the sound of rain hammering on the bedroom window.

This winter had been wet and miserable beyond belief, and there were still a couple of months to go until we'd see any visible improvements in the weather. I really didn't want to do another lambing season in torrential, freezing rain, not after the one we'd had four years ago. It had been the closest I'd ever come to wanting to give up.

Heaving myself out of bed, I quickly threw some clothes on and headed downstairs. It was still dark outside with only the faintest line of grey starting to appear on the horizon as I filled the kettle and went to chuck some logs on the burner.

The farmhouse I called home was several hundred years

old, and despite attempts to modernise it over the years, I still found the best way to keep the place warm was the large, cast-iron wood burner that sat in the small sitting room connected to my kitchen.

"Out of the way, Mog," I said, carefully stepping over the ancient grey cat sprawled out in front of the fire. Mog opened one eye and looked at me disdainfully before stretching out her old bones as far as she could. Nobody really knew who she belonged to, but she'd turned up when I was fifteen and had made herself at home. It had been more of a case of her adopting the house than anything else since she'd refused to move down the road with my parents when they'd decided to hand over the reins of the farm to me.

I'd been convinced she'd be more comfortable with them, but Mog had staunchly dismissed any attempts to leave, and eventually, I'd given up. I didn't mind having her around. She didn't require much other than two meals a day, a fire to snooze in front of in the winter, and a patch of sun in the summer. And she was happy to listen to me grumble.

"I'll leave your breakfast out," I added as I carefully added some logs to the burner and coaxed the dying embers back to life. "Mum's popping in about ten-ish too. She wants to refresh the cottage welcome packs."

Mog let out a meow, and I chuckled to myself. I didn't know why I was talking to the bloody cat, but at that point, it was habit. I knew she didn't really understand me, but it was nice to get some acknowledgment.

With the fire roaring merrily and Mog happily toasting

herself, I walked back through to the kitchen to make myself some tea and check the weather. The rain may have let up, but it looked like we were in for freezing temperatures and snow instead. And the long-term forecast suggested the whole of February was going to be a mess of freezing rain, snow, subzero temperatures, and gales.

Great, that was all I bloody needed. Just once I'd like a cold, dry winter with the odd smattering of rain, not torrential downpours that turned everything into a quagmire.

"Looks like we might need the lambing barns," I muttered as I sipped my tea. Usually, we let the ewes lamb out in the fields and on the hills where they spent most of their lives.

It was where they felt safe and comfortable, but when the weather was really shit, we made sure we had the option to bring some of them into the barns. There they'd be protected from the worst of the elements, and the lambs would be warm and dry. It was a pain in the ass to set up, but it meant we lost fewer ewes and fewer lambs.

None of the ewes were due to lamb until the end of March at the very earliest, which was two months away, but I liked to be prepared.

And the sooner we started on the prep, the easier it would be.

I made a mental note to tell Higgs when he came in so we could make a plan. Higgs didn't really have a job title, but like Mog he'd arrived one day when I was about twelve or thirteen and stayed.

These days, I didn't know what I'd do without him. He could do anything from calming a worried ewe in labour to remembering a litany of dates and details at the drop of a hat to fixing the quad bike, or perfectly levelling the outdoor riding school to keep the livery clients happy, or fixing fence posts, or a million other things. He was a quiet, serious man who always seemed to know what the farm needed at any given time.

I'd asked him once if he'd ever considered taking over a farm of his own—because I was convinced he was a better farmer than me—but he'd just given me a small smile and said that it "weren't right for him," and he was happier without the responsibility over his head.

I knew what he meant. This was my family's farm and had been for five generations. And with every one, it seemed harder to sustain. I loved this farm with my heart and soul, but every week it found new ways to keep me up at night, wondering how I was going to keep it going. No wonder my hair was already starting to thin on top.

And I was sure at least some of my pubes were going grey from stress.

"Come on," I said to myself. "Let's be having you. You've got work to do."

Draining the last of the tea, I headed towards the door and pulled on my waterproof overalls, heavy boots, and a thick hat and gloves. I knew I'd probably end up taking the gloves off again when I got moving, but my skin was already starting to redden and crack from the cold, and it was only January. I'd rather not lose all feeling in my fingers before I was thirty-five.

The air was crisp and cold as I stepped out into the early morning, my breath fogging in front of me. Closing the door behind me, I ran through my mental checklist for the day as I headed towards the pair of old stables where my two sheepdogs, Nell and Moss, slept.

Predictably, as soon as she heard my footsteps on the icy stone outside, Moss's head appeared over the door. She was the younger of the two, at four years old, and was full of boundless energy that seemed to go on for days.

"Yes, yes, I'm coming. Hang on," I said with a smile, knowing that what Moss wanted more than anything was feeding. I ducked into the second stable, where I kept their food and other odds and sods, to make up their breakfasts and returned two minutes later to see Moss bouncing up and down with glee.

Opening the stable door, I saw Nell emerge from the nest of blankets she'd made herself. She stretched and wagged her tail before giving a full body shake and trotting over to me. I put their bowls on the floor, watching for a minute to make sure Moss didn't try to steal Nell's considering she pretty much inhaled every meal as soon as it appeared.

By the time they'd finished, the moon was starting to hang lower in the sky, and the line of grey on the horizon had stretched into a thick band edged with gold. That was the only perk to winter—I was up so early that I got to see the sun rise over the moors every morning. And it was stunning each and every time.

I was just loading Nell and Moss onto the back of the quad bike when Higgs appeared, materialising beside me like some sort of ghost. Luckily, I was used to it by now, but the first few times he'd done it, he hadn't half made me jump.

"Morning, Higgs," I said.

"Morning. You need a hand?" he asked, his voice soft and gruff. Nell wagged her tail, and he put his hand out for her to nuzzle. Neither of my collies were pets, and they weren't the friendliest or cuddliest pair, but Nell adored Higgs.

"No, should be fine. I'm going to do the rounds and put some hay out. We'll need to look at getting some silage out there too."

Higgs nodded and looked up at the sky. "Aye, best be doing it soon. We'll have snow by Monday."

"We can do it this afternoon, then," I said. If Higgs said there'd be snow by Monday, there'd be snow by Monday. I'd never known him to be wrong about the weather in the nearly twenty years I'd known him. "Get it up there before the roads get blocked."

"Aye. I'll get it ready and finish those fence posts while you're out."

"Cheers," I said. "Think we're going to need the lambing barns again this year. Long-term forecast is proper shit, and I'd rather we have options if push comes to shove."

"Can start on that next week, then," Higgs said. "Allus best to be prepared." He gave Nell a final pat on the head and stepped back. "All reight, in a bit then."

I knew I was being dismissed and pulled the keys out of my pocket before climbing onto the bike and starting it up. The cold nipped at my exposed skin as I headed out the farm gate and onto the narrow road, carefully avoiding the oncoming Land Rover, which belonged to Dylan, who managed the livery yard for me.

The yard had been one of my more recent investments after I'd realised we needed to diversify if we were going to stand any chance of keeping the farm running.

After a lot of thought and research, I'd decided that if we were going to have a yard, we needed to do it properly if we were going to stand any chance of making money. So that had meant fixing up two of the old barns and building large, airy stables to go inside them, where any horses would have plenty of space to walk around and lie down. We'd added a secure tack room that was more like a vault, a washing off area so horse's legs could be hosed and scrubbed to get rid of any mud when they came in from the fields, lots of outside space to tie up, and made sure there were plenty of electrical sockets available for kettles and clippers and anything else people might need.

I'd refenced some of the low-land fields closest to the farm to create plenty of turnout and doubled our hay production so we produced enough for the sheep, Dad's cows, and the horses, although we occasionally still needed to buy some in along with straw.

The biggest and most expensive project, though, had been the enormous outdoor arena we'd built two years ago. Although Higgs, Dad, and I had managed to do a lot of it ourselves, there were some things we just couldn't do, and we'd needed to get a specialist arena builder in to finish the project, including providing the top-of-the-line sand and rubber surface. But now the arena rivalled anything you'd find anywhere and came complete with floodlights and a selection of colourful poles and show jumps, some of which Higgs had made himself in the workshop.

From start to finish, the yard's construction had cost a hell of a lot of time and money, but it had been worth it. The place was thriving, and we had a permanent waiting list.

I'd known from the start I wasn't going to be able to manage it, not with the farm as well, which was where Dylan came in. He'd been there from the beginning and took absolutely no shit from anyone. He dealt with all the day-to-day details while I did the billing and the maintenance. It meant one less thing for me to worry about, and I trusted Dylan to let me know what he needed.

I pulled the bike up alongside the window of his car and Dylan's smiling face appeared. He had reddish-blond hair sticking out from under a beanie, and he was wrapped in a puffy, dark coat that had a wisp of hay sticking to the collar.

"Morning, Will," he said cheerfully as a wave of warm air from the car washed over me. It smelt distinctly of horse. "I know you're on your way out, but I just wanted to let you know the hay barn is getting low. We could do with some more straw too."

"No worries. Higgs is around if you want to ask him to top it up."

"Perfect, I'll do that."

"We're going to get snow by Monday too," I added. "Might want to limit turnout. There's salt in the bin as well if you need it for the yard."

Dylan frowned. "The forecast I saw said it wouldn't be until next week if we get it at all."

"Higgs said by Monday."

"Monday it is then," Dylan said with a knowing smile. "I'll get it sorted."

"Cheers. Any problems, just let me know. We're going to be taking silage out later, and I've got some fencing to repair, but I'll have my phone if you need me."

"It'll be fine. It hasn't snowed yet. Besides, it can't be worse than last year."

"Don't bloody jinx it," I said with a chuckle. "I don't want another winter like that."

Dylan grinned and pretended to zip his mouth shut. "I won't say a word. At least not about that. Also, don't you have football this afternoon?"

"Tomorrow," I said, mentally adding that back in to my rapidly growing mental list. "Although, if the weather gets bad, they'll probably cancel it."

"Do you really think that, or do you just want them to cancel it so you can do more work instead?" Dylan asked pointedly. I shrugged. While I did enjoy playing in the rec league my friend Spencer had dragged me into, it did take up a lot of my limited daylight hours over the weekend during the winter. And while part of me knew it was good to get away from the farm and do something other than work, the rest of me worried that I should be using those hours to get stuff done instead.

"I'm not answering that," I said, and Dylan grinned.

"Exactly."

"All right, you've made your point. Go sort your horses."

"I'm going," he said. He went to roll up the window,

then stopped. "Seriously, though, Will, you need to take breaks. The farm won't stop if you take a day off once in a while."

He drove away before I could respond. I watched him go before continuing up the road towards the narrow track that would take me onto the moors.

Dylan wasn't the first person to tell me to take time off. All my other friends constantly said the same thing. Even my parents had started muttering that I worked too much.

The problem was, none of them could see what I saw.

They saw a family farm that worked like a well-oiled machine, one that required care and attention but wasn't likely to break that easily.

I saw a crumbling legacy teetering on the edge of a precipice, where one wrong move would send it hurtling into the abyss.

CHAPTER THREE

Jamie

As I PULLED the hire car up outside the seaside hotel I'd chosen as my escape for a week of introspection, I couldn't help thinking I'd made a mistake.

I was sure this place would be lovely in summer with a quaint seaside charm that went over well with locals and families, but I wasn't sure it was for me. Perhaps I should have just hired a ski chalet or gone to Bali or the Seychelles.

The grey sky was thick with clouds, threatening more of the snow I'd seen dusting the moors as I'd driven across. The sea was an equally stony grey with roiling waves that crashed onto a thin strip of dark sand. The only colour I saw was the locked-up beach huts, their backs pressed against the concrete front as if they were trying to escape the freezing water that inched ever closer.

The only thing that stopped me turning around and driving back to London was that I was tired, and even I wasn't careless enough to risk my own life by driving on tiny, icy roads when I could barely think straight.

One night in Heather Bay wouldn't kill me. The hotel had looked perfectly nice online, so as long as the reality matched the pictures, I'd survive for a day or two.

Leaving the car in the small, designated car park, I pulled my suitcase out of the boot and headed for the reception of the Heather Sands hotel, which several travel websites had informed me was one of the UK's hidden seaside gems.

The boutique hotel was right on the water, and I had to admit the outside was quite pretty. It looked like a Victorian building that had been well looked after and restored, and as I approached, the heavy, wooden front door swung inwards as a smartly dressed member of staff pulled it open.

"Good afternoon," the man said as he welcomed me inside. He was wearing a dark suit and had a thick York- shire accent, although I supposed that was to be expected since Heather Bay was right on the Yorkshire coast. "Are you checking in?"

"Yes," I said as the man smoothly took my suitcase from me. I glanced around at the reception area I'd stepped into, trying hard to hide my surprise.

The floor was made up of slate grey tiles, and there was a large rug in the centre with a round, wooden table placed in the middle of it. The table held a large bouquet of flowers with two plates of small biscuits on either side. There were several doors leading off the entrance hall, and through one, I saw a cosy-looking lounge with large windows that looked out over the water. At one end was a large set of stairs with plush carpeting I assumed led to all the rooms, and not far from that was the reception itself, set behind a large counter made of the same wood as the table.

"Perfect," said the man. He gestured over to the reception desk. "If you go and see Tracey, she'll get you sorted out. Did you want me to take your case up to your room?"

"That would be lovely. Thank you," I said. The man nodded, and I headed towards the desk. At first impression, this was as nice as any hotel I'd stayed in before.

Perhaps people were right when they said there were nice things available outside London.

It didn't take me long to get checked in, and Tracey quickly informed me of breakfast times, the details of the restaurant, and where I could find more information about the local area. I thanked her and took the key cards she offered me before heading up the stairs to the third floor. It didn't seem like the hotel was particularly large, which I appreciated, and it didn't take me long to reach the door to room 302.

I'd booked a small suite since I intended to be there for a while and wanted to be comfortable, and I was pleasantly surprised to find a good-sized, open space with wide windows overlooking the sea on the far wall. The front part of the room was comprised of a small living area with a coffee table, desk, television, and a comfortable-looking sofa. To my right was a raised area where a large bed sat, made up with white sheets and deep purple scatter cushions, alongside some wardrobes in a similar dark wood as the desk and coffee table.

All in all, it was a charming space that would give even London's bougiest boutique hotels a run for their money. The only difference was that a lot of those hotels often screamed *trying too hard*, as if they were desperate for guests to notice how cool and unique they were, while Heather Sands seemed to exude a warm elegance that invited you inside and asked you to take it as you found it.

There was a knock on the door, and I opened it to the man with my suitcase. I thanked him and gave him a tip before I sent him away, then I slipped off my shoes, slung my coat over the back of the sofa, and padded over to the window.

From up here, with the last of the afternoon sun shining on it, even the icy, grey sea looked appealing. I began to think I hadn't made a mistake after all. Perhaps this really was what I'd needed.

Over the last two weeks, I'd debated about whether I actually needed a break or whether I was just running away. It was probably a little of both, but staying in London would have made it so hard to sit down and have a serious think about what had got me feeling so off-kilter. Even in the time since my first realisation that something was off, nothing had changed. I'd still gone out for dinners with friends, spent endless hours in bars and clubs, and fallen into bed with Kai and whoever else offered.

It was like I couldn't do anything different until I got out from under the city's spell.

I'd been worried Kai or Daisy would want to come with me, but neither had expressed any interest in somewhere so unglamorous. I'd thought for a brief minute that Kai might miss me, but then he'd just shrugged and told me he'd be fine. The last I'd heard from him, he'd been shacked up with some newly arrived Hollywood actor who was in London for a few weeks.

His casual dismissal didn't even sting. It was just part and parcel of who Kai and I were to each other.

As I gazed out the window, noticing the impressive castle on the cliffs, I tried to remember the last time I'd had anything that resembled a relationship, but nothing and no one sprung to mind. I wasn't sure if that bothered me or not.

I stared out at the scenery for a few more minutes before turning back to the room. I had no idea what to do now. Usually, my evenings in London followed a regular pattern: food, drinking, partying, and sex. Wake up, rinse, and repeat. But I'd come here to get away from that.

The only problem was, I didn't know how.

"Well done, Jamie," I muttered to myself. "You've really fucked yourself over here."

I supposed dinner at the hotel would be a reasonable place to start, perhaps followed by watching something on Netflix, and an early night. It was only half-past four, though, and still too early for any of that.

Okay, so maybe Netflix first. Or a bath.

I shook my head and paced up and down the room. Why the fuck was this so hard? Why did I feel so lost at the idea of spending one measly night on my own? God, the idea of being alone for a whole week seemed impossible.

I wanted to rescind my earlier thought that this had been a good idea. This was a horrible idea. I had no idea how to do *anything* that didn't involve drinking, dancing, and fucking any and every man I wanted.

"Get a fucking grip," I said as I stopped walking and flopped onto the bed. It was ridiculously comfortable, and I sprawled out like a starfish, staring at the ceiling. "It's not like it's the end of the fucking world."

This was ridiculous. I was nearly thirty fucking years old. I shouldn't need someone to babysit me or keep me company like I was a puppy in need of attention. I needed a distraction.

Maybe a walk would do me some good. Yes, that would clear my head and blow away some of my swirling doubts.

But I did let myself lie there for a few more minutes, just enjoying the sound of the sea outside my window and the soft bed underneath me.

And before I knew it, I found myself drifting off.

When I woke an hour and a half later, I felt a lot calmer, and my internal freak-out about what the fuck I was doing seemed to have abated.

I still felt unsure but more in a Bambi-on-ice way rather than a the-world-is-ending way. It was probably the natural reaction to totally uprooting my life and deciding to do some intense internal soul-searching at the drop of a hat, especially after I'd pretended it wasn't happening until last night when I'd finally packed for my trip.

The whole room was pitch black and the sky outside was similarly so.

When I got up and peered out the window, I saw glimmers of stars and a sliver of moon through the gaps in the clouds, and I smiled. It was virtually impossible to see the stars in London most nights. That, and I barely ever bothered to look.

Feeling renewed, I slipped my shoes back on and grabbed my coat. I still wanted to take a walk and gather my thoughts before I found food, and I assumed it would be easy to find a path to the front from the hotel.

Slipping my key card into my pocket and wrapping up against the cold, I headed downstairs and into the evening air. The wind had a stinging bite to it that made me jump, but it wasn't bad enough to force me back inside.

As predicted, it was easy enough to follow the streetlights to the front, where a mixture of closed shops and open takeaways studded one side of the road with the beach on the other. The golden glimmer of the streetlights bounced off the edges of the high tide, and I found myself mesmerised as I walked. My stomach rumbled as I passed several fish and chip shops, and I realised I hadn't eaten in hours.

I'd told myself I'd get dinner in the hotel, but the temptation of fish and chips was growing stronger by the second. Perhaps I'd get some on my way back and just eat it in my room.

I reached the other end of the front and realised the road curved round a little farther, heading slightly up the hill before slightly splitting in two directions. Intrigued and not ready to go back, I followed the pavement until I heard laughter and noise spilling out of a building on the corner.

The faded sign swinging in the wind had a picture of a

fat, sleeping, white goose in the middle, and the Sleeping Goose painted in gold lettering around it. I stared up at it for a second, wondering whether to go in. Pubs were always a bit hit or miss, especially if you didn't know the area. They could be charming gold mines, or they could be dodgy as fuck. And while the sounds pouring out of establishment were loud and joyful, it didn't mean I'd be welcome.

As I hesitated, I heard a gleeful, bouncing voice behind me on the wind and turned to see two men approaching.

"A chess set, Laurie. A chess set! All the mice have got little hats too and props. Just think how fucking delightful it would look in the living room," said one of the men, who was wearing knee-high boots with chunky, knitted tights, a tartan skirt, and a pink coat that seemed to have white fur around the collar. As he got closer, I was sure his face looked vaguely familiar, but I couldn't work out why.

"You don't even know how to play chess," said the other, a gothic-looking man with a long, dark coat and leather boots. I assumed his name was Laurie from what his companion had said.

"Yes, but I could learn. And even so, it would be worth it for the aesthetic," the first man said before he sighed dreamily. Then he added, "Do you think we'll be the last ones here?"

"We usually are. Everyone expects it now."

"Well, if people could please stop dying, I could finish work earlier."

"I know," Laurie said dryly. "It's very rude of them."

The pair of them had reached me now, and I had to pull

my phone out of my pocket so I didn't look like I was staring at them. They slid past me and into the pub. I turned slightly to let them by, and as I did, I noticed the progress pride sticker stuck in the window nearest the door with swooping letters above it that read *Everyone Welcome*.

I smiled to myself and followed the two men inside.

CHAPTER FOUR

Will

"I NEED you to settle something for me," Theo said as he dropped into the seat next to me in our crowded corner of the Sleeping Goose.

"What's that?" I asked, wondering what I should mentally prepare myself for. I never really knew with Theo.

Across from us, Laurie slid into a free chair and sighed.

"I'm sorry," Laurie said. "He won't stop harping on about it."

"I'm not harping on about anything. I'm just trying to convince you that it's a fabulous idea."

"What is it?" I asked as I drained the last of my first pint. "Am I going to need to forget this conversation ever happened?"

Theo giggled. "No, I promise it's not that bad."

"You said that the last time you wanted me to settle something." Being asked to compare monstrous dildos was not anything I'd ever thought I'd be doing, and I was sure I'd never be able to get the idea of Theo using one of them out of my head. There were some things you didn't need to know about your friends.

"Okay, it's *definitely* not like that," Theo said. "I found a taxidermy chess set on Etsy, a full chess set made of mice with little hats and costumes and props, and I want to get it for our flat, but I need you to convince Laurie not to be such a stick-in-the-mud."

I glanced over at Laurie, who'd unbuttoned his dark coat to reveal an equally dark shirt and waistcoat, and wondered if I should tell Theo it wasn't my job to convince his boyfriend of anything. But they'd probably been having this argument all day and wanted a third party to settle it once and for all.

"Can you play chess?" I asked, and Theo sighed forlornly.

"No, but I could learn. And even so, it would be perfect for the aesthetic."

"You also forgot to mention that it's over a grand," Laurie said pointedly.

"Seriously? A fucking grand?" I asked, turning to stare at Theo.

"What's over a grand?" Lane asked from his seat on my other side. He was a builder and one of my best friends. I didn't realise he'd been listening since our group was so loud and noisy, but now he seemed fully invested.

"A chess set Theo wants," I said.

"Is it made of fucking gold?" Lane asked.

"Better," Theo said with a grin. "Stuffed mice."

"Fuck no," Lane said. "You can't spend a grand on a chess set made with dead mice."

"Exactly," Laurie said. "Thank you! That's my point exactly. And we don't have room for it."

"But it's so cute," Theo whined, his lips starting to form a pout. "And I want it."

"I want doesn't get," Laurie said.

"You're so mean."

"I'm not mean. I'm practical."

I watched the pair of them bicker and smiled to myself. I wasn't getting involved with this any further. I'd never known Theo not to get his way, and the fact that Laurie could say no to him was astounding. The fact that Lane had backed him up was even more so, although I knew Lane's views on any sort of taxidermy had been set when Theo had gifted him and his boyfriend, Oliver, a stuffed frog last year.

"I'm sorry, Theo," Lane said, giving Theo a sympathetic smile. "I don't know if you're going to win this one."

"I'm not giving up," Theo said. "Just you wait."

"I'd like to see you try," Laurie said with a raised eyebrow, and I bit back a chuckle.

"And that's my cue to go to the bar," I said. "Anyone want a drink?"

After collecting the extensive drink order from our small horde of people, I slipped through the crowd towards the bar. The Sleeping Goose was always packed on Friday nights as people came to relax and unwind, and the fact that it was Heather Bay's unofficial queer bar and designated safe space meant it was filled with a huge variety of people rather than the traditional pub crowd.

I'd started coming here with Lane a few years ago when the current owners, Soren and Colin, had taken it over. Since then, it had become our regular meeting place, and every week, we assembled for a few drinks and to catch up. Our group had grown over the years, but our plans had never changed, and it was one part of the week that I always looked forward too.

"Excuse me," I said, sliding past a man I didn't recognise who stood at the bar.

"I'm sorry," he said in a smooth London accent that instantly flagged him as someone who wasn't from around here. I assumed he was a tourist, despite the fact it wasn't the season, or someone to do with the upcoming period drama that was supposed to start filming up at the Castle any day. "I keep getting in the way."

"You're fine. It can't be helped."

"Yes, it is rather like a can of sardines in here."

My lip twitched into a smile as I let my eyes roam over him. He was about my height with artfully styled honey-blond hair and hazel eyes framed by long lashes. He had a strong jaw lightly dusted with stubble and full lips I couldn't stop staring at. He was stylishly dressed in a dark pea coat over a jumper, and the cut of both screamed money.

"I'm Jamie," he said, giving me a wry smile and cutting the silence between us. I swallowed and blinked, feeling like I was being snapped out of some sort of mesmerised state.

"Will," I said. I wasn't sure if I should stick out my hand or not. I wasn't used to random encounters with strange men in pubs. I had a few regular hook-ups, but they were all locals I already knew.

"Can I buy you a drink, Will?" Jamie asked as he slid a step closer.

"Er, maybe? I've just gotta get a round for my table first." I glanced back towards my friends, praying none of them could see us because otherwise I knew I'd be the sole focus of their attentions. I'd hoped the crowd would keep us covered, but it parted at just the wrong second, and I saw Lane look up and over to us, and I knew I'd been spotted.

"Maybe afterwards, then? I'll wait here."

"Yeah, maybe," I said as I tried to get my head to stop spinning. Soren chose that moment to come to my rescue, and a few minutes later, I had a tray laden with drinks in my hands.

"I'll see you in a minute," Jamie said with a smile that made my stomach drop. I nodded and let my feet carry me back towards the table and the pack of wolves hungry for gossip awaiting my arrival.

As if it wasn't bad enough I'd been spotted, they all went silent when I arrived—a rare feat I'd only seen happen once before when Lane had brought Oliver to the pub on a whim last summer and introduced him to us.

At that point, Oliver had been Lane's mythical teenage ex-sweetheart who'd ruined him for all other men. He'd turned out to be a charming, funny man who was the perfect match for Lane, and even at that point, when they'd claimed to just be reconnecting as friends, it had been obvious to me that they'd end up back together.

Which they had. And they were now more in love than ever.

"Who's that?" Lane asked because he was always straight to the point.

"Tourist," I said, handing him his pint before distributing the rest of the drinks. "Sounds like he's from London."

"He's really cute," Theo said. "What did he ask you?"

"Nothing much."

Alex, one of the other members of our group and the most cynical man I'd ever met, scoffed. "It didn't look like nothing."

"Mmmhmm, it definitely looked like something," Lane said with a grin that meant nothing but trouble.

"He just offered to buy me a drink," I muttered.

"Then why the fuck are you still here?" Lane asked. "Go. Get laid."

"I'm not…"

"Will, darling," Theo said sweetly, "when a gorgeous man offers to buy you a drink, you accept. Then you find somewhere with a lockable door and let him fuck your brains out. Or vice versa, depending on your personal preference."

"What have you got to lose?" Alex asked as he picked up his pint. "If he's a tourist, it's not like he'll be sticking around."

"Exactly," said Spencer, Alex's older brother who I'd known since school. He gave me his attempt at a stern expression, which was like being frowned at by a golden retriever. "You need to have some fun, Will. When was the last time you got laid?"

"I'm sorry," I said, slightly sharper than I'd intended. "I didn't realise this was a group decision."

"It's not," Noah said. He was Alex's best friend, Spencer's boyfriend, and probably one of the most sensible men at the table, but even he was giving me an encouraging smile. "We just worry about you."

"You don't need to. I'm fine."

"Of course you are," Theo said, his sweetness now laced with sarcasm. "And let me say, one workaholic to another, you need some downtime, and one night of fun with Mr. Sexy over there will not kill you. Besides, you can leave straight after."

"Mr. Sexy?" I raised my eyebrow, and Theo shrugged.

"You didn't give us his name, so I had to improvise."

"Theo has a point," Oliver chimed in from his seat on Lane's other side. "Go and talk to him, and if you're not comfortable, then you can leave."

"Exactly," Lane said. "And if he won't leave you alone, we'll set Alex on him."

"Why me?" Alex asked indignantly.

"Because you're our resident asshole and could probably kneecap him without a second thought," Lane said. Alex thought about it for a second, then shrugged.

I was still standing in front of them, unsure what to do. I wasn't going to admit it, but it had been a while since I'd gotten laid. The brutal winter days didn't exactly leave me with a lot of energy to leave the house, and I very rarely invited hook-ups over since it would be easy for both my parents and someone at the yard to see an unfamiliar car and start gossiping.

But I was in town, and if Jamie was just visiting, then he had somewhere we could go. I glanced over my shoulder and saw him watching me, a smirk on his plush lips. Various parts of me warred with each other over whether this was a smart decision or not, but in the end, my libido won.

"Fine, I'll go talk to him," I said. "But if *any* of you come over and say anything, I'm leaving. And I'm not telling you what happens either."

Theo opened his mouth, then winced and closed it quickly, and I had a strong suspicion someone had kicked him under the table.

"We won't say a word," Lane said and picked up his pint. "Thanks for the drink."

"Yeah, yeah, you all owe me," I said, shaking my head and taking the tray back to the bar. I slid it over the polished surface to Soren, then walked round to where Jamie stood. He'd tucked himself around the other side of the bar from my friends, away from their prying eyes.

"Hello," he said, his smile widening into something dangerous and charming that made my stomach flip. "All sorted?"

"Yeah. Apparently a two-minute conversation is enough to require a full interrogation."

Jamie chuckled softly. "I'm glad they let you escape."

"Me too," I said, flagging Colin down to order some drinks. "So are you just visiting?"

"Yes," Jamie said. "I wanted to get out of London for a bit."

I nodded, quietly wondering why, of all places, he'd chosen coastal Yorkshire at the start of February. "You're definitely out of it here. Heather Bay isn't exactly Kensington."

"That is very true, but it seems nice enough," he said. I wasn't sure if he was just being polite or not.

"It's pretty in the daylight. In the sunshine, the whole place comes alive," I said, suddenly feeling defensive. I knew Heather Bay wasn't the most glamorous of places, but it was my home and well loved by everyone who lived here. "And the moorland is beautiful. You won't find anything else like it."

Jamie looked at me for a second as if he was trying to figure something out. "I'll have to try and get out there before I leave. I didn't get in until mid-afternoon, and it was a bit late to do anything by that point."

"Just make sure you stick to the paths if you go out walking," I said. "Don't go in bad weather, and don't bother the sheep."

"Okay. I'll remember that." He picked up his drink off the bar and took a long, slow sip, his eyes never leaving me. I couldn't work out if this was the most awkward conversation with a man I'd ever had or just a close second. I thought the honour of the most awkward went to the time some drunken lad had tried to chat me up at university, then vomited on my shoes.

"Sorry," I said. "I'm really not good at this."

Jamie chuckled softly. "Conversation or flirting?"

"Both."

"If you want, we can skip both of those and get to the fun part." He leant closer and lowered his voice, his breath ghosting against my skin and sending shivers down my spine. "Come back to my hotel with me."

CHAPTER FIVE

Jamie

I WATCHED Will's face as he processed my suggestion, waiting for him to give in and say yes.

He was incredibly handsome with eyes that seared into my soul, dark hair swept back off his face, and a dusting of stubble along his jaw that I wanted to feel against my inner thighs. His hands were broad, and I saw cracked skin and calluses when he picked up his drink, so I was going to assume he did some sort of manual labour.

He was very different from the men I usually shacked up with, and just the thought of him pinning me to the bed made my cock throb in anticipation. I'd tended to top more when I was fucking Kai, but one look at Will's broad shoulders and well-muscled thighs had me wanting to bend over there and now.

All I needed him to do was say yes.

"Okay," he said finally, and a pleased spark rushed through my chest. "But I can't stay."

"Honestly, I wasn't expecting you too." I wouldn't have wanted him to either since mornings could be so awkward with new hook-ups, but I wasn't going to say that.

Will nodded. "Where are you staying?"

"The Heather Sands hotel. Do you know it?"

"I know where it is. But since I live just up the road, I don't really have much need for a hotel."

I chuckled. He seemed a little less nervous now, like the anticipation and worry of saying yes to this had dissipated and had been replaced by a dry sense of humour. "I'm guessing you don't regularly pick up visitors, then?" I asked, casually fishing for more details. I'd assumed from his awkwardness he didn't do this very often.

"Sometimes in the summer, but not many of them are Heather Sands kind of men," he said.

"Exciting. I get to be your first."

Will laughed, and the warm sound made something lurch in my stomach. "If you want it, it's yours."

"Good." I downed the rest of my drink. "Come on, this is more than enough conversation for me."

"Really?" He smirked, something flashing in his eyes. And for the first time since I'd bumped into him, I felt a shift between us like he wasn't just going to give me every-thing I wanted the way Kai would. "What if I want you to talk to me?"

"It depends what you want to talk about?" I lowered my voice. "What I want and what feels good, that's a definite yes. My life story or why I'm here, that's a no."

"Good," Will said. "We're on the same page." He leant closer and plucked the empty glass from my hand. "I bet you make the sweetest noises when you come. And I'm betting you're loud too."

I swallowed, letting my eyes lock onto his and feeling the searing heat between us. "Would you like that?"

"Yes. I thought that was obvious." He put our glasses on the bar. "Come on, show me this posh hotel room of yours. I promise not to make conversation while we walk."

I chuckled and followed him out of the crowded pub, wondering if, for once, I'd actually met my match.

As we reached the door, I threw a quick glance across to Will's friends, who all looked like they were trying very hard not to stare at Will's disappearing behind. They looked so different from the crowd I usually found attached to me, but it wasn't just in appearance.

There was something... genuine about the way they seemed so involved in his life. It had almost been funny watching him with them earlier, like it was a group decision whether Will was allowed to leave with me.

Apart from Daisy, I didn't think I'd ever had a friend like that in my life. And Daisy was happy to let me cavort around with whoever I wanted without batting an eyelash.

Shaking all thoughts of Daisy and London away, I stepped out into the night, gasping as a rush of freezing air whipped into my face. "Fuck, that's cold!"

Will chuckled. "It comes straight off the North Sea. Just be glad it's not raining too. If the wind's right, the rain comes at you sideways."

I pulled my coat around me tighter as we started

walking back towards the hotel. Despite my previous embargo on all non-sex related conversation, I found myself saying, "If that happened, I would be staying indoors away from it. I'm assuming that's what you do?"

Under the glow of a passing streetlamp, I saw Will smirk. "I thought we weren't talking."

"I changed my mind."

"No, I don't," Will said. "I'm out in all weathers usually."

"God, that sounds horrific. What possesses you to do that?" I couldn't imagine ever being outside in the cold and wet unless it was to go somewhere else, and even then, I usually went as far as I could inside a car. The only vague exception was when I went skiing, but even then, if the weather was horrible, I tended to stay inside the chalet with a nice bottle of wine and some excellent company.

"I'm a farmer. It's part of the job description."

I looked at Will for a moment as we walked along the front. That explained the callused hands and his wardrobe, which would definitely be called more functional than fashionable, even if he wasn't currently wearing wellies. "Hmm, that fits."

Will glanced at me and grinned, one eyebrow raised. "What about you, posh boy? Banker?"

"Not really," I said, suddenly wishing I hadn't opened my mouth. Because even though I didn't want to continue this line of conversation, it wasn't exactly fair of me to shut it down. Although, Will had offered his occupation more willingly than I'd expected. Perhaps it was because I was used to the London scene, where unless you were in finance or consulting, very few people led with their careers.

Especially because a lot of people I knew didn't actually *have* them. They had passion projects instead.

Fuck, even in my head that sounded obnoxious.

Will didn't push, though, and I wondered if he'd already worked it out. Most of the time, being a trust-fund brat hardly registered in my consciousness, but now it felt like a searing brand on my forehead.

I was nearly thirty for fuck's sake, and I had nothing to show for my existence except an art history degree and a collection of stories that would have made Oscar Wilde proud. But hedonism tended to rack up bills rather than pay them.

As we rounded the corner on the final stretch to the hotel's front door, I paused for a second, my gaze catching on the bobbing waves in the harbour and the little fleet of boats moored there. The warm light from the town glinted off their hulls and danced across the water, mixing with the pale light of the thin, crescent moon hanging just above us. It was picturesque in a way I'd not seen before, and it momentarily caught me off guard.

"You okay?" Will asked, pausing just ahead of me.

"Yes. I was just… looking at the boats." It sounded ridiculous when I said it out loud, but Will just gave me a soft smile that made my stomach drop again and reached for my hand.

"Don't they have boats in London? Or Ibiza? Or wherever else you spend your time."

"They do, but I don't tend to look at them."

"Not a chartered party yacht kind of man?" Will asked, his voice gently teasing in a way that made my insides twist. I'd barely known him an hour, and he already had me more tangled up than anyone I'd ever met. What the fuck was wrong with me?

"No," I said as I slipped my hand into his, trying to ignore how warm his skin felt against mine. "To be completely honest, I get horrifically seasick, which does not make days on yachts particularly fun, even if the sea is calm."

"Don't worry. I won't tell." He shot me a wink, and I swallowed.

There were only a few people around as we slipped into the hotel, and nobody made it their business to notice us as we climbed the stairs. We were still only holding hands, and I couldn't remember the last time one of my hook-ups had moved this slowly. Even if I'd been taking them back to mine, we'd have been all over each other on the journey home.

Will's teasing and the crawling pace of this encounter was making my head spin. I just wanted to get a locked door between us and the rest of the world so I could forget what was going on in my head and focus on what I was good at: making men come.

As soon as we reached the third floor, I pulled the key card from my pocket and steered Will towards the door. It clicked open, and I dragged him inside, barely remembering to flick a light on before I was backing him against the nearest wall. Need boiled within me, and I was desperate for his touch. I wanted to get out of my head and think about nothing but the way my body felt.

Will let out a muffled sound as his body hit the wall, his hands coming up to wrap around me as my lips crashed against his. It wasn't the smoothest kiss, and it took him a second to respond, but when he did, I melted against him.

His hand slid up my spine to cradle the back of my neck, gently moving and holding me in place. His lips were rough and chapped, and he tasted like the beer he'd been drinking, but fuck did he know how to use his mouth.

His kisses drew me in, making me hungry for more, and I groaned. Will let out a pleased growl as his tongue caressed the seam of my lips before pressing inside. I pushed against him, desperately wanting more, my hands reaching out to fumble with his buttons. Shit. I was *never* this uncoordinated. I suddenly felt like a fumbling teenager instead of a man renowned for having a revolving door to my bedroom.

"What's the rush?" Will asked, his mouth still brushing against mine.

"You're still dressed."

"So are you." Will smirked. "Did you want me to change that?"

"I thought that was obvious."

He kissed me again, languidly this time, like he was taking great delight in making me wait. When he released me, my head was spinning, and I could barely focus enough to dump my coat on the sofa and kick off my shoes. The rest of my clothes went to the floor as I focused on watching Will strip down.

There was something meticulous and methodical about the way he pulled off his fleece and reached for the buttons on his shirt, slowly popping them open to reveal a furred chest and a toned torso I wanted to lick. I bit my lip and wrapped my hand around my cock, stroking myself as he dropped his shirt on the floor and reached for the button on his jeans. They were already starting to bulge at the crotch, and my mouth watered at the thought of getting him inside me.

Will's eyes seared into mine as he unbuttoned his jeans, but I tore my gaze away to watch as he began to push them down, taking his underwear with it. His cock was only half-hard, but fuck, it looked good—flushed and thick in a way I knew would fill me up. I hadn't bottomed for a while since Kai hated topping, and it had been too long since I'd been stuffed full.

If I'd been on the fence about letting Will fuck me, I wasn't any more. I needed him to pound me until I couldn't think of anything but him, then leave me dripping with his cum.

"Fuck," I said finally, filling the silent room. "You're really hot. And you have a really nice dick."

Will chuckled softly and stepped out of his jeans. For all his teasing about being in a rush, he was happy enough to take his time to get naked with me. "Thanks, I guess."

I stepped closer and ran one hand across his chest. "You sound like you don't believe me."

"I mean, I guess I look all right."

It was my turn to laugh now. "Trust me, when you've

seen as many naked men as I have, you learn to be discerning. And you are, like, top ten percent hot."

"Top ten percent?" he asked wryly.

I smirked and brushed my mouth against his, my other hand reaching between us to grasp his cock and pump it slowly, loving the way it grew hard in my hand. "You'll get up to five if you know how to use this."

"I'm honoured." One hand came up to cup my jaw, keeping me close to him. There was a dark fire burning in his eyes, and it made my breath catch in my throat. "But what makes you think I don't?"

"I've been with a lot of men who think that having a nice dick means they don't have to do shit," I said, trying to keep my voice level and like I wasn't about to drop to my knees to give Will whatever he wanted. "And I'm really hoping you won't turn out to be one of them. I don't want to be disappointed with what Yorkshire has to offer."

Will snorted, his lip curling at the edge. "I think I'd be better off showing you, then," he said, drawing me closer and into a blistering kiss.

All my thoughts melted away as lust consumed me. My fingers danced across Will's skin as his lips worked magic on mine, drawing out soft moans and needy groans from deep in my chest. I felt my feet moving as he steered me backwards in the rough direction of the bed.

He broke away and muttered, "How far away is this fucking bed?" I wanted to laugh, but then he leant down and wrapped strong arms around my thighs, lifting me up so I could wrap my legs around his waist as he carried me across the room and up the step I'd forgotten was there before dropping me onto the bed.

"Are you going to join me?" I asked as I looked up at him, drinking in every inch. "Or do I need to start by myself?"

"You can start," he said. "I was just going to grab lube. Assuming you've got some?"

I smirked. "I'm never without it." I hadn't actually unpacked, and my suitcase was still where I'd left it. "It's in the suitcase," I said. "Do you mind? I can get it if it's easier."

"It's fine." Will walked over and quickly opened it, following my directions to retrieve the slim, black bottle. "Do you have condoms?"

"I do if you really want them, but I'm on PrEP, and I get tested regularly. It's your choice."

"I'm on PrEP too," Will said as he closed the suitcase and stepped up onto the raised platform, dropping the bottle beside me.

"Good, in that case, you can fuck me raw and fill me up," I said.

Will groaned, climbing onto the bed and blanketing me with his body. His lips felt like a brand as they trailed down my neck. "Mmm, I can't wait to be inside you."

I wrapped my legs around him, pulling him closer to me. "Fuck yes, I need that." My hand scrabbled on the bed beside me, searching for the lube. I grasped it and practically threw it at his head as I added, "Get the fuck inside me now."

"Are you always this demanding?" Will asked, plucking

the bottle from my hand before resuming trailing kisses across my skin, completely ignoring my demands. Was he intent on torturing me or something? I couldn't complain, though, because I was loving every second.

"Usually, I don't have to be."

"You always get what you want then?"

"Yes. And I'm not used to having to ask twice."

"Mmm, you know you can't push me around, don't you, posh boy?"

I grinned because I had definitely realised that, but I wasn't going to admit it. As much as I loved being thrown around, I adored bringing men to their knees. "I bet you'd love it if I did," I said.

Will chuckled darkly, circling his hips and grinding his cock against mine, making me moan. "Keep telling yourself that."

"I will. Now can you please just fucking fuck me?"

"If it'll shut you up, then yes." Will sat up and ran a hand down my thigh. "Roll over."

I happily complied, rolling onto my stomach and pushing my ass into the air. My cock was achingly hard and dripping precum onto the sheets as I reached one hand back to slowly stroke myself. The lube bottle clicked, and I groaned as a cool, slick finger pressed against the sensitive rim of my hole. Will pressed kisses to my cheeks as he circled my entrance before pushing one finger inside.

"Fuck," I groaned. "More. Give me more."

"In a minute," Will said as he gently slid his finger all the way in before starting to pump it in and out. "I don't want to hurt you."

"That's very chivalrous, but you won't. Seriously. Just give me another." It was sweet that he wanted to be careful, but I wasn't going to break. It wasn't like I was asking him to suddenly start fisting me.

Either Will couldn't be bothered to keep arguing, or he didn't mind me bossing him around as much as he'd said because a second later I felt the soft, sweet burn of him sliding another finger in. I groaned, gripping my cock tightly as I pressed back onto him. Will moaned softly as I began to rock my hips, fucking his fingers and taking them as deep as I could.

"Fuck, you have a nice ass," he said in an almost reverent tone as he ran his hand down my back.

"I know. You should get your cock in me," I said, squeezing my hole around his digits and making him groan. "It'll feel so fucking good."

"Do you want another finger first?"

"No," I said. "You can fuck me."

I stilled my hips as he pulled his fingers out, a shiver running across my skin as he drizzled more lube onto my hole. The bed dipped as he moved closer, his hand gripping my hip as he guided me back onto his cock. I moaned, grasping my own erection tightly as Will's cock breached me, sliding deep inside. He went slowly, giving my body time to adjust as he filled me, and by the time I felt his balls against my ass, I was ready for more.

Will gasped as I began to roll my hips, fucking myself on his perfect cock. His fingers dug into my skin as I milked his shaft, angling my hips so his dick tagged my prostate with every thrust and squeeze. Pleasure burned through me, and I chased the sensations with every move of my body.

"Shit," Will groaned. "Jamie... Fuck... that feels..."

"Yeah? Like me milking your cock like this?" I asked, twisting my head to watch the way desire and enjoyment etched themselves into Will's expression. "Like how good my tight hole feels around you?"

"Yes... Fuck... God, you feel incredible."

"Mmm, so do you. Told you you had a nice dick," I said with a groan as I thrust backwards. Will grasped my hips, pulling me all the way onto him and holding me in place for a moment while circling his hips.

"Fuck!" I cried. "Do that again."

Will let out a low moan and circled his hips again, his cock rubbing over my sweet spot and making my dick jerk in my hand. "Like that?"

"Yes! Just like that." I gripped my cock tightly and started to jerk myself hard. "Now fuck me. Just fucking pound me."

Will gave a deep, tentative thrust like he was testing the waters to make sure it wasn't too much. I groaned, pushing back harder, practically begging for more. He seemed to get the idea because he held my hips tightly and started to fuck me so perfectly I thought I was seeing stars. God, he really did know how to use that gorgeous cock of his, and it was made even better by the way he sweetly did as he was told.

There was something there for me to think about, except not at that moment because I could barely remember my name.

All I heard was the sound of skin on skin mixed with

my own moans and Will's deep grunts as he pounded me hard and deep, sending endless waves of heat through me until my whole body felt hotter than the sun. Sweat dripped down my skin, and my muscles burned as I jerked my cock, desperate for release.

"Will!" I cried out as every one of my muscles tightened, raw pleasure consuming me as my dick pulsed in my hand, shooting thick ropes of cum across the soft, white sheets.

I heard Will curse, but his voice sounded far away. Every desperate thrust he made drew out my orgasm until I could barely tell what universe I was in, then, just as it was on the verge of too much, Will gave one final, perfect thrust and growled out his release, filling me with his load.

"Mmm," I hummed, stretching my arms out in front of me and arching my back. "That was…"

"Fun?" Will supplied, his voice hoarse and breathless as he released my hips. He pulled out gently before leaning down to press a kiss to my spine. It was such a sweet gesture it momentarily stunned me.

"Yeah, that works." I sighed happily as I felt his cum start to trickle out of my hole, running down my thighs in a way I'd always loved. It just satisfied some deep need within me, an itch that occasionally I desperately needed scratched. I rolled over and flopped down onto the mattress, looking over at Will who was now sitting on the edge of the bed. "I take it you enjoyed it too?"

"I did," he said. "Thanks. I needed that."

"My absolute pleasure." I stretched again, lazily thinking I needed to shower before I fell asleep.

"What are your plans for the rest of the night?" Will

asked, standing up and helping himself to a tissue from the decorative box beside the bed.

"I don't know. Shower. Food. I might see if they do room service. Then sleep."

Will nodded and wandered over to start collecting his clothes. "And tomorrow?"

"I don't know. I suppose I should find something to do rather than just staying in bed. Especially since I've come all this way." I hadn't really made any plans beyond getting there, and while I'd vaguely thought about having a wander around the town, that was about as far as I'd gotten.

"You should go up to the Castle," Will said. "Town's nice too. A lot's closed this time of year, but it's still worth exploring. Go for a walk on the beach or out on the moors if we don't get more snow. Don't just sit here."

There was an earnestness to his voice that couldn't be ignored, and it made something in my chest clench. It was a request I couldn't say no to.

"Okay," I said, watching as he dressed himself. "I promise I'll explore."

"Good." He gave me a warm smile that made my chest even tighter. Then he reached for his boots and pulled them on, the picture of well-fucked decorum. He gave me another smile as he headed for the door. "See you around, posh boy."

I watched him go, tucking the evening's events into my memory.

I really hoped he meant it.

CHAPTER SIX

Jamie

OVER THE NEXT FEW DAYS, I made good on my promise to Will to get out and explore Heather Bay.

I tried not to think about why I felt so beholden to a man I'd only met once and told myself it was just part of getting away from everything in London. After all, how was I supposed to work out what was bothering me about my life if I just moped around the hotel room, gazing out the window?

On the Saturday, I woke up late and had a leisurely breakfast at the hotel, delighted to find that the restaurant had beautiful views over the bay. I ate my food while watching the fleet of fishing boats heading out to sea. The day was cold, but it was bright and sunny, and I decided it would be a good day to explore the town itself.

I'd wrapped up warm and spent the day pottering around the narrow, cobbled streets and sticking my nose into all the tiny shops. Many of them were closed for the winter season, but a few were open for a couple of hours, and I delighted myself by finding a small art gallery dedicated to local artists.

Some of the work was truly exquisite, and it hadn't taken any convincing for me to hand over my credit card. I'd bought two pieces: one depicting the bay during a storm and one that showed the moors glittering under the snow with sheep picking their way through the heather.

It made me think of Will.

The next day, Sunday, I'd gotten into my car and driven up the narrow roads towards Hareford House, the castle-esque building on the cliffs above the bay. A lot of people I knew found country houses terribly dull, especially because some of them lived in them and said they all looked the same after a while. But after university, where I'd spent a lot of time looking at various paintings in various houses, I'd developed an appreciation for them.

Hareford House wasn't one I'd visited before, and I declined the guided tour to spend a glorious few hours walking around and taking in every detail. One of the staff members informed me that some of the house was closed because they were starting to set it up to film for a new period drama, something the staff seemed very excited about.

The only period drama I'd watched was *Bridgerton* because Daisy had insisted I watch it with her. I'd protested loudly, telling her it was tedious, but at least some of the men had been hot enough to make it worth it. I made a mental note to mention this one to Daisy to see if she knew anything. If the cast was sexy, I'd probably agree to watch it, if only for the prospect of seeing the actors naked.

After I'd finished exploring the house, I walked around the gardens, stopping by a low stone wall to look out over the fields and moorland beyond. There were a few sheep grazing, and I wondered if they belonged to the house's estate or to another farm. It made me think of Will again.

I assumed he'd be working today based on the knowledge of farming I could dredge up from the depths of my memory. I'd loved books about animals and books set on farms when I was younger, and I remembered sitting in bed with my nanny, Julia, while she read to me, and then, when I was old enough, sitting next to her on my sofa as I stumbled through reading them back to her.

Thinking about Julia reminded me that her birthday was coming up, and I made a mental note to send her a present. She'd moved back to Germany a couple of years ago with her husband and their daughters, so I didn't see her as much as I used to, but I still called her every couple of weeks and sent her the most beautiful presents I could find.

I actually spoke to her more than my own mother these days.

I watched the sheep for a little longer, until I couldn't feel my fingers or toes, then I kept walking.

Even from the hints he'd given me, it was obvious Will's life was completely different from mine. But there was something intriguing about that. I had no idea what it was like to dedicate your life to something in the way that farming required. I could barely grasp what it involved beyond long hours in all weather.

To be that dedicated to something was an utterly alien concept to me.

It was just starting to snow when I reached my car, and as I drove back to town, I wondered if the weather would make Will's life more difficult.

It kept snowing all night, and by Monday morning, the whole town was covered in a thick blanket of snow. It was incredibly picturesque, and even though I hated being cold, I wrapped up warm after breakfast and went for a stroll.

Everything was just as beautiful outside with the snow sparkling under the late morning sunshine and crunching under foot. It reminded me of something from a Christmas card or one of those photos in the luxury travel and home magazines we'd had at home. I'd always assumed those pictures had been Photoshopped beyond recognition, but clearly, I'd been wrong.

The feeling of joy lasted for all of ten minutes. Then I started to lose feeling in my feet. Apparently, the incredibly expensive boots I was wearing were more aesthetically pleasing than warm.

Turning down a side street, I saw the sign for a coffee shop and quickly ducked inside. A bell rang as I pushed the door open, warm air and the smell of coffee and cake enveloping me in a cosy hug.

"Morning!" called a voice from behind the counter. It belonged to a tall man with blond hair pulled back into a small bun, whose welcoming smile perfectly matched the shop's atmosphere. "Bit nippy out, isn't it?"

His face rang a bell of familiarity, but I struggled to place him. I knew I hadn't been into the shop before, and it hadn't been at Hareford House or in any of the other shops either. Then, as I walked towards the counter, it hit me. Friday night. The pub. He'd been sitting with the group Will had been talking to.

Was everything in this town determined to remind me of him?

It was too late to leave now, though, and I just had to hope the man wouldn't say anything. If it were London, I'd know for sure, but in Heather Bay, everyone seemed so much friendlier.

"Just a little," I said, giving him a small smile as I looked up at the large chalk boards on the wall behind the counter. Above the top of the drinks menu, the words *Novel Tea* were written in sweeping cursive. My first thought was that it was a cute name for a coffee shop, my second was how cheap the drinks were in comparison to my local Starbucks.

"What can I get for you?" asked the man. "We've got all the regulars up there and a few specials over there." He pointed at the second board, and I noticed a list of monthly specials.

"Can I get a pot of tea, please?" I asked, my eyes turning to scan the counter in front of me, which was full of delicious-looking cakes and pastries. It hadn't been too long since I'd had breakfast, but I was cold and miserable, and I was sure some of the snow had seeped into my shoes. "And one of the cinnamon buns too."

"Sure, what tea did you want?" He gestured to a shelf behind him, which had a line of jars, each of them with neatly written labels stuck to the front.

"English breakfast is fine, thank you." I didn't drink a

lot of tea, tending to prefer coffee, but this just seemed like the place for it.

I reached into my pocket to pull out my wallet, glancing around the shop as I did. It wasn't that busy, but that was hardly surprising considering it was barely eleven on a Monday and the whole town was covered in snow. There were a variety of tables scattered around, each surrounded by a collection of mismatched chairs, and one wall was covered in floor-to-ceiling bookcases, each shelf over-flowing with paperbacks.

In another scenario, the whole thing might have looked messy, but there it just looked oddly charming and eccentric. It welcomed you into the rabbit hole and invited you to make yourself comfortable for as long as you wanted to stay. All it needed was a hookah-smoking caterpillar or a grinning cat.

"So," the man behind the counter said as he rang everything up on the till, "just visiting for a few days?"

"Yes," I said, wondering if he was just making polite conversation or trying to dig. "Just a short break. Although, I might not have picked the best time of year."

"Oh, I don't know. It's cold, but it's quieter, and Heather Bay is bloody beautiful in the snow."

"That's true," I said. "It's very picturesque."

I tapped my card on the reader and slipped it back into my wallet while the man reached into the counter for a cinnamon bun and slipped it onto a plate. "Grab a seat," he said. "I'll bring it over with your tea in a second. Help yourself to a book if you want one. They're free to read while you're here, and if you want to take one, we just ask for a small donation, or you can swap it for one of your own."

"Thanks." I smiled and looked around the room, eventually choosing a small table near the window. It had just started snowing again, and I liked the idea of watching it fall. It felt like such a simple, childlike thing to do, but right then, it was all I wanted. I'd spent so much of my adult life indulging my every whim, but it had very rarely involved small things like watching rain on the window or the sun setting over the horizon, the little wonders that made the world beautiful.

"Here you go," the man said a few minutes later as he set a pot of tea on the table accompanied by a cup and saucer, a little jug of milk, and my cinnamon bun.

I tore my eyes away from the window, where the snow was quickly filling up the footprints that had been left on the cobblestones. "Oh, thanks."

"No worries." He paused like he wanted to say something, then added, "I'm not being nosy, but you were in the pub on Friday, right?" I stared at him, and he continued. "I'm not trying to be weird, I promise. I was just there with my friends. We go every week. I, er, I think you might've met one of them. Will."

"And if I have?" I asked, trying to work out what the fuck was going on. Will had muttered something about being interrogated when he'd joined me at the bar, and from what I'd seen, this man had been part of that group, so it was probably useless pretending I hadn't left with Will. In fact, it seemed like his friends had practically thrown him at me.

"Sorry, I don't mean anything by it. I just... I don't know whether you wanted to see him again, and if you do, if you had a way of getting hold of him."

Was he offering to give me Will's number? I didn't know if that was sweet or brazen. Still, I had regretted not asking for it before Will left.

Sometimes with my hook-ups, I knew I wasn't interested in another round as soon as we'd finished, but when I was interested, I always tried to make sure I could find them again to ask, even if it was just grabbing their Instagram handle or finding them on Grindr. But with Will, I had nothing. I didn't even have a last name so I could do some casual social media stalking.

"No, I don't have his details." I knew I sounded frosty, but it was more from shock than anything. I'd always loathed the idea of fate or the universe having a plan or any of that bullshit, but even I had to admit this felt a tiny bit like a sign. Even if it was just being in the right place at the right time. Although, since this was a small town, it was possible I would have bumped into him again anyway.

"Do you want them?"

"Will he mind if you give them to me?"

The man frowned and pursed his lips. "Okay, hang on a second. I'll be right back." He shot me a grin. "I'm Spencer by the way. Welcome to Heather Bay."

CHAPTER SEVEN

Will

HIGGS and I were hefting bales of hay out into the snow when my phone rang. I pulled it out of my pocket and was surprised to see Spencer's name on the screen. He usually never called me, so I could only assume it was an emergency, but why he was calling me instead of one of the guys in town was a mystery.

"Hello?" I asked, tucking my phone between my ear and shoulder so I could pull my pocket knife out to cut the bailer twine off some of the hay. The snow had covered a lot of the more nutritious grazing and I needed to make sure my pregnant ewes got enough to eat as they entered the final stages of their pregnancies. They were already waddling towards us, eagerly awaiting the new delivery of food.

"Will," Spencer hissed, his voice barely above a whisper. "I need to ask you something."

"What's wrong? Why are you whispering? I can barely bloody hear you."

"Sorry, I can't talk too loudly because I don't want to be overheard. Hang on." I heard him moving and muttering something to someone about being in the back. I assumed he was at Novel Tea. "Okay, that's better. I'm in the stock room."

"Can you tell me what's going on now?" I asked, sticking the knife back into my pocket and starting to shake out some of the hay. It was still snowing heavily, making the golden strands look like they were being enthusiastically dusted with icing sugar.

"You know how you left with that guy on Friday?"

"Yes..."

"Did you, er, did you give him your number?" Spencer asked in a way that was far too casual to be casual. He was fishing for something.

"No... Why? What've you done?"

"Nothing!" I didn't believe him, and disapproving silence filled the line until Spencer cracked and continued. "Okay, so he just came into Novel Tea, and I recognised him from Friday, so I might have asked him if you'd given him your number, and he said you hadn't, and I was just wondering—"

"Spencer," I said, cutting him off, "did you give it to him?"

"No! I wasn't going to do that without asking you."

"Is that why you called? To get me to say yes?" I straightened up and brushed some stray snow from my face. Sometimes, I really wished my friends weren't so bloody interfering. I knew they meant well, but this was my life, and I didn't need my dating decisions made by a committee.

"Yeah, it is," Spencer said. "I know you're busy, especially with this weather, but come on, Will. Some no-strings-attached fun would be good for you. This guy isn't going to be here forever, and it would be good for you to have a distraction."

"A distraction? Is that what you're calling him?" I tried to stop myself from smiling, but it was hard. Spencer meant well, and I appreciated him not randomly handing out my number, but that still didn't mean I had time for Jamie, especially since the snow was supposed to get worse.

"I mean, I don't know his name, so it's that or Theo's suggestion of Mr. Sexy."

I snorted and shook my head. "His name's Jamie."

"Yeah, that fits," Spencer said, more to himself than me. "Come on, Will. I don't even know if he'll message you, and if he does, you don't have to do anything about it."

"Are you going to keep nagging until I give in?"

"I don't know. Probably. I could always get someone else to nag you instead. Lane would make you do it."

Spencer was right there. Lane was one of my best mates and didn't take no for an answer.

Lane and I had been there for each other through a lot, and I'd been the one he'd come to when he'd first started to realise he wasn't over Oliver.

It had been painfully obvious the pair of them were just dancing around their feelings and trying to pretend it was nothing more than a casual summer fling. I'd breathed a sigh of relief that I didn't have to watch them pretend nothing was happening when they'd finally admitted they were back together.

I loved Lane, but he could be really obtuse at times.

"Fine," I said, knowing I wasn't going to win. "Do whatever you want."

"Awesome, you're the best! Keep warm out there. Let us know if you need anything."

I said goodbye and hung up, shaking my head as I stuck my phone back into my pocket. I had no idea if this was going to amount to anything. I tried to tell myself I didn't care if it did.

But as I opened the rest of the bales Higgs had dragged out of the old stone barn, I knew it was pointless to deny how I felt.

That night with Jamie was the most fun I'd had in years, and if he offered me another opportunity to see him, I'd take him up on it in a heartbeat.

The conversation with Spencer floated around my brain for the rest of the day while I worked. It was an annoying distraction, but I couldn't make it go away.

When I tried to think about something else, my imagination helpfully supplied snippets of Jamie gasping and moaning in pleasure while I was deep inside him. And that wasn't helpful when I was freezing my balls off on the moors, trying to make sure all the animals had enough to eat. Several feet of snow didn't suddenly mean I could pack up and spend most of the day indoors. In fact, it almost doubled my workload because everything seemed to take twice as long.

By the time I got back to the farmhouse for a quick break late that afternoon, every part of me was cold and aching. I desperately wanted to slide into a scalding hot bath and soak my troubles away, but I still had a few things to finish up.

Dylan had messaged me about getting more salt for the yard to make sure nobody came a cropper, and they needed more hay too since the horses were only allowed out for a few hours a day to avoid injuring themselves and turning the fields into icy mud pits that would take months to repair. Plus, I had Nell and Moss to feed and make sure they were toasty enough, then final rounds.

As I flicked the kettle on to make a quick cup of tea, noticing with joy that Mum had been in and left me a whole cherry loaf cake at some point, I pulled my phone out of my pocket to see if I had anything from Jamie.

I dismissed the notifications from the group chat because I didn't have time to read through the hundred or so messages I'd missed throughout the day as well as the various emails—I'd look at them tomorrow—until finally I saw a message from an unknown number at the bottom.

JAMIE *Hey, it's Jamie. Your friend from Novel Tea gave me your number in case I fancied getting in touch. He promised me he'd checked with you. Hopefully, he has actually given me the correct one, and I'm not messaging some total rando.*

I chuckled to myself, unsurprised Spencer had

attempted to make it clear to Jamie that he'd gotten my permission. The kettle boiled, and I threw a teabag into a mug, adding the water and leaving it to stew. I cut myself a chunk of cake while I tried to think of a response.

WILL *Yeah, this is the right number, so you're not messaging a total rando, only a partial one. And Spencer called me to ask, so you're good there - Will.*
JAMIE *Thank God for that. Although I do like meeting the odd randomer, especially if they're sexy. I recently met this one guy in a Yorkshire pub, and he was a really good fuck.*
WILL *Was he now? Sounds like you had fun.*
JAMIE *He was, and I'm hoping he'd be up for another round tonight.*

I glanced out the window at the darkening sky, frowning as I tried to think everything through the same way I always did. I still had things to do before I could call it quits for the day, and none of them were things I could just put to the side. But after that...

It wasn't like I had any plans for my evening beyond soaking myself until I shrivelled up and watching whatever I could find on Netflix until I fell asleep. I wouldn't exactly be missing out on anything if I went to see Jamie. And I could just leave again afterwards to make sure I was back for the morning. I didn't really want to be stuck in town if we had more snow overnight since the tiny back roads up to the farm could easily get blocked or become treacherous to drive. My Land Rover would be fine, but it would be everyone else that was the problem.

WILL *He might be. Depends on when and where.*
JAMIE *Come to Heather Sands about nine?*
WILL *Make it eight, I have to get back and get up at five.*
JAMIE *Seriously? Five?! Eight it is.*
WILL *I'll see you then.*

A smile slipped onto my face as I put my phone down and cut off a second piece of cake to eat with my tea. I'd been tempted to tease him and say that some of us actually had jobs to get back to, but I wasn't sure if that would be too much.

If this was just an ongoing series of hook-ups, I didn't want to get too involved or share too much since Jamie probably didn't care. It wasn't like the casual thing I'd had with Andrew, who was a mate of mine and Spencer's, where we'd both shared stuff about our lives. Andrew and I both knew we were never going to be more than casual fuck buddies because we just didn't work that way together, but we'd still become friends along the way.

If Jamie was leaving soon, I doubted he'd want that with me, and I wasn't sure how comfortable I felt sharing parts of myself with a man who just considered me another name in his book, someone to be remembered fondly when he thought about that time he'd decided to piss off to Yorkshire in February.

That was another reason for me to hold back. It wasn't like Jamie had been exactly forthcoming with any details about himself beyond his name and what I'd worked out for myself. Like the fact he was likely some sort of trust-fund brat who just partied and fucked his way through life while spending money like it was water. His life was completely different from mine, and I wasn't about to give him the opportunity to shit all over it when he'd probably never done a day's work in his life.

But none of that meant I couldn't go and get off with him. Jamie had been right when he'd called it a really good fuck, and maybe Spencer was right. Maybe I did just need some mindless, meaningless sex to distract me from the long slog through the rest of winter I had ahead of me. February was always the worst month, and every year it seemed to drag on forever.

Perhaps getting off with Jamie as many times as I could was exactly what I needed.

CHAPTER EIGHT

Will

I MESSAGED Jamie as soon as I parked in the hotel car park, wanting to make sure he was still happy to meet up before I walked inside. I didn't fancy hovering in reception with everyone watching or worse, heading up to his room and then getting kicked out.

His response was almost instantaneous.

JAMIE *Good. Come to my room? I'm in 302. I'm waiting for you.*

Another message came through underneath it, and I smirked. This time it was a picture of Jamie lounging on top of the bed. He was shirtless with his jeans popped open to reveal the waistband of his underwear.

It was difficult to tell from the angle of the picture whether he was hard or not, but my money was on yes. That thought made my cock throb in my jeans, and I reached down to adjust myself before I climbed out of the car. I didn't want to go walking through the hotel lobby with an obvious hard-on. Now that I was there, all my previous doubts had been silenced by my desperate desire to get laid.

WILL *I'll be there in a minute. Lose the jeans.*

Locking the car behind me, I strode towards the hotel. I was trying to look casual, but I knew I was failing. Anyone looking at me would've thought my ass was on fire. I slipped into the lobby, pulling out my phone in the hope that it would make me looked relaxed and like I belonged there, even though I was pretty sure I'd seen the woman behind the desk in Tesco several times.

I'd tried to dress a bit nicer tonight, which for me meant my least scruffy jeans, my cleanest jumper, and the pair of boots I kept for the pub and any other non-work things since nobody wanted me walking round Tesco in shoes that smelt like sheep shit. I didn't do fancy clothes, not in the way Jamie seemed to, but it had been good enough the other night, so it would do now.

It didn't take me long to reach the top floor, and there were only a few doors there. When I found 302, I wasn't sure whether to go straight in or knock. Jamie had told me to come straight up, but I didn't want to assume.

Then I noticed the door was slightly ajar, resting on the deadbolt that had been locked open. I smiled to myself.

I guessed I wasn't the only one who was desperate.

"You know," I said as I pushed the door open and

stepped inside, unclicking the lock behind me so the door shut properly, "you shouldn't leave the door open like that. Strangers might come in."

"I hope so," Jamie said, a pleased note in his voice. "Anyway, you don't count as a stranger."

"I don't?" I asked teasingly as I walked into the room, looking at him spread out on the bed in just a tiny pair of skintight boxers that clung to his erection. He looked so fucking delicious I knew I wasn't going to be able to keep my hands off him for very long.

"No. I have your name and number. We're practically engaged."

I chuckled and started stripping off my clothes. "My mum'll be thrilled. Are we getting married here or in London?"

"London, obviously," Jamie said, his hungry eyes watching me as I pulled off my t-shirt and jumper and threw them onto the back of the nearby sofa. He slid one hand across his thigh and palmed his cock through the thin material, letting out a little sigh as he did. "Then we can honeymoon somewhere exotic. Not that the location really matters because we won't spend much time outside. I'm planning on keeping you in bed as much as possible."

"Is that right?" I asked, toeing off my boots and reaching for the button on my jeans.

"Yes." He grinned. "Now fucking get naked and get over here. I'm desperately sex starved."

"It's been three days."

"I know. It's a travesty," he said, sarcasm lacing his words as he watched me strip off the rest of my clothes. He moaned softly as I freed my cock, and I couldn't resist reaching down to slowly pump it. "Fuck, I missed your cock."

"Do you want me to fuck you again?"

"Maybe," he said, his eyes still locked on my cock. "Do you switch?"

"Yes. I'm vers."

"Mmm, this just keeps getting better." He looked up at me and shot me a teasing smile that made my stomach lurch. It made me feel off-balance but not in a bad way. It had been the same on Friday. Whenever I thought I'd figured out something about Jamie, he'd flipped my expectations and thrown me off-kilter.

It was like I was standing on a vibrating balance platform and trying to keep my footing, but if I fell off, I knew the consequences wouldn't be bad. It would just mean this round went to Jamie, and a small part of me didn't mind that.

"Does it?" I asked, trying to school my face into a nonchalant expression. "Do you want to actually ask me the question then, or are you just going to dance around it all bloody evening?"

"Don't you like me teasing you?"

"No."

"But you like teasing me?" he asked with an almost infuriating smile. I wasn't sure if I wanted to kiss him to make him shut up or just make him get on with it.

I walked over to the bed and looked down at him. Jamie was almost at eye level with my cock, and I saw the way his eyes dropped down to it, his mouth falling softly open like he was thinking about sucking it. "Yes," I said. "Because you're fun to tease."

"So are you." He licked his lips, then looked up at me, eyes wide with desire. "Can I fuck you tonight?"

I pretended to think about it for a second. "Yeah, you can fuck me. If you suck my cock first."

Jamie huffed out a laugh. "Oh no, what a hardship."

"I didn't think it would be. You've been staring at it since I came in."

Jamie shrugged and shuffled across the bed, reaching out to wrap his fingers around my shaft, pumping it slowly. "Like I said, you have a fantastic cock, farm boy."

I chuckled. "Is this where I'm supposed to answer 'as you wish' to every request you make?" Jamie raised an eyebrow, and I snorted and shook my head. "Are you seriously telling me you've never seen *The Princess Bride*?"

"Are you seriously asking me about my film knowledge when I'm about to suck your dick?" he asked with what I assumed was supposed to be a withering expression. It didn't work though because I just thought it was cute.

"Apparently so," I said. "But—"

Whatever else I was about to say vanished from my brain as Jamie leant forward and flicked his tongue over the head of my cock before enveloping the silken head with his lips. I groaned as he slowly slid me deeper into his mouth, his fingers covering what he couldn't take until my entire shaft was wrapped in tight heat.

Jamie moaned around me, sending a wave of heat through my body, and I glanced down to see him looking up at me with wide eyes full of want. I reached out and slid my fingers into his hair, gripping it softly in an attempt to anchor myself before Jamie sucked my brain out through my dick. He must have realised the effect he was having on me because I could have sworn he smirked before he started to work my cock.

"Hnngh, fuck… Fuck that's good," I said, unable to tear my eyes away as my shaft slid in and out of his pretty, plush mouth.

Jamie hummed in a way that sounded like, "I know," and if he didn't have a mouth full of cock I was sure he'd be saying it to my face. Usually, I didn't find arrogance attractive, but there was something about Jamie's that turned me on. Maybe it was because I'd seen hints of vulnerability from him too, like when we'd been walking back to the hotel and he'd avoided my questions about his life and the way he'd stared at the boats on the water like he'd never seen them before.

I barely knew enough about him to fill a Post-it Note, but there was something about Jamie that screamed there was more to him than met the eye. I just didn't know if he'd let me dig. Or if I even wanted to. It wasn't like he was going to be around long enough to make it worth my while to get involved, but even though I knew it was probably pointless, part of me wanted to know what was going on under the handsome, carefree picture he showed to the world.

"Shit," I groaned as Jamie sucked me deeper, making it impossible to think about what else might be going on. His fingers caressed my balls, and my hips gave a tiny, aborted thrust. I wanted so much more, but I didn't want this to end either. It was going to have to, though, because I wanted Jamie deep inside me when I came, and soon that wasn't going to be an option.

"Jamie," I growled, my grip tightening on his hair. "Fuck… Fuck, Jamie… I… I'm getting close…"

He pulled back, releasing my cock with a wet pop and looking up at me with a devious smile. "Does that mean you want me to stop?" he asked, wrapping his hand around my shaft and continuing to pump it slowly.

"No, not really. But if you want to fuck me, then you'll have to."

"Why?" He kissed the head of my cock again, sending another ripple of pleasure through me before he added, "You don't have to tell me. I'm just curious. Do you prefer to be hard when you get fucked? Can you not get it up again that quickly? Or did you want to be filled when you come?" He must have seen my face twitch because his smile widened. "Is that it? Do you desperately need to feel my cock inside you when you shoot? Do you like the idea of milking me with your hole? Mmm, I bet you get so tight when you come. God, I can't wait."

"Don't look so fucking smug, posh boy," I said, trying to pretend his pretentious smile wasn't making me even harder. "It doesn't suit you."

"I know it does, though," he said. "And if you didn't like it, you wouldn't be looking at me like that."

"Like what?"

"Like you want to fucking devour me." Jamie tightened his grip on my cock and twisted his palm over the head, making me groan.

What was it about his teasing that made me feel like this? Was it the fact that he wasn't afraid to push my buttons just to see what happened? Or was it because he let me tease him and gave as good as he got in return?

"Why don't you fucking get on with it, then?" I asked as I leant down to brush my lips against his. "You said you wanted to fuck me, so fuck me."

"Are you always this bossy?"

"Comes with the territory when you've got a business to run," I said.

"Does it? I've met some guys who are desperate to get away from being the boss when they have sex. All they want to do is submit and have all their decisions taken away for a while," Jamie said softly, his tone shifting from teasing to thoughtfully serious as if he was trying to ask me if I wanted the same without actually asking the question.

"What are you trying to ask me? You don't need to act coy. I'm a simple man, Jamie. If you want something, just ask."

Jamie pulled back, his eyes searching mine before they narrowed and he looked at me with an emotion I couldn't place. "You're not a simple man, Will."

"Fine," I said, trying not to focus on the way his words had made my chest flutter. "Just be honest with me, please. It makes things so much easier." I gave him a little smile. "Just ask me the question you want to ask."

"Do you like the amount of control you have right now, or do you want to give some up? I don't mind either way, and if you want to submit, even just a little, then you can do that, and I promise I'll make you feel safe," he said as he reached up to brush my jaw. "You don't have to be in control all the time if you don't want to be."

"I... I know..." I swallowed, trying to pretend I didn't feel like I'd just gotten off one of those weird gravity rides that spun you so fast you ended up pinned against the wall. "This is fine, though."

"Are you sure?" Jamie asked. "I won't think less of you or something. It's okay if you want to let go for a bit." He kissed me gently, his thumb running across my jaw. "I won't tell. It'll just be between us."

"I don't... I..." I couldn't even find the words to describe what I was feeling because I wasn't sure I could name the emotions. "I can't..." I said finally.

"Can't what?" Jamie asked, releasing my cock to reach out and tap my thigh, indicating I should climb onto the bed with him. I realised I still stood next to him, bent over with my head in his hand. I straightened, debating for a second whether I should just leave to avoid whatever the fuck this was. But then he gently grasped the back of my thigh, and I found myself sliding onto the bed next to him.

Jamie moved over, and I went with him until we were in the middle of the bed. Then he rolled over until he was blanketing me with his body, his arms on either side of my head as his gaze pierced mine. "Can't what?"

"I can't let go," I said quietly. "It's not possible."

"Yes, you can. And I promise you, it'll help."

"You can't know that." I could never let go, never take a night off, never relax and just be. There was too much at stake in my life for that, and if I took my eye off the ball, even just for a second, there was a chance everything would come crumbling down around me. I couldn't let that happen. My family had struggled for too many generations for me to throw everything away.

I was all that was left. And even if it broke me, I wouldn't let them down.

"True," Jamie said softly, his voice calm and reassuring in a way that soothed the sudden tightness in my chest. "There's a lot I don't know. There's a lot I'll never know. Sex might even be the only thing I'm good at. So please, Will, let me take care of you. Even if it's just this once. And if you want to stop at any point, we can, but trust me. I think you need this."

I looked at him and saw the desire in his eyes. It was laced with concern, but I didn't know why. Maybe… maybe it wouldn't hurt, just this once, to let someone else take the lead.

"Okay," I said with a nod of my head. "What do you want me to do?"

CHAPTER NINE

Jamie

"YOU DON'T NEED to do anything," I said, looking down at the beautiful man underneath me and trying to dismiss the way my heart was aching for him.

I wasn't even trying to dig when I'd first mentioned to Will that I knew several high-flying men who preferred to submit in bed because it gave them a chance to just *be* for a bit rather than have to hold everything together, but his reaction had immediately told me I needed to push just a little. And seeing the way he'd unconsciously tensed, as if his body was fighting every ounce of desire to give in when I'd nudged, had been enough.

I hardly knew Will, but it was already clear to me that he was barely holding everything together. I'd seen it before in men who had crushing responsibilities on their shoulders, and over the years, I'd learnt that sex was one way to lessen their burdens if only for a little while. And selfishly, it gave me a sense of purpose too.

I'd told him sex was the only thing I was good at, which was true unless you counted drinking and spending money like water. But at least helping Will let go for a while actually made a positive difference to someone other than myself, and it wouldn't end with yet another lecture from my father's accountant about my shopping habits.

"Don't think about anything," I continued as I leant down to brush my lips across his. "Don't think about work, or the farm, or what you have to do tomorrow, or anything like that. Just focus on me and the way you feel. Can you do that?"

"Yes," he said. "I can do that."

"Good." I kissed him deeply, revelling in the taste of him and drawing it out until I felt him relax underneath me. "Focus on me and only me."

"What are you going to do?" Will asked as I began to trail kisses down his neck and onto his chest.

"I'm going to take you apart," I said, looking up at him with a teasing smile. "But I suppose you want specifics?" Will nodded. "I'm going to kiss all down this fucking gorgeous body of yours, then I'm going to suck your cock again because I fucking love the way you feel in my mouth, but you're not going to come. I already know you want me inside you for that, so when you're hard and desperate for more, I'm going to spread that gorgeous ass of yours wide and eat your hole. I want to taste you as I get you all wet and loose for me, then I'm going to slide my fingers in deep and stretch you wide because I'm betting you haven't bottomed in a while."

"H-how did you know?" Will asked, his voice catching and his breath already coming in shallow pants as I rolled my hips and brushed my cock against his just to tease him.

"Lucky guess," I said. Because I wasn't going to tell him it was always the same way with men like him who were wound so tightly from everything going on in their lives that they couldn't imagine letting anyone fuck them, even if they wanted it.

Or because the men they hooked up with took one look at them and expected them to exert the same control over them in bed as they did over the rest of their lives. Which never helped and all it did was to make them even more stressed because they had something else to worry about.

"I'm not sure I believe that."

"You don't have to. But I'm not giving you another answer."

"What if I want one?"

"I want doesn't get," I said teasingly, giving him another soft kiss. "Unless you ask *very* nicely. And even then, I'm still not answering you, not now anyway."

"Why not?" Will asked, sounding genuinely curious.

"Because I don't want you to think about that. I don't want you to think about anything except the way I'm making you feel."

Will let out a derisive chuckle. "You seriously want me to stop thinking about everything else?"

"Yes," I said. "I want you to try at least. I know it can be hard at first when you're not used to it—when your whole life is literally just work—but you need to try."

"Fine. But you'll have to distract me."

I grinned at him. "Is that a challenge?"

"I don't know? Is it?"

"Don't push your luck," I said, nipping his lip and soothing it with a kiss. Will gasped, a needy moan escaping his lips, which I filed away for later.

I'd been expecting him to try to push back again, but the playful nip seemed to have distracted him. I smiled as I did it again, drawing another deep moan from Will's mouth. He really did make very pretty noises.

We kissed for a long time, and I didn't mind that this supposedly quick and dirty hook-up had turned into more. There was something electrifying about drawing Will's focus to me, and it wasn't just the usual thrill of taking a man so used to being in charge apart.

I doubted Will had let himself be this vulnerable with anyone in a long time, if at all, and the realisation was both heady and touching. I was barely more than a stranger, so what was it about me that had allowed him to open himself to the idea of giving up control. Was it because I was the first man who'd actually asked him about it? Or was it something more? Something about *me*?

Will moaned softly, the sound drawing my focus away from my self-centred questions and back to the man who needed me. I could think about myself later. Right now, I had to make good on my promise to Will. If he was going to give up even a modicum of control, I needed to show him it was worth it.

I ran my lips down his body, kissing every inch of skin within reach until I reached his hips. His cock had softened during our conversation, but now it was hard against his hip, precum beading at the tip. I hadn't been lying when I said Will had a nice dick. I flicked my tongue out, collecting his precum on my tongue and drawing another groan from deep in Will's throat.

I loved how responsive he was. The more he started to relax, the more noise he made, and I was relishing every tiny gasp and moan.

"F-fuck," Will murmured as I sucked his cock into my mouth for the second time that evening. Some nights, I could take or leave sucking cock, but there was no doubt in my mind that I loved having Will in my mouth. His hands made fists on the bed beside me like he wasn't sure if he was allowed to touch me or not. My lips curled into a smile around his dick because despite his reservations, he was already giving in just a little.

"You can touch me," I said, popping off his cock for a moment and slowly pumping it with my hand. "You can put your hands in my hair, and I don't mind if you pull it either, but you're not allowed to direct me or fuck my throat. You'll get what I give you, okay?"

"Okay." Will nodded, an earnest look in his eyes. It was clear he was enjoying this.

"Good." I kissed the head of his cock again, keeping my eyes on his as I began to take him deep. My many years of sucking cock had done wonders for my gag reflex.

Will moaned as one hand reached out, but instead of my hair, he grabbed my other hand that I'd been resting on his hip. It stunned me for a second because I'd never expected him to want to hold my hand. He interlaced our fingers together, squeezing tightly in a gesture that felt surprisingly intimate.

I wasn't used to intimate. Not in this way.

I shook the feeling off and focused on his dick instead. Now wasn't the time for me to start experiencing all sorts of internal weirdness. I was just there for sex and to make Will feel good, nothing more. And judging from the sounds he was making, I was doing a good job.

"Spread your legs for me," I said. "I want to play with your ass."

Will nodded again, letting go of my hand to spread his thighs wide. I ignored the sudden feeling of loss as he released my fingers and focused on nudging his legs where I wanted them.

"If it's easier, you can roll over," I said. "Whatever is most comfortable for you."

"I... er... I don't mind. What do you..." He trailed off, looking at me with uncertainty. I'd thought giving him an option might help, but now that he'd really started to give in to the idea of me taking the lead, the decision seemed to have thrown him.

"I want you like this," I said, sitting back on my heels and running my finger down the inside of his thigh. "Just lift your legs for me and hook your arms underneath your knees. Good... show off your hole for me. Mmm, I can't wait to be inside you."

My cock throbbed as I looked down at Will, all spread out and on display for me. His hole was rimmed with dark fur, and I was desperate for a taste. I knew once I started, I wasn't going to want to stop until I was buried deep inside him, hearing him moan and beg as I fucked him. And for that, I needed lube.

It was easy enough to retrieve the small bottle off my bedside table before returning to the bed and making myself comfortable between Will's thighs. I trailed kisses down his inner thighs, where the dark hair was softer and finer, until I reached his cock. I gave it a teasing lick as I passed before laving my tongue over his balls. Will groaned, and I smiled to myself.

"If you want to stroke your cock while I get you ready, you can," I said. "But only enough to keep you hard. You're not allowed to get yourself off."

"Is that an order?" Will asked.

"It's a reminder. After all, you were the one who said you wanted my cock inside you when you came. I'm just making sure you get that." I shot him a wink before lowering my head to press a teasing kiss to the furled skin of his hole. Will gasped and swore, but I didn't give him any time to think before I began to eat him out, savouring the earthy taste of him.

I pressed my tongue against the tight ring of muscle, slowly teasing it open. Will groaned, his hips jolting like he was trying to chase the sensation, and when I glanced up, I noticed his head was thrown back and buried in the pillows, one hand fisting the sheets. I reached for the lube and clicked it open, my patience starting to run thin as I poured some onto my fingers. Even though I wanted to fuck him, I wasn't going to rush prepping him.

"Just relax for me," I said, glancing up at him. "Try to bear down. Hopefully the lube isn't cold."

Will gasped as I slowly pressed a finger into him. "Fuck!"

"Good fuck or bad fuck?"

"Good." He chuckled softly. "That lube is bloody cold, though."

"Sorry, but take it from someone who knows that you do not want that warming lube anywhere near your ass. It's like rubbing chilli flakes on your butt."

Will snorted. "I'll take the cold one, then."

"As long as you mean this one and not the one that is supposedly cooling…" I shuddered at that memory, and Will chuckled. "I'm glad you think it's funny."

"Wasn't me who suffered," he said with a note of dry humour in his voice that made my heart fizz like I'd put too many Haribo Sours on my tongue.

"Your sympathy is appreciated." I slowly began to work my finger in and out of him, letting Will get used to the feeling. I adjusted my position so I could keep my eyes on his face, watching his expression for any flash of discomfort, and when I was sure he was ready, I added a second. Will groaned and pressed back onto my fingers.

"J-Jamie…"

"Yes?" I asked softly, my other hand reaching out to tease his cock. I wrapped my fingers loosely around it, providing just enough sensation to drive him wild but nothing more.

"I need… Please, Jamie… I need you inside me."

"Patience." I pressed a kiss to the inside of his thigh. I

wasn't going to rush him because I needed Will to know I could take care of him. That he could let go with me and feel safe. That he didn't have to do anything for me because everything I wanted I got from doing this.

I made Will take three fingers before I considered fucking him, and by that point, I knew neither of us could take much more. I slid my fingers gently out of him, kissing the inside of his thigh before tucking my knees under me so I was kneeling between his legs, looking down at the gorgeous man spread out beneath me. My cock was hard and aching between us, and I quickly added a little more lube to my shaft before guiding it to press against his rim.

"Breathe for me," I said. "It's probably going to burn at first."

"I'll be fine," Will said. "I'm not going to break."

"I know," I said, leaning down to take his mouth in a soft kiss. "But I don't want to hurt you. I told you I'd take care of you, and I meant it."

I sat back so I could watch his face as I pushed inside him at an achingly slow pace. Will exhaled deeply, letting out a deep moan as he took every inch of me. I loved glancing down and seeing my cock inside him. He felt so fucking perfect around me—hot and tight like he was pulling me into him.

"Fuck," Will said. "That... Fuck, that feels good."

I smirked. "It'll feel even better in a second."

Reaching down, I pulled one of his legs up to rest on my shoulder, allowing me to push deeper into him. Will groaned, his cock jumping against his abdomen as I started to grind into him, using small strokes and rolls of my hips to drive him wild.

I turned my head to kiss his calf, running my hand down his thigh to grip his hip as I began to use longer strokes, pulling nearly all the way out, then driving back in. I lifted his hip slightly to change the angle and drag him deeper onto my lap, and Will cursed, his head rolling back on the pillows.

"Do you like it when I hit there?" I asked teasingly, repeating the motion over and over to drive my cock against his prostate.

"Yes! Ugh... It... Fuck, it feels so good."

"Lift your other leg for me." It was a statement not a question. Will nodded and lifted his other leg, and I guided it onto my free shoulder before wrapping my arms around him, one on his thighs and one on his calves. It didn't allow me the biggest range of movement, but it would allow me to fuck and grind against his sweet spot until he couldn't breathe.

Sweat dripped down my skin as I focused all my energy on Will's pleasure. Time seemed to fall away as I lost myself in him. I trailed kisses down his legs as I thrust into him over and over, my senses filled with the sound and sight and smell of us. Heat filled my muscles as my orgasm began to build, the familiar pressure running down my spine as my balls tightened.

"Touch yourself," I growled as my thrusts grew harder and more erratic. "I need to feel you come."

Will groaned and nodded, wrapping his hand around

his cock and starting to jack himself hard and fast, thrusting up into his grip as he chased his release.

"That's it," I said, pulling him deeper onto my cock. "Fucking come for me."

Will's eyes were full of desperation as they met mine, his mouth falling open. He cried out as his hole suddenly tightened around me, squeezing my cock as his body stiffened and ropes of cum painted his skin.

"That's it," I said, my voice low and rough and full of pleasure as I watched him. "Fuck, you look so good when you come."

"N-now you," Will said, gazing up at me with a fucked-out expression that only heightened the heat building inside me. I'd given him that. I'd given him the release he truly needed.

That was all it took to send me hurtling over the edge, growling out my release as I filled him with my cum.

CHAPTER TEN

Will

"YOU'RE ALIVE, THEN?" Lane said, grinning at me from the farmhouse doorstep. He was wrapped in a thick coat with the collar pulled up and a beanie pulled down over his short hair, leaving only his face exposed. Behind him, outside the pool of light cast by the house and the security light above the door, I saw more snow falling.

"What made you think I wasn't?" I asked as I stepped back to gesture him inside before all the heat disappeared out the door.

"You haven't answered your fucking phone in four days. I was getting worried."

I grinned and raised an eyebrow. "Were you? Or are you just here because you want to ask about Jamie?"

"Who?" Lane asked as he shed his coat and hat, hanging them on the rack before toeing off his heavy, steel-capped boots.

"You're a piss-poor liar, you know that?" I sighed, walking into the kitchen to flick the kettle on. Then I thought better of it and went to the fridge to dig out a couple of beers.

We'd had another day of nonstop snow, and it didn't show any signs of letting up. I was tired and stressed, and it didn't help that I couldn't get Jamie off my bloody mind. Monday night had been incredible and had cracked open some doors in my brain I'd bolted and boarded tightly shut so I could pretend they didn't exist.

Now it was Wednesday evening, and it was still all I could think about. I'd have been back to his hotel without a second thought if it wasn't for the snow and my bone-deep exhaustion.

"How long was it before Spencer cracked?" I asked, digging out a bottle opener to pop the tops off the bottles before handing one to Lane.

"Cheers." Lane took a swig and glanced around the kitchen. He really was fucking awful at trying to feign innocence. "How do you know he cracked?"

"It's Spencer. The man's lovely, but he's not great at keeping secrets. If you ask him the right question, he'll crack like an egg, and he won't even realise he's done it."

My guess was Spencer had told his boyfriend, Noah, since I hadn't expressly forbidden him from saying anything and after that his brother, Alex, since they owned the coffee shop together.

Noah was better at keeping things to himself, but he and Alex were thick as thieves so as soon as they realised the other knew, they'd both be talking about it. They'd also both grown up with Lane and Oliver, so Alex had probably told Lane. If I was lucky, it would've just stayed with that lot. But Theo was nosy as fuck, and what he knew Laurie knew too, and then there were Oliver's friends Anders and Bastian, who were both regulars at Novel Tea.

Honestly, that coffee shop was like the spawning site of all our gossip.

"Would it be better if I told you I didn't actually hear it from him?" Lane asked, giving me a half-smile.

I sighed and took a long drink of my beer. "Let me guess, Alex told you?"

"Yeah... Spencer told him and Noah."

"I thought so," I said, scrubbing my face. I didn't know why I was irritated since I hadn't told Spencer not to say anything. Maybe it was because this thing with Jamie wasn't anything more than a fling and would be over as soon as he went back to London.

That thought soured my stomach, and I pushed down the grimace threatening to contort my face.

"You're pissed," Lane said. "Is it because he told us? Or is it because I told you we know?"

"I don't know." I tried to think of how to put my feelings into words because I wasn't even sure what they were.

"Come on." Lane tilted his head in the direction of the living room. "Let's sit down."

I followed him through and carefully stepped over Mog to stick another log on the burner before I sat down. I didn't think she'd moved much all day, especially not since my mum had insisted on bringing her food bowl into the living room so she didn't have to go far when she wanted to eat. That cat was so bloody spoilt it was almost unbelievable.

Lane didn't say anything, he just sat and watched me while I twisted the beer bottle in my hand. "I'm not pissed because he told you," I said eventually. "I don't even care that you know whatever you know." I turned to look at him. "What did Spencer even tell you anyway?"

"Not much," Lane said. "Just that Jamie had come into Novel Tea on Monday and that he'd recognised him. And that he'd asked Jamie if he had your number, which apparently he didn't, so Spencer had asked you if he could give it to him."

"Did he tell Alex that he badgered me into it by calling me when I was out on the moors trying to get hay out of the barn?"

Lane shook his head and chuckled. "No, he skipped that part."

"I figured as much," I said, taking another swig of my beer.

"Does this mean you haven't seen him again since Friday?"

"I didn't say that." I looked over at Lane, and he grinned.

"You had fun then? Let off some steam?"

"Something like that." I wondered how much I should tell him. Lane was my best mate, and we'd talked about a lot of stuff over the years, but I'd always held back a little. It wasn't like I didn't want to share; I just didn't know how. Learning to talk about the farm was one thing but talking about my suppressed sexual fantasies was another. I could barely even admit to myself what I wanted, let alone say it out loud.

Lane raised an eyebrow as he sat back into the cushions, his eyes fixed on me like he was trying to work something out. "Do you want to talk about it?"

"Not really," I said.

"I promise I won't tell a soul," Lane said. "Not even Oliver."

"It's not that. There's not much to talk about really. He'll be going back to London at some point, and that'll be it."

"Do you want him to stay?" Lane asked. "Is there something else going on, or is it just that he's a really good lay?"

"I don't know… definitely the second. Maybe the first. He's just different, that's all. And like I said, it's not really worth thinking about since he's not sticking around."

Lane nodded. "Do you think it's just that the sex is really good and you don't want to go back to shagging your regular hook-ups?"

"Maybe." I chuckled and took another drink. "Maybe it's just because he's been a good distraction since the weather's been so bloody awful."

"It's a pain in the fucking ass," Lane agreed. "I bloody hate snow. I slipped on a patch of ice under the snow this morning while I was walking across the yard. Nearly broke my neck and got a wet ass. Had to get Ollie to bring me some spare boxers so I wasn't sitting around in wet underwear all morning. Do you know what it's like having cold, wet boxers stuck to your balls? It's like sitting on fucking ice cubes."

I snorted. "Not your sort of thing, then?"

"Definitely not." Lane shuddered, then thought for a second, a small smile pulling at his mouth. "Guess it'd be different in bed, though. Like one carefully applied ice cube is not the same as falling on your ass in the stuff. Maybe I'll ask Ollie to see what he thinks."

"Don't let me stop you," I said, and Lane grinned.

"Are you trying to get rid of me? Is Jamie secretly hidden here? You haven't got him tied to your bed, have you?"

"No. I don't think he's the tying down type." I tried not to think about the idea of Jamie tying me to the bed and why that was suddenly making my pulse race. "And I'm not sure if I'll see him again."

The thought of texting him and asking for another round resurfaced like it had multiple times over the past few days. Everything had felt like twice as much work, as it always did in the snow, and it was wearing me down like water on rock.

I had people on all sides needing things from me and pelting me with questions, from Higgs asking about feeding schedules and repairing one of the fences that had come down in last week's wind, to Dylan asking about water supplies for the yard since the pipes were freezing, to my dad asking endless questions about his beloved trio of Highland cows, even though he could just walk down the bloody road and check on them himself.

But ever since his hip replacement last year, my mum had tried to make him be more careful about going out in the ice and snow since one bad fall would be enough to cause him some serious damage, and this year, he seemed to have taken her words to heart. Either that or she'd hidden his boots.

When I thought about Jamie and what he'd given me on Monday, all those voices pulling me in different directions seemed to dull like they were far away. I knew seeing him again would give me another chance just to let go and switch off for an hour or two, but it frightened me. Jamie was leaving, and I didn't want to get attached to him and what he was offering only to have it ripped away.

I knew he had a life to get back to, whatever that was, and it was selfish of me to expect him to give me more. But I didn't know if I'd be satisfied without one more taste.

"Can I ask you something?" Lane said, his voice laced with a soft, serious note.

"Sure."

"Are you happy? And I don't mean just like surface level happy or happy today, but I mean, are you happy with your life? Because these past few months... I know you've said in the past that this job is hard and that you always knew this farm would be yours, but I just... I know it's fucking impossible with a job like this because it's your whole life rather than something you just do day-to-day, but there's more to life than work, Will. I know I've said it before, and I'll probably say it again, but you deserve to be happy, possibly more than anyone I know. And I don't know if you are."

I opened my mouth to tell him everything was fine, that of course I was happy. Why wouldn't I be? Except even in my mind those words sounded like a lie.

Things were fine, good even, and I didn't have anything

to complain about beyond the weather, the stress, and the farm's constant lack of money. But that was the same as normal, so it wasn't anything I wasn't used to. But happy? That I wasn't so sure about. Not anymore.

"I'm fine," I said because it was all I could think to say. "I think I'm just tired at the moment. Winter always takes it out of me, especially when it's like this."

Lane's expression told me he didn't believe me, but he didn't push. Instead, he totally changed the subject and started asking about the dogs and telling me that he was starting to get a little worried about his elderly collie, Sparrow, since the winter was making her stiff and pottery.

I welcomed the change, and we spent another hour just chatting about dogs, the small projects he was working on in the cottage that he and Oliver owned, whether Noah and Spencer would finally actually move in together, and about the upcoming period drama that was supposed to start shooting at the Castle but had apparently been pushed back because of the weather.

When Lane finally stood up and said he needed to get back because Oliver was making dinner, the snow was still falling and was now lying a good couple of feet deep across the garden.

"You going to be all right driving back?" I asked, looking up at the sky and seeing nothing but dense clouds.

"I'll be fine," Lane said. "I'll go slow, and if I run into any problems, I'll give you a call, and you can come tow me out."

"All right. Let me know you get back okay, or I'll spend all night thinking you're stuck in a hedge somewhere."

"I will." Lane pulled me into a hug. "Don't leave it another four days or I'll be back. Just let me know you're alive for Christ's sake so I don't have to worry about you turning into a snowman or something."

I followed him out to where he'd parked his van, waving him off and watching him trundle slowly out onto the drive, heading towards the lane that would lead him back to town.

While I was out, I stuck my head over the dog's stable door to check they were both warm enough. I'd hung an old heat lamp that we'd used in the past for lambs and the litter of puppies Moss had had last spring and smiled when I saw the pair of them snuggled up together in one bed underneath it. They were buried under enough blankets I could only see parts of their faces sticking out. Nell opened one eye and looked up at me but didn't seem inclined to move.

"Good girl," I muttered. "You stay nice and warm in there."

If the weather stayed like this, I'd bring them into the house, and they could sleep in the kitchen since Mog would refuse to share the log burner, but if they were happy in the stable for the night, they could stay there.

My footsteps crunched on the snow as I walked back to the house, my mind half thinking about what to make for dinner while the other half thought about what Lane had said. I wasn't convinced I deserved happiness more than any other person, but I knew he was right that there was more to life than just an endless slog, even if I wouldn't admit it out loud.

And even if Jamie was only here for a little bit longer, maybe I needed to take what I could from him. Maybe it would be okay for me to be selfish for once and think about what I wanted, even if it was only for a couple of hours. It would give me something to hold on to as I approached lambing season—the busiest time of the year, when sleep became a thing of the past.

I leant against the kitchen counter and pulled out my phone, tapping out a message before I lost my nerve.

WILL *What are you doing tomorrow?*

CHAPTER ELEVEN

Jamie

"WHAT THE FUCK are cheese sauce granules?" I muttered to myself as I walked around the large Tesco on the outskirts of Heather Bay, clutching my basket in my hand like it might try to bite me if it got loose. I couldn't remember the last time I'd set foot in a supermarket that wasn't the Little Waitrose down the road from my flat, and even then, it was only when I had a dire emergency.

Michael bought all my food for me, and anything else I needed was acquired by the housekeeper. So why I'd thought it was a brilliant idea to turn up at Will's this evening with dinner was beyond me.

Will had invited me for another hook-up, nothing more, but that still hadn't stopped me from spending all day traipsing up and down the beach deep in thought. I'd never gone to this much effort for a fuck buddy, and I was trying not to look too closely at my reasons for wanting to do something for Will.

I tried to reason with myself that he was likely to be tired and stressed, especially because of the bad weather, and me bringing him dinner would be a nice gesture before I took him to bed and fucked him senseless. Although, given my hideous lack of cooking skills, he might prefer it if we went straight to the latter.

Giving up on the idea of making something from scratch, I wandered across a few more aisles in search of something more suitable.

"Okay, this will do," I said, stumbling across a bay that had some sort of dinner-for-two deal. The choices weren't terrible, so I picked up a main, a side dish, a pudding, and one of the bottles of red wine they had on a nearby rack.

I wondered if I should also get something for a starter, so I continued perusing the aisles until I'd added a couple of bits to make a charcuterie plate, which I didn't think would be too hard to throw together. And if all else failed, we could just eat things out of the packets.

I grabbed another bottle of red wine too, just in case, then stuck a bottle of white in for good measure and in case Will preferred white over red. I'd seen him drinking beer in the pub, and I hadn't bothered to ask much about his likes and dislikes outside of sex. In fact, we hadn't really talked about much at all.

That realisation pulled me up short just as I was shoving things into a newly acquired bag at the checkout.

Despite the fact this had only been an invitation for sex, I was turning it into a date.

I looked at the cashier, who was scanning my second bottle of red wine, as the blood drained from my face. Was it too late to put everything back and pretend this had never happened?

It wasn't that I didn't do dates. I just hadn't done one in a while. I very rarely had long-term boyfriends, and most of the men I hooked up with didn't care if I bought them a drink or dinner first. When I did do dates, they were always firmly on my terms—nice restaurant with good wine, then back to my flat where I could easily turf them out in the morning.

But this… this was completely different, and what made it worse was that I'd done all of it without a second thought. There'd been no consideration about what I'd get out of it, only that it might make Will happy.

Fuck me. What the hell was this place doing to me?

I know I'd said I'd wanted to get away to do some soul-searching, but I'd never expected it to actually happen. Not like this anyway.

In a daze, I paid for my purchases and headed out to the hire car. At some point overnight, it had stopped snowing, but it hadn't warmed up enough during the day to get rid of what had settled. I'd been nervous about driving in it, but I figured as long as I went slowly, I'd be all right, especially because the roads were likely to be gritted. I'd driven a little bit in France in the snow when we'd gone skiing in the past, so it wasn't like I was a complete beginner when it came to difficult road conditions.

Although, I wasn't going to say that out loud because it would probably make me sound like a prat.

Will said the farm wasn't too far out of town but that the road got quite narrow, and the turn could be quite easy to miss. I'd been adamant that I'd be fine and turned down his numerous offers to come to the hotel, mostly because I was nosy about the farm but also because a tiny, rarely used part of my brain had quietly suggested that it was selfish of me to expect Will to finish working, get cleaned up, drive to me, then drive back again when all I'd done today was walk up and down the beach and eat room service while sprawled out on my bed.

I entered his postcode into the car's SatNav, remembering what he'd said about it only getting me in vaguely the right place, and headed out onto the road. The sky was a cold, leaden grey and thick with clouds, and the car dashboard said it was barely above freezing. I was glad the farm wasn't far because for all my bravado, it wasn't fun driving up the narrow roads. The roads in Heather Bay had been fairly clear, but the farther out I got, the more snow was left on the roads.

"Is that it?" I said, bringing the car to a gentle stop as I stared at a gateway between two low stone walls. There was a name-plaque on one side, but the snow had covered half of it. I saw a small cottage a bit farther down the road, and Will had mentioned his parents lived nearby, so I could only assume I was in the right place. If not, hopefully someone here could redirect me.

"It's an adventure," I muttered to myself, carefully turning the car onto the snow-covered drive. It at least had tire tracks for me to follow, so there had to be something here. "God, this is a new one for me. Since when have I ever been *this* desperate?"

The car bumped along the track, occasionally hitting potholes I hadn't even realised were there while I cursed myself for ever leaving London. Nothing like this ever happened in Chelsea.

Eventually, after what felt like forever, I rounded the corner to see a low, stone farmhouse with smoke drifting out of a chimney and light illuminating the windows. There was a Land Rover parked outside it, which I assumed was Will's, so I slipped my little hire car in next to it. There were a couple of outbuildings close to the farmhouse, but when I got out, I saw that the road continued round, presumably to the rest of the farm.

I grabbed the Tesco bag off the back seat and then jumped out of my skin when loud barking erupted behind me. "Shit!" I spun on the spot, nearly losing my footing on the icy stone as I spotted two collies bouncing up and down in a nearby stable.

A door in the farmhouse opened, and a warm, familiar voice drifted out of it. "What are you two barking about?"

"It's just me!" I said, trying to appear vaguely dignified as I walked around the car, hoping I didn't lose my footing and end up on my ass.

"I thought it might be," Will said, standing in the doorway and giving me a gruff smile. He looked more relaxed than I'd seen him before, dressed in a thick jumper, old jeans, and woolly socks, but as I got closer, I could feel the exhaustion radiating off him. "What's with the bag?"

"I brought dinner." I grinned at him. "And wine."

"You didn't have to do that."

"I know, but I wanted to." I stepped up into the doorway and pressed a kiss to his lips. They were chapped and cold, but somehow, I'd never found a pair sweeter. "I thought you might be tired, and this would mean you ate something. You'll need at least a little energy for later."

"Thanks," he said, gazing down at me with the most beautiful deep-chestnut eyes. There were dark circles underneath them that I could've sworn were more prominent than they had been before. Either that or I was horrifically unobservant, but I couldn't be blamed for that since the last time I'd seen him my eyes had gone straight to his cock.

"You're welcome. Can I come in now? It's fucking freezing out here."

Will chuckled and moved to the side so I could slide past him into a surprisingly modern country kitchen. It had a flagstone floor and cream walls with wooden countertops and grey-blue cabinet doors. There was a large, old-looking table in the middle, and beyond that, through a stone archway where two rooms had clearly been knocked together, I saw a small sitting room with a cast-iron log burner whose core was glowing like the inside of the sun.

There was a coat and boot rack on the other side of the door, so I toed my shoes off and hung my coat on top of one of Will's. It stood out starkly against his well-used gear, practically screaming city boy. If I ever came back to the countryside in winter, I'd have to invest in some more appropriate clothing.

"What did you get?" Will asked, finally closing the door

and turning to look at me as I put the Tesco bag on the counter.

"Nothing super special, just one of those Tesco Finest dine-in things, so I don't know how good it'll be, but it's better than my cooking." I pulled out the lasagne and the side of peas with pancetta that I'd grabbed along with the pack of chocolate and orange cheesecake slices. "They didn't do a starter with it, and I wasn't sure if that would be enough food, so I grabbed us a couple of salami and prosciutto selections, some olives, and some cheese. I don't know how good the burrata will be, but I'm sure we'll manage. I got a couple of bottles of red too, one came with the meal deal, and then I got us another. I got white too since I wasn't sure if you drank red."

I looked up at Will, who was giving me a wry smile. "What?" I asked as I emptied the rest of the bag. "Is it too much? Not enough? Oh my God, please don't tell me you'd have preferred a rosé."

"It's great," he said, stepping forward and drawing me into a gentle kiss. "I didn't expect you to go to all this trouble."

"I mean, you did make me step foot in an actual super-market for the first time in years. It was horrible."

Will snorted. "Seriously? Do you just live off takeaway and dinners out?"

"No, I actually have a housekeeper and a personal chef," I said. "I'm a terrible cook, and this way, I actually eat things that are good for me. Although, I do still go out a couple of times a week just for fun. I have so many favourites, and there's always somewhere new to try." I picked up the package for the lasagne and turned it over. "How do you cook this? Do you just have to stick it in the oven?"

"Yeah," Will said, leaning over my shoulder and pointing to a set of instructions. "See? Thirty-five to forty minutes at one-seventy." He plucked it out of my hand and walked over to the large range cooker that sat in the centre of the short wall to my left. "I can't even remember the last time I had dinner out. I mean, sometimes we'll grab a few bits in the pub, but not like a proper dinner."

"Really? Why not?" The idea of not going out regularly baffled me. "Do you just not have good restaurants around here? Surely you must have a few."

"There are some great places round here," Will said. "But even if they're not expensive, I can't afford to drop money on meals out two or three times a week, not when I've got food here. I'll get a takeaway every so often, and sometimes a couple of us will go and grab some food, but it's not something we do regularly. I just can't afford it."

He said it matter-of-factly without any hint of condescension or patronisation, and that almost made me feel worse. He wasn't challenging me or snapping at me just quietly pulling me up and reminding me that not everyone had the same lifestyle I did. I spent so much time in my own world that I forgot sometimes that very few people actually lived like me and that the real world was utterly different from my diamond-encrusted bubble.

"Maybe... maybe if we have time, we could go to one of them?" I asked casually, watching as Will twisted one of the dials on the oven. "I'm here until Saturday... but only if you're not busy. I guess with all the snow you're rather swamped."

Will turned to look at me, his mouth curved into a soft smile that made my heart race. "I'd like that."

"Cool," I said, trying not to focus on the way my face was burning. "Cool. You can show me where's good." I swallowed and looked at the bottles of wine on the counter. "Do you want a drink?"

CHAPTER TWELVE

Will

"Y‍EAH, A DRINK WOULD BE GOOD," I said, trying to push down the strange feeling bubbling away in my stomach. "Why don't you open one of the bottles of red?"

"Perfect," Jamie said. "Where do you keep your wine glasses?"

"Just in there." I pointed at one of the cupboards on the opposite side of the kitchen before grabbing a tray out of the cupboard next to the oven to stick the lasagne on. It might have only been a posh set of ready meals, but I appreciated Jamie's gesture since my plans for dinner had reached as far as seeing what was in the freezer or failing that, cheese on toast.

Seeing him with the Tesco bag had thrown me for a second, and despite Jamie's attempted blasé attitude, it was easy to see he was nervous. Whether that was because he didn't think I'd appreciate him bringing food and think he was overstepping or because he simply wasn't sure I'd like his choices, I didn't know.

But what I did know was that this posh boy from London, who by his own admission didn't know anything about basic life skills, had willingly gone to my local supermarket to make sure I was fed. And there was something about that that made me stop dead in my tracks.

"Here you go," Jamie said, handing me a large glass of wine as soon as I turned around from shoving the food into the still-heating oven. "Hopefully it's okay. It hasn't really had time to breathe, but honestly, I'm far too lazy to decant wine most of the time."

"You'd have a hard time finding something to decant it into here," I said, accepting the glass and giving him a smile over the rim. "Not unless you want to use a vase or something."

Jamie shuddered and took a sip of his drink. "No thank you. Let's avoid all forms of botulism."

I chuckled. "Probably for the best." I lifted the glass to my lips, admiring the deep, rich colour of the wine. I wasn't the biggest wine drinker, but I didn't mind the odd glass when the occasion arose, and this felt like a very fitting one. Jamie was watching me carefully but in a way that desperately tried to suggest he wasn't.

"What do you think?" he asked in a faux casual tone as I took a long sip.

"It's good," I said, nodding. "I like it. You have good taste."

"That has been said." He grinned, visibly relaxing again. "On more than one occasion. Apparently, I also have expensive tastes, at least according to my father's accountant. He and I don't exactly see eye-to-eye."

Looking at Jamie, I could well believe that, but I wasn't going to spoil the evening by saying it. I got the feeling Jamie already knew that he lived a life most people could barely dream of. Or at least, he was starting to realise it.

"Oh, aye?" I asked casually.

"Yes. Apparently, my spending habits would rival even Kim Kardashian. Although I think there are a lot of people who'd give me a run for my money, but apparently, that argument is pointless. Even if I did say he should attempt to go shopping with my best friend, Daisy, one day to put my habits into perspective. I have never seen anyone spend so much money on shoes, and that's coming from me."

"I think I own about four pairs of shoes," I said with a grin. "No, wait, maybe five. I'm sure I've got a pair of smart shoes somewhere that Mum made me buy for my grandad's funeral a couple of years ago."

"I think I brought more pairs than that in my suitcase," Jamie said. "They've all been awful in the snow, though. I've nearly ruined my Bottega boots."

"I don't even know what that is." I'd never been into clothes or fashion in any way, shape, or form. Clothes were clothes to me; they just did a job. The only thing I ever spent good money on was work boots because decent boots were a lot more comfortable and lasted a hell of a lot longer. I'd learnt that very quickly as a teenager when I'd bought a pair of boots for the bargain price of twenty quid and gone through them in two weeks.

"It's a brand. A very expensive one." Jamie glanced

down at his wine, looking almost contemplative. "Sorry, you must think I'm a right fucking bore. You invited me over to fuck, and all I've done is stand here and bitch about money and shoes. I must sound like such a twat."

"A bit," I said, stepping a little closer to him. I put my arm around his waist, drawing him against me. "But you're fine. You're like a little frog outside your pond for the first time, and it's quite funny seeing your view on the world."

"A frog? Seriously?" He was smiling now, and that was all I'd wanted.

"Do you want to be a fish instead?"

"God no, I don't want to be either."

"Fish or frog, take your pick."

"Fine, I'll be a frog," he said, his mouth forming a grumpy pout. "But only because I don't get any other options."

I laughed because I'd never seen a pout look so attractive, not even on Theo who'd made it into an art form. "Don't pout, posh boy. It doesn't suit you."

"Then why are you staring at me?" Jamie asked, his lips curling into a smirk.

"Because I'm trying to work out why a grown man is pouting," I said, leaning down to brush my lips against his in a teasing kiss.

"You just told me I was a frog. What did you expect?"

"I'm not sure, but you're cute either way." I deepened the kiss, tasting the wine on his mouth. It was rich and full-bodied with an underlying note of spice and something that suggested it was expensive.

"You think I'm cute?" Jamie asked. He'd barely pulled away, and his lips kept caressing mine as he spoke.

"I do. I wouldn't have said it otherwise."

Jamie hummed. "Are you always this honest?"

"Mostly," I said, "but not always. I'm honest as long as it's not going to hurt people. I hate it when people use being honest as cover for being a right twat. There's just no need for it." I tilted my head back to look down at him, studying his expression. "Why do you ask? Do you think I'm lying?"

"No... It's just..." He grinned and shook his head. "I just don't think I've been called cute before."

"Really?"

"Yeah. I'm usually the one calling people cute."

"Well, now it's my turn," I said. "You are cute, Jamie. And handsome. And bloody sexy too."

"Thanks." He glanced down for a second, the bridge of his nose tinting slightly. "You're sexy as fuck too." He leant in and kissed me again. It was soft and lazy—the sort of kiss that didn't have any goal except to be enjoyed.

"If you hadn't put dinner in, I'd suggest we go upstairs," he said. "Or I can blow you right here. I'm not picky. I can make you come by the time everything's ready."

It was tempting, especially imagining Jamie on his knees in front of me. But hard, cold flagstones weren't the best to kneel on for any length of time beyond a few seconds, and since he'd gone to so much effort to organise all the food, I didn't want to let it go to waste. Besides, I was curious about spending time with him outside of a sexual setting.

This was the closest thing I'd had to a date in years, and there was a small part of me that wanted to enjoy it, even if it would only be just once.

At least this way when my friends asked me when I'd last been on an actual date, I'd have an example to throw at them.

"It's tempting," I said. "But no."

"Seriously?" Jamie's eyes were wide with surprise. "You're seriously turning down a blow job right now?"

"Yeah, I am." I sipped my wine again and smirked. As much as I'd enjoyed letting Jamie take control when we fucked, I wasn't going to let him win everything. I didn't think either of us would like it.

"Why? I mean, you're fully within your rights to do so, and I'm not going to push, but I'm just curious."

"Never been turned down before?"

"Not recently," he said. "A few times in the past but not for a while. Then again, I usually spend time with men whose sole desire is to get laid."

The more I heard about his life, the lonelier it sounded. Did Jamie really only spend time with rich, vapid assholes and men who wanted to fuck him, filling his days with nothing but spending money and partying? To each their own, I supposed, but it just sounded so empty. My life might have been hard and stressful and exhausting, but I wouldn't change it. Even on the days when I was *this close* to giving up.

"You brought all that food," I said, diverting away from my thoughts about Jamie's life. "Would be a shame to waste it."

"You know it'll keep."

"I know. But I want to eat it with you."

"Okay… Yeah, let's do that." He sounded completely stunned like he couldn't fathom the idea of me wanting to spend time with him like this. "Do you want me to make a board? Or a plate will do… Do you have…"

"Let's just eat it out of the packets," I said, giving him a soft kiss before stepping away to reach for the wine bottle. "You open everything, and I'll see how long those peas need."

"I might need a plate for the burrata," he said. "It doesn't really work in the tub."

"Sure." I walked over to the other side of the kitchen, pulled a small side plate out of the cupboard, and handed it to him. Jamie nodded and turned back to the counter to start opening everything while I grabbed the peas and flipped the packet over, quickly scanning the instructions. It wouldn't take long, so I could just stick them in the microwave before the lasagne was ready.

"That looks good," I said, casting my eyes over the immense selection of food Jamie had laid out. It was more like a mini banquet than a starter for two.

"Good. I wasn't sure it would be enough as I was walking round, but now I'm wondering if it's too much."

I chuckled. "Don't worry. It'll keep." I reached over and plucked a piece of salami out of one of the packets, popping it into my mouth. Jamie did the same, although his eyes were still fixed on me.

"When did you say you go back to London?" I asked as

I reached for one of the delicate slices of prosciutto. One day, I wanted to go to Italy and eat as much as I could find.

"Saturday afternoon," Jamie said. "I only booked a week. I thought that would be enough."

"For what? Or am I not allowed to ask?"

"You are, but I'll warn you now, it'll sound ridiculous when I say it out loud."

"Even more ridiculous than the fact you've never been to Tesco?" I teased, giving him a sly wink as I reached for the burrata. The cheese was so soft and creamy it had easily fallen apart, and even though Jamie had brought some posh toasted crackers for it, I ignored them in favour of picking up a bit with my fingers. Jamie stared at me as I licked the rich, salty cheese off my finger, his mouth open in a soft *O* like he'd forgotten what he was about to say.

"I... er... You're very distracting when you do that."

"Do what? I'm just eating cheese."

"Don't be a twat," he said, a new note of fondness in his voice. "You know exactly what you're doing." He gestured at the posh crackers. "I bought those to eat with the burrata."

"I know, but I don't want one."

"You're a menace to society," he muttered, rolling his eyes, but the warmth in his expression was unmissable.

"I think that's you," I said as I picked up more of the cheese. "Come on, tell me about this ridiculous reason that made you leave London."

CHAPTER THIRTEEN

Jamie

WATCHING WILL EAT charcuterie in the most sexual way imaginable, I was having a hard time putting my thoughts in a coherent order, let alone finding a way to voice them. I was never going to allow Will near cheese again.

"Everything was starting to feel pointless," I said, tearing my eyes away from Will to look down into my glass of wine. Then I wouldn't have to see the disdain on his face when I inevitably sounded like a spoilt prick. "I don't know why. I just started to feel hollow. Nothing really appealed anymore."

I sighed and took a long sip of wine, trying to figure out my next words. Despite the fact I'd come to Heather Bay to figure this shit out, I'd gotten no closer to the source of my emptiness. Maybe it was because I hadn't actually tried. For all my insistence that this week would be about self-reflection, I'd done very little. The prospect was too painful to consider because I wasn't sure I'd like the outcome if I actually started looking at myself and my life with a critical eye.

"How do you mean?" Will asked. "In a bored of your routine kind of way or in a life is pointless kind of way?"

"Is there a difference?" I asked, attempting to play off the moment with levity, but when I glanced up, Will looked more serious than I expected.

"Yeah, actually, there can be a big one."

"I suppose it's more of the boredom one," I said as I mulled the question over. "My life is the one everyone wants, but I'm bored of it. I'm bored of the parties and the clubs and the endless hedonism, which isn't a phrase I ever thought I'd say aloud, but... I am. Everything just feels the same, and I'm tired of it. I want something different... something more. I just have no idea what that is or how to find it. It's not something I can just walk into Selfridges and buy, although it would be so much easier if I could."

"Purpose," Will said quietly. "You're looking for purpose, something to give your life meaning. To give you a reason to get out of bed in the morning."

His answer caught me off guard because it was so simple and yet so stunningly true. The closest I'd ever had to a purpose was being good at sex and making my partners feel good, but I doubted that counted. "Yes, I suppose I am. But, like I said, I don't think I can just walk into a shop and hand over my credit card to acquire some."

"No, not really." Will shook his head, his lip twitching, and I wondered what he was thinking.

"Well, if you have any advice on how to find a purpose, I'm all ears."

"I don't know if I'm the best person to talk to."

"Why not? You seem to have an abundance of the stuff. Doesn't farming give you purpose?" I frowned, unsure where I'd gone wrong in my thinking. Was there a hidden stumbling block I'd missed?

"It does, and I wouldn't change it, but there's a difference between getting to choose what you do and where you go in life and having it chosen for you." He looked at me with such a heart-breaking expression that I felt my chest clench.

"You're rich, Jamie, so rich I don't think you even understand how much most people would kill for what you probably spend on a night out. Now, I'm not judging you for it because that's not for me to do, but you've never had to do a day's work in your life, and if it wasn't for this sudden crisis of faith, you'd probably never have to. And that means you get to choose what you do with your life, with the unconscious knowledge that you have the money and freedom to do whatever you want because even if it goes wrong, it's not going to be the be all and end all. You can just try again and spend your time finding something you enjoy doing without having to worry about whether it makes you money or not because you don't have the threat of bills and financial insecurity hanging over your head."

Every word of what he was saying rang clearer than a bell, and even though, deep down, I'd known it all along, it was like I was hearing it for the first time.

A small part of me wanted to be angry and lash out like a wounded animal backed into a corner, but the rest of me knew there was no point in fighting. What would I be fighting about? The fact that I hated that every word Will was saying was true? Or was it the fact that he'd turned a spotlight on my life, shining a light into all the dark crevices I'd ignored.

"You can hate me for saying it," Will continued, clearly expecting a certain reaction. "And whether that would be right or wrong of you isn't for me to say. But you have to understand that most people don't get the choices you do and that most of us have to weigh up a lot more factors before we make decisions about our lives. For some of us, there aren't even that many options: it's do this or perish. Nobody's coming to our rescue if we don't."

"You said you wouldn't change it," I said. "The farming. But does that mean it isn't something you wanted? Sorry, I know I must sound like I'm trying to avoid your point, but I'm just... Fuck..."

I knew I sounded ridiculous. How could I not? How could I have gotten to this point in life without going through any of these realisations? Had my bubble of privilege protected me to the point that I couldn't even see outside it anymore?

I didn't need to answer that question. I already knew it was true. I'd always been so wrapped up in my life that I'd never stopped to really consider how different things were for other people outside the superficial differences I could judge in the blink of an eye. It was so easy to assume everyone had the same level of choice as the people in my social circle when the reality was anything but.

Maybe that was why so many of the people I knew were so judgemental of the rest of the world. They just assumed everyone's reality was the same, and that a lack of "success" was someone's fault for not trying hard enough.

I was starting to understand what people meant when they said eat the rich.

Will grimaced, picking up a couple of plump green olives and popping them into his mouth one at a time. "It's complicated."

"Can you explain it? Please."

"Are you sure? It's a heavy topic for an evening that was just supposed to be about food and sex."

I chuckled. "Seems a bit late to stop now. You've already pointed out my staggering inability to grasp the way the world functions for everyone outside my champagne bubble, so we might as well keep going. Then we can drink all the wine and fuck to forget all our problems. It's always worked for me."

Will huffed out a laugh and shook his head. He walked over to the oven and opened the door to check the lasagne. I poured the rest of the first bottle of wine into our glasses and helped myself to a couple slices of salami. For all the heaviness of the conversation, I felt weirdly liberated.

This was a discussion I'd never expected to have, and yet here I was with a man whose warm, gruff charm belied the way he seemed to be able to see straight through me and cut through my carefully composed exterior with a verbal accuracy that could only be compared to the sharpest precision of Japanese kitchen knives.

"This farm has been in my family for generations," Will said eventually. "My father ran it and before that his father, and his father before him, and at least another two generations before that. Every one of them has had their struggles, but the farm is still here, and it even belongs to us now since my great-grandfather managed to cobble the money together to buy it off the Hareford family when they were on the verge of bankruptcy and sold off the land to make ends meet."

"It's an impressive legacy," I said.

"Aye, it is. And there's always been a Foster on this farm, and I won't be the one to break that chain."

"Don't you have other family who could take it over?"

"No. I'm an only child since having me was enough of a struggle for my parents, and although I've got a couple of cousins, only a couple are interested in farming, and one already runs one down in the Dales. With my parents getting on in years, it's mostly on me to keep the place running," Will said. "I could have walked away, and I won't lie, I considered it once or twice, but I don't know what else I'd do with my life. Farming is in my blood."

I nodded, still wrapping my head around what he'd said. I knew plenty of people with family businesses but none that had been built like this one had—with blood, tears, and sheer stubbornness. Finally, I said, "Can I ask you something?"

"You'll find a way to ask it anyway," Will said, a glimmer of dry humour in his voice. "Might as well ask it now."

"What made you want to walk away? Was it just the money? The amount of work?"

"No... It was seeing the way it broke my father." He sighed and took a long sip of his wine like he was considering whether to continue. "Do you remember the foot-and-mouth outbreak back in 2001?"

"Maybe?" I tried to search my memory for something that fit, but nothing came to mind.

"I was nearly eleven," Will said. "I don't remember much about the start, but I remember Dad being worried. Then it started spreading across the country. It's highly infectious you see, so it spreads quickly and is easily transmissible. Mostly it affects cloven-hoofed stock, so cows, sheep, pigs, goats, things like that. The government shut down rights of way, livestock sales, and then they started culling."

I could see where this was going, and I knew it was going to break my heart. I almost didn't want to hear Will say it.

"We didn't have any cases here, but it was a contagious cull policy, so any animals within a couple miles of known cases would be slaughtered to prevent the spread. Dad brought everyone in, but then we got word there was a case at Long Hill, just up the road, and that was it. Mum made me stay in the house when they came, but they burned all the bodies on-site, piled them up in a trench Dad had to dig and made a pyre... Sometimes I can still smell it on the wind..." His voice trailed off, the matter-of-fact tone he'd started off with replaced by one full of sorrow.

I put my arm out and pulled him into a hug, squeezing him as tightly as I could manage. "I'm so sorry," I said. "That must have been horrific."

"The worst part was afterwards," Will said. "Couldn't buy any more sheep to start with, and everything had to be deep cleaned. And my dad just... He withdrew. It was like there was nothing there. I know now he was depressed, but back then I was so scared and confused. In the stroke of two months, everything changed, and I didn't know if he was going to come back."

"Did he get help?" I asked quietly. "Did you?"

"Me? No, I was just expected to be good and help out where I could. Dad, yeah eventually. I think my mum eventually told him that she'd already lost the farm, she wasn't going to lose him too. They don't really talk about it, at least not to me." He was still wrapped in my arms, his head resting on my shoulder. "That was the thing that made me want to walk away—the idea that everything could be taken away so quickly and leave nothing behind but ash. I didn't want to get my heart broken again."

"Then what made you stay?"

"My parents rebuilt this farm into what it is today. I still remember the first lambing two years after we lost everything, and I remember my dad giving me one to hold that he'd had to bring in and telling me this was our legacy. That we had to hold on to it and take care of it, no matter what happened. And I wasn't going to end that. It might not make sense to you, but it's something I won't change." He lifted his head, a tiny smile curling at the corner of his mouth. "I'm a stubborn bastard, and whether I like it or not, this place is mine to protect, so I'm going to do just that."

"You're an incredible man, Will Foster. I don't know many people who'd do what you do."

"You stay round here and you'll meet plenty of them," he said. "I'm nothing special."

He kissed my forehead and slowly pulled away, walking over to the oven to check on our food while a new sensation bubbled in my chest.

Will might not have thought he was special, but I did. It was clear his family's legacy weighed heavily on his shoulders, a crushing pressure he refused to give in to. He was the complete opposite of me in so many ways, and I was utterly intrigued.

And as he bent down to retrieve our dinner from the oven, I already knew I didn't want to go back to London. There was something about Will pulling at my heart, and I wasn't leaving until I figured out what it was.

CHAPTER FOURTEEN

Jamie

I WAS HELLISHLY DEEP in a vivid dream about being on *MasterChef*, sweating with fear while trying to prepare a five-course meal, when an alarm sounded from somewhere behind me. That was odd because I never set an alarm, and when I cracked my eyes open, the whole room was pitch black.

It was also cold as fuck. I wiggled deeper under the thick duvet, almost wishing I'd had the sense to put clothes on when Will and I had finished fucking late last night. I hadn't been expecting to stay, but after dinner we'd ended up watching *The Princess Bride*—since Will thought I needed educating—and making out lazily on his sofa.

By the time we'd dragged ourselves upstairs to fuck, it had been late, and Will had refused to let me leave afterwards because he'd said it was dangerous for me to drive back in the dark and the snow. And considering how little

I'd enjoyed driving up to the farm in the first place, I hadn't been about to argue with him.

"S'okay, go back to sleep," Will said gruffly from beside me. He was still naked, his body radiating warmth as I slid myself across the small gap between us and wrapped my body around his.

"Or you could stay here," I said, pressing a kiss to the back of his neck. What was the fun of waking up naked if we didn't take advantage of it? "It's still dark, and it's fucking freezing. You should stay here and fuck me instead."

Will rolled over, pushing me onto my back and lying half-across me. His soft cock was hot against my thigh, and I knew it wouldn't take much to get him hard. It would be so easy for him to slide inside me and fuck me deep and slow the way I was craving.

"I could," he said as he leant down to brush his lips against mine. "But I have sheep to feed, and they won't wait just so you can get laid."

"How rude of them." I wrapped my arms around his neck, pulling him against me. "I can't even convince you to let me jerk you off?"

"Mmm, it's tempting, but no." He kissed me softly. "Go back to sleep. It's only half five. I'll come back in a few hours and fuck you then."

"Half five?" I groaned as Will climbed off me, throwing the duvet off so he could climb out of bed. "No, I refuse to believe it. That's an utterly absurd time of day to get up."

"That's why I told you to go back to sleep," he said with

a soft chuckle. "I'll just grab some clothes and get dressed in the bathroom."

"No, it's fine. I'm awake. And if you're going to walk around naked, it would be rude not to let me watch."

Will chuckled again and flicked on the small lamp beside the bed before standing. He didn't seem to notice the cold as he walked over to a large chest of drawers and began fishing things out, his body illuminated by the soft glow of the lamp.

Sitting up enough to get a good view, I watched him closely and pulled the duvet close around me, trying to draw every smidgen of warmth out of it. This situation was so unfamiliar to me. I'd had hook-ups get up and leave first thing but never this early. And it had always been them leaving my house, not leaving me *in* their house.

"Are you okay with me staying here?" I asked, suddenly unsure. "Would you rather I left before you came back?"

Will looked over his shoulder and raised an eyebrow. "No, I want you to stay. I'm not turfing you out. Besides, I said I'd fuck you when I got back, and I thought that was what you wanted?"

"It is… I'm just…" I sighed. "Ignore me, I'm still half-asleep."

"Stay," Will said softly, walking around the bed to kiss me and still holding a pair of boxers in one hand. "You're not intruding, and it's not weird. I promise."

"As long as you're sure."

"I wouldn't have said it otherwise."

"I'm not convinced," I said with a wry smile. "I think you're too polite to tell me to fuck off."

Will snorted. "If you say so, posh boy." He kissed me again and stood up, starting to get dressed. As he walked back to the chest of drawers, he passed the window and stopped to look out between the curtains. "I don't think you'd be leaving anyway."

"Why? Has the apocalypse arrived?"

"No, just another two foot of snow."

"You're shitting me." I stared at him, convinced it had to be a lie.

"I'm not," he said, turning away from the window, his mouth set into a hard line. "I'll try and be back as soon as I can, but it might take me a while. I'll have to help Dylan with the yard as well as doing the rounds. We'll need to clear the drive too."

"It's fine," I said. "Just do what you need. I'll be here."

I watched him pull on the rest of his clothes, wondering whether I should offer to help. I didn't exactly have a suitable wardrobe for the occasion, but I was sure I could borrow a coat. And even I could lift a shovel or something. Did you even use shovels to move snow?

"I've got my phone if you need me," Will said, leaning over the bed to give me a quick kiss before he headed towards the door.

"Stay safe," I called as the door closed, then I heard his footsteps echoing on the landing and down the stairs. Will had left the lamp on, but I didn't lean over to turn it off. Instead, I just slid across to his side of the bed and buried myself in the duvet, breathing in the scent of him on the pillows while I let my gaze linger on the room.

It was simply decorated with plain cream walls and

wooden furniture. There were a few trinkets here and there, and a stack of books on a small bookcase, but no pictures on the walls or massive personal touches. It was clean and tidy too without even a stray t-shirt lingering on the floor. The room felt almost unlived in. Maybe Will was so busy he only viewed his room as a place to sleep and occasionally fuck, but to me, it felt like a reflection on Will's life, practical but empty of joy and love.

If I lived here, I thought as I sank back into the pillows, sleep threatening to pull me under, I'd have to fix that.

When I woke again, the room wasn't any warmer, but there was now light in the gap between the curtains where Will had peered out earlier. The old alarm clock on the bedside table said it was nearly eight, which seemed like a more reasonable time to get up, even if I usually considered it far too early.

My one problem was that I hadn't brought anything with me except food.

I could stomach wearing most of the same clothes as yesterday, but I drew the line at rewearing underwear. I had some standards.

Scooting quickly across to the other side of the bed, I grabbed my phone and returned to the warm bit I'd been snuggled in. Will had said he'd be back in a few hours, but I could only guess what time that would be, and I thought it would be rude to still be in bed when he got back. I could at least attempt to make myself presentable.

JAMIE *Random question, but can I borrow some underwear, please? I don't have anything with me. Hope you haven't frozen to death yet!*

I wasn't expecting an instant response, so I scrolled through social media while I waited, casually liking various pictures from bars, clubs, and restaurants as well as Daisy's newest handbag and some photos from her recent trip to Verbier. I noticed she hadn't posted about her boyfriend recently, and I was really hoping she'd seen sense and dumped him. She deserved so much better.

As I was pondering Daisy's romantic life, another message flashed up on the screen.

WILL *Sure, help yourself. They're in the top drawer. If you need anything else, t-shirts are in the second drawer and jumpers in the bottom. Not frozen yet but might be soon. Should be back in about an hour for a bit.*

JAMIE *Thanks! I'll see you soon. Do you want breakfast?*

WILL *I can just grab some toast or something.*

Toast didn't really seem like it would be enough, and I was sure it wouldn't be that hard for me to throw together something a little more substantial. It didn't have to be Michelin-star worthy just edible. I didn't want to be responsible for Will getting food poisoning.

But that did mean I'd have to get out of bed…

"Fuck, it's cold," I grumbled as I slid out from under the thick duvet, practically sprinting across to Will's chest of drawers to retrieve some clean underwear. We were about the same size, so I grabbed a pair of soft blue boxer-briefs and a thick pair of socks, pulling them on at a record pace. I dragged my jeans on, hopping up and down to pull them over my frozen thighs. Then I paused.

I'd worn a stylish grey cashmere jumper last night, and while it was absolutely gorgeous in the most understated and elegant way, it wasn't the most practical or warm. If the rest of Will's house was as cold as his room, I was going to need something thicker. Especially if I planned on venturing outside.

Opening the second drawer, I found a selection of t-shirts and folded shirts. Will was a little broader in the shoulders than me, but with a bit of digging I found a black t-shirt that fit reasonably well and would be fine as a base layer, especially tucked into my jeans.

The bottom drawer was a pain the ass to open, but eventually, I heaved it out far enough to see a few thick, woolly jumpers all wedged together. I grabbed a chunky, cable-knitted one in dark green, which had little flecks of colour splattered throughout the wool. It was a bit big, but hopefully it would be in a stylish way rather than making it look like I didn't know how to dress myself.

Finally dressed and feeling a little warmer for my efforts, I shoved my phone into the pocket of my jeans and headed downstairs, making a quick pit-stop in the bathroom as I went.

The ground floor was considerably warmer, and I assumed Will had relit the log burner before he left. I stuck my head into the living room to check, and sure enough, there was a fiery glow dancing in the burner's little window. The grey cat that had been there last night was still stretched out in front of it, and I wondered if she'd actually moved.

"Mog," I said softly, hoping I was remembering her name correctly. "Mog! Are you alive? Shit, please tell me you aren't dead."

I watched to see if she was breathing, but it was virtually impossible to tell from this angle. I shuffled forward a step or two, intending to give her a gentle nudge to check for signs of life. As I bent down, praying that I wouldn't have to break the news to Will that his cat was dead, Mog lazily opened one eye, staring at me with clear disdain.

"You could have moved," I hissed. "Or, you know, breathed visibly."

Mog huffed and closed her eyes, clearly over this very one-sided conversation. I stood and looked at the fire. It seemed like the logs on it were starting to burn out, but I didn't know whether I needed to put another one on the fire or not. There were a few in a nearby basket, but I didn't know whether they were for the burner or something else.

I'd just have to wait for Will and ask.

Walking back to the kitchen, I tried to think about what I could easily make for breakfast. Will had said he'd just make toast, so I assumed he had bread somewhere. And I saw a few eggs sitting on the windowsill in a wire basket shaped like a chicken.

How hard would it be to make scrambled eggs? I hadn't made them before, but surely it wouldn't be that difficult to figure out.

I pulled my phone out of my pocket, thinking through my options for a second before I tapped a couple of buttons.

"Hello?" Daisy's voice was thick with sleep and full of surprise. "Jamie? You okay?"

"How do you make scrambled eggs?" I asked, putting the call on speaker as I walked up and down the kitchen trying to work out where Will kept the bread.

"Did you seriously wake me up to ask about scrambled eggs? I thought you were staying in a hotel?"

"I am."

"Then why are you making your own breakfast? Just ask the chef to do it."

"I'm not at the hotel," I said as I lifted the lid on a large, rectangular metal tin and found half a loaf of soft-looking white bread inside.

"Where the fuck are you then, darling?" She gasped. "Oh my God, Jamie. You didn't have to go self-catering did you? Because I would literally die if that happened to me. Don't you remember that awful mix up when Totty and I went to Ibiza? I swear, I will never let her book another holiday again."

"No, it's nothing like that. I just... I met this guy, and I stayed at his house last night. I thought it might be nice to make him breakfast."

"That's awfully sweet of you," she said. "But isn't that what the housekeeper's for?"

"He doesn't have one."

"Seriously? Who doesn't have a housekeeper? He's not, like... poor, is he?"

I frowned, an uncomfortable feeling rising in my chest.

Daisy was my best friend, and I knew her definition of *poor* was basically anyone with a net worth of less than several million, but the way she'd said it... "He's a farmer."

"Jamie, are you sure you're okay?" she asked. "I know you said you wanted to, like, find yourself, which I totally get—it's why Binky and I are going to Bali next week—but, like, you're acting so weird. Do you need me to call someone?"

"I'm fine," I said. "I'm sorry, just forget I called."

"No, please just tell me what's going on. I'm so worried about you." I heard the concern in her voice, and maybe she actually meant it. I hadn't exactly told anyone why I was disappearing for a week beyond vague phrases of needing space and finding myself.

"I promise I'm okay. I was just feeling super cooped up and getting bored, and I wanted a change of scenery—somewhere completely different—and it's been good. I've been doing some thinking, some exploring, and I met this guy."

"Oh my God, is it serious? Are you thinking of moving there?"

"No, I just... I've barely known him a week. But he's working this morning because there's been a lot of snow, and I wanted to do something nice for him when he gets back. I can't do much, but I figured I could make breakfast or something."

Daisy let out this soft sighing sound. "That is the sweetest thing ever, Jamie. Oh my God. That's like Hall-mark-level romantic. But you can't even cook."

"I know. That's why I rang you."

"But I can't cook either."

"I thought you had to learn at school?"

"Yeah, but that was stupid things like fruit salad and cake and, like, pizza," she said offhandedly as my hope for help disappeared down the drain. "Just Google it or something. I bet you can find something on TikTok or Insta."

Why the fuck hadn't I thought of that already? It hadn't even crossed my mind, even though I'd seen videos of people making things hundreds of times. It had just never clicked.

"I'll do that," I said as I glanced out the window and looked at the crisp, glittering white world outside. It looked gorgeous, but that didn't mean I wanted to go anywhere near it. "And don't worry about me. I promise everything is great."

I chatted with Daisy for a few more minutes while she told me about her next trip and bemoaned the cold, and I promised to catch up with her soon. When she hung up, I looked at the loaf of bread in my hand, my mouth setting into a firm line.

Seriously, how fucking hard could it be to make scrambled eggs?

CHAPTER FIFTEEN

Will

THE SMELL of something burning hit my nostrils before I'd even opened the kitchen door.

"What the hell?" I muttered, throwing the door open and stepping inside, not even remembering to remove my boots as I stared at the chaos before me.

Jamie stood in front of the hob, prodding at something in a pan that was smoking. There was some blackened toast sticking out of the toaster, and there was a small puddle of water around the kettle where it had been overfilled. There were at least three dirty bowls on the side with another two saucepans in the sink and a pile of eggshells on the counter next to the open tub of butter.

"What on earth… What happened?" It looked like a fucking bomb had hit my kitchen, and I had no idea how one man had managed to make this much mess.

"Funny story," Jamie said, turning to me with a sheepish

grin. "It turns out scrambled eggs are not as easy to make as the BBC Good Food website would have you believe."

I stared at him. "You tried to make scrambled eggs?"

"*Tried* being the important word there. I, er, I thought you might be hungry when you came back, and I wanted to make you something more substantial than toast. I didn't think it would be this difficult." He prodded the burnt, misshapen lumps in the pan in front of him. "Sorry."

He sounded totally bereft, and it reminded me of the time when I was seven and had tried to make Mum breakfast in bed for Mother's Day. I'd done my best, but that had also involved two broken plates and a bottle of milk going all over the kitchen. And considering Jamie had openly admitted he had no idea how to cook, I couldn't be mad at him for trying.

"It's fine," I said as I gathered my wits about me. "Turn that hob off and let's clean up, then I'll teach you." I reached down to unlace my boots, leaving them on the mat and hanging my coat on the rack. I hadn't anticipated adding teaching basic cooking skills to my to-do list for the morning, but what was one more thing.

"You don't have to. You're busy, and I don't want to make more work for you. Even though I suppose I already have." He sighed, and it was only then, as I walked across to him, that I registered what he was wearing.

"You borrowed my jumper," I said.

"I hope you don't mind. I thought it would be warmer than mine since your house is freezing. Also, I wasn't sure if I needed to put more logs on the fire. I think it was still burning, but I'm not the best judge."

"It's fine. It looks good on you." It was one my mum had knitted for me a couple of years ago, and I wore it a lot in the winter because it was warm and comfortable and long enough in the torso that I didn't get a cold breeze rushing up my back when I bent down.

It was a deep forest green with speckles of colour dotted throughout, and I remembered how excited my mum had been when she'd found the wool in the craft shop in town because she'd always loved including pops of colour in things.

And seeing Jamie wearing it did something strange to my insides.

I'd never had a partner who'd worn my clothes before. Now I never wanted to see him in anything else.

I closed the gap between us and wrapped one arm around his waist, pulling his back against my chest and pressing a kiss to his neck. "I like seeing you in my clothes."

"If this weather keeps up, you'll be seeing a lot more of it," he said. "I can't drive back to town in this."

"If you want to leave, I can take you. It'll be easy in the Land Rover." I didn't want him to leave, but I didn't want him to feel like he was trapped.

"No, it's fine. I'll stay."

"Are you sure?"

"Yes." He twisted his head around and kissed me. "But only if you give me more of your jumpers to wear. Your house is really fucking cold."

"Done," I said with a chuckle. "You do know it's about six hundred years old, right? It's not exactly easy to keep warm."

"I guess we'll just have to keep each other warm, then," he said. "Like penguins."

"You didn't want me calling you a frog yesterday, but now you're happy to be a penguin?"

"That was then. This is now." He grinned against my mouth, relaxing back against me. "Sorry again for ruining your kitchen."

"It's okay. You didn't burn it down or break anything," I said. "Now you just have to clean it up. And before you say you don't know how, I'll teach you." I tilted my head back and looked past him at the sorry pan of eggs. I'd never seen anything look so god-awful, and I was almost pleased he'd burnt them so I didn't have to try and eat them.

"You must think I'm such a prat. I'm nearly thirty, and I can't even make fucking scrambled eggs."

"Everyone's got to start somewhere." I patted his butt and added, "Come on, let's get it done. I can't be here all morning, and I'd actually like to eat something."

While Jamie threw away the burnt eggs, cremated toast, and mountain of eggshells, I nipped through to the sitting room to chuck more logs on the fire. Mog opened one eye and looked at me, then glanced towards the kitchen as if giving her opinion on Jamie. I wasn't sure if she was impressed or not.

Once the fire was stoked, I walked back to the kitchen and showed Jamie how to load the dishwasher and stick it on before getting him to wipe down the sides while I washed the frying pan and refilled the kettle. Despite my initial fears that Jamie had used everything in his repeated attempts to master scrambled eggs, there were still a few eggs left in the basket and enough bread for toast, and before long, I stood behind Jamie again as I gently helped him fold eggs with a wooden spoon.

"You don't want the heat too high," I said, gently moving his arm. "Otherwise, it all sticks to the pan and burns or turns into rubber."

"Or, if you're me, both."

"That's called talent."

Jamie laughed and shook his head. "I'm guessing cooking it on a higher heat doesn't just make it cook quicker?"

"It does, but not in the way you want. You need to control the heat." I helped him stir them again, watching as they came together into beautifully soft and fluffy golden clouds. "See?"

"Oh my God, they actually look like eggs!"

"Ta-da." His excitement was adorable, and I'd never expected to find a grown man so fucking endearing. "Turn the heat off to let them finish cooking. I'll get the toast."

"Is it ridiculous that I'm excited about this?" Jamie asked. "It feels like this is something I should've learnt years ago. I think most students can make breakfast."

"You'd be surprised," I said, thinking back to my own university days. "I lived with this one guy in my first year who couldn't even boil an egg and thought you could eat chicken rare."

"Even I'm not that stupid."

"How did you manage at university? Didn't you live in a house share?"

"Sort of, but I actually just lived with a couple of friends from school in a house my father bought for us, and it was just easier for us to have a housekeeper and someone to sort food for us. And when neither of them were around, we just lived on takeaway, restaurant meals, and alcohol. And before university, I was at boarding school, so I've always had someone looking after me."

I reached for what was left of the loaf of bread, cutting it into thick slices and popping them into the toaster while I tried to think how to respond. It sounded like such a strange life to me to be so used to other people doing things for you that you had no concept of how to do things for yourself. I didn't pity Jamie, but it wasn't a life I'd want for myself. "Did you never fancy learning?"

"Not really. I never saw the point of it. Although, this morning may have altered that. Perhaps I should ask Michael to give me a few lessons so I can make the basics," Jamie said. "I should probably be able to fend for myself in case of the apocalypse. Or, heaven forbid, if I find myself in self-catering." He shot me a cheeky smile, his tongue poking out of the corner of his lips.

"Don't knock it until you've tried it," I said. "We've got half a dozen self-catering properties around the farm, and they're always popular. I think they're all booked for the summer already."

"As charming as that sounds, I'm not sure they're for me. How else am I supposed to find sexy men in pubs and convince them to come back to my room to fuck me?"

"Just use Grindr like everyone else."

"True, but then they'd have to come and find me, and I'm so impatient when I'm horny." He grinned at me.

"Although… it would mean I was closer to your house, and having a sexy farmer on tap sounds ideal."

"Maybe it would be best if you didn't stay in one, then," I said teasingly. "You'd just be here all the time wanting food and sex. I'd never get you to leave."

"Come on, you can't tell me that doesn't sound fabulous. I'm wonderful company and an excellent fuck. You'd love it."

"If you say so," I said as the toast popped. I pulled it out and dropped it onto the old wooden chopping board, reaching for the tub of butter, which was considerably emptier than when I'd opened it yesterday.

"I do."

I glanced over at Jamie, who was smiling at me. It made my insides twist and bubble. I tried to push the feeling down, but as soon as I tried, it just slipped through my fingers like I was trying to catch water. I'd never felt like this before, and I wasn't sure it was welcome. I didn't even know what it was, only that it was connected to Jamie and the way he looked at me.

I looked down at the toast, hoping that focusing on the thing right in front of me would free me from distractions. But all I could think about was how rarely I made breakfast for two.

"Can you grab some plates?" I asked, looking over my shoulder and gesturing at one of the cupboards. "Do you want tea too?"

"I would kill for some coffee if you've got some."

"I have. It's nothing fancy, but it's got caffeine."

"Right now, that's all I need," Jamie said with a smile

that turned the bubbling feeling in my stomach into a rolling boil. He was holding the plates in his hand, and there was something about seeing him in my kitchen, wearing my clothes, and helping make breakfast, that called to some long-lost part of my soul. One I thought I'd given up years ago when I'd accepted my lot in life.

It was like a whisper on the wind over the moor, like a summer breeze through the heather and an autumn chill from the sea. It frightened me in a way that nothing else had before because I knew it would be impossible to keep. All I would be able to do was watch it pass me by and feel the caress of it on my skin before it danced away and left me where I always was. Alone.

"Are you okay?" Jamie asked as he put the plates down beside me, and I forced a smile.

"Yeah, sorry, just thinking about work. Not sure how long I'll be able to hang around unfortunately." Was I running away from my emotions? Probably. But at that moment, I didn't know what else to do. "Do you want a lift back to town?"

"Maybe... or... Can I come with you? I don't know if I'll be any help, but I, er... I want to try. And I'd love to see more of the farm. I just might need to borrow some boots. And a coat if you've got a spare one."

I stared, trying not to let shock register on my face. Of all the things I'd been expecting Jamie to say, offering to help hadn't been on my bingo card. I hadn't even thought it was an option.

"Yeah," I said, forcing the words out before the silence hung in the air for too long. "Sure. That'd be great."

"Perfect, and I promise not to complain about the cold. If I do, you can... I don't know, throw snowballs at me or something."

I chuckled and shook my head as I put the toast on the plates, wondering what other surprises the day would bring.

CHAPTER SIXTEEN

Jamie

I'D PROMISED WILL I wouldn't complain about the cold, so I didn't. At least not out loud.

Freezing wind whipped my exposed skin as the quad bike bumped over the snow, and my gloved hands clutched at Will's waist as I held on for dear life. The seat wasn't really designed for two, and it meant an uncomfortable ride, but I'd been told it was the easiest way to get where we were going. Behind me, the two sheepdogs, Nell and Moss, sat in a small, flat bed. Both of them had been eager to get back to work, bouncing around Will's feet and climbing onto the bike with a single word when Will and I had emerged from the house.

Will had warned me they weren't pets and to let them be. If they wanted to talk to me, they would, but they weren't the sort of dogs who'd come looking for cuddles and belly rubs.

"How're you doing back there?" Will called as we slowed for a moment.

"I'm good," I said, hoping it didn't sound like my lips were numb. "Glad you leant me your coat."

"Yours wouldn't have done you any good up here."

I had to agree. My coat was another pretty but not practical part of my wardrobe. Before we'd left, Will had handed me one of his old coats and told me to put it on. It was a bit ragged and worn and smelt vaguely of what I assumed was sheep, but I had to admit it had done the job. He'd also given me a pair of boots and another pair of thick socks to put on since the boots were about a size too big, along with a tweed flat cap and a pair of gloves.

I'd caught sight of my reflection in the car window as we'd passed and realised I looked completely unrecognisable, like an alternative-universe version of myself.

"I'm just going to get the gate," Will said as he brought the bike to a halt in front of a large, metal gate set into a stone wall. As he dismounted, I saw where we were headed and gasped.

Beyond the gate lay the moorland. It was covered in a thick blanket of snow that glittered in the cold morning sunlight and seemed to stretch out beyond the horizon, which fell away in the distance. The landscape was bleak and wild with strands of heather and the odd bush or tree poking out from the snow. In one direction, it seemed to rise impossibly steeply, and in the other, it seemed to curve into the earth.

I had never seen anything so beautiful.

Will turned back from the gate and must have seen me

staring because I caught the hint of a smile on his face. "God's own country," he said as he climbed back onto the bike and rolled it through the open gateway.

"It's… it's incredible," I said.

"Aye, that it is." He dismounted and went to shut the gate. "Not far now. There's an old barn just over that hill that we use for hay storage. Ewes'll be up there waiting."

"Don't they get cold?" I asked as we started moving again, my hand tightening on Will's waist.

"No, they've got a nice thick fleece, and they know where to find shelter if they need it. They're a hardy breed my Swaledales. They're born and bred on these moors. It's where they're most at home, and I'll only bring them in if I need to."

"Will they give birth out here?"

"Aye, they will. Like I said, they're at home here. It's where they feel safe. If the weather's proper shit, I might bring them in, and if any get into trouble, we'll bring them into the lambing barn, but we try to get them out as soon as possible. Sheep worry, and it's not good for 'em. That's why lambing's so hard. Someone's got to be up here at all hours in case something goes wrong."

I gripped his waist tighter, gazing out over the landscape. "How does that work? Do you have to set up a rota? Do you have to camp?" God, I couldn't imagine camping out here, certainly not in this weather. Camping was very high on my personal 'nevers' list, and it didn't appeal in the slightest.

Will laughed, the sound bold and joyous. "Mostly Higgs and I'll take it in turns to run shifts. Usually, we get another pair of hands in too. Sometimes we'll come and stay out here. We used to bring one of the old shepherd's huts out, but they all got turned into holiday lets for our posh glamping stays, so mostly we'll just camp in one of the old barns. They're warm and dry, and there's a couple of them about depending on where we lamb."

I couldn't think of anything to say because all I could think about was how Will had given up some form of potential comfort to give himself another income source, and from what I knew about Will, that wasn't something he'd have done without a lot of thought. He'd shown me a couple of them as we'd driven up the road towards the moor, and from a distance, they'd looked very cute and cosy. I could see why people liked them.

I tucked myself in closer to Will and held on tight, watching the moorland roll past us.

As we got a bit closer, Will slowed and gave a single command to the dogs who hopped off the bike and began to lope alongside us, easily keeping pace.

"There we are," Will said. "Right where I knew they'd be." He chuckled and turned his head. "I came up here this morning to do a quick headcount and throw out some pellets, but they want more hay, and I'm late getting it out, so they're waiting for me."

I glanced past him, and sure enough, on the gentle slope below us, I saw a flock of sheep spread out around an old stone barn that seemed both at odds with and part of the landscape.

Will gave another command to the dogs, and they slowly cut down the side of the hill. "We'll just bring them in a little, then you can put some hay out, and I'll give a few of them a once-over. One of them looked like she might be limping earlier, and I want to get a better look."

"Sure, I can do that," I said, uncertainty rising in my chest. I was sure it couldn't be that difficult, but my experience with both animals and anything resembling physical labour was nonexistent.

"Don't worry, I'll show you what to do," Will said. "I'm not just going to dump you there and expect you to figure it out."

"You'd be within your rights to do so."

"No, I wouldn't. You've not done this before, and I want it done right."

Will pulled the bike to a stop not far from the barn, where the dogs were holding the sheep in a loose circle. I'd never seen sheep up close before. Will's had black faces with distinctive white markings across their noses and eyes that almost looked like goggles or eyepatches. They all had little curled horns that tucked over their narrow ears, and long, shaggy-looking coats over their round middles. They were watching us closely with what I could've sworn was suspicion.

One of them let out a demanding bleat, and the rest took up the call. Will chuckled, shaking his head as he climbed off the bike. "All right, all right. Hang on. Honestly, more demanding bunch I've never met."

I swung my leg off the seat, my feet crunching in the snow. Was it silly that I was a little afraid? I'd not spent any time around animals besides the occasional cat or dog before.

"Don't pay them any mind," Will said, seeming to sense my hesitation. "You pay them no mind, they'll pay you no mind. And don't be afraid to push them off if they get too demanding when we get the hay out. Come on, let me show you what we need to do."

He led me over to the barn door and pulled a key out of his pocket. The door was solid and in better repair than I'd expected, but then again, I supposed it had to be well maintained to be of any use.

"We'll get a couple of bales out," Will said as he pushed the door open and gestured for me to follow him. I got a waft of dried grass as I stepped inside, the smell reminding me of the long, hot days of summer. It was warm and almost comforting. The bales were large and stacked on top of each other from wall to wall, but a lot of them were already missing where they'd been used.

"Think you can carry one?" Will asked.

"I can try."

Will nodded and walked over to part of the stack, bending down to grasp what I realised was two thick strands of orange string holding the bale together. He hefted it upwards and started to carry it towards the door. I stepped quickly out of the way and went to fetch another.

It turned out hay was a lot heavier than it looked.

"Shit," I muttered as I gripped the string and heaved it off the floor, feeling the twine digging into my hands. "How the hell does grass weigh this much?"

I staggered, the bale swinging in my hands as I struggled to keep my grip. The journey to the door felt like a mile, and I was already sweating inside my layers.

"Do you need a hand?" Will called, looking up at me as I took a tentative step into the snow. He'd already gotten his bale open, and there were sheep clustered around his feet.

"I'm fine," I said, my voice coming out as a strangled yelp. "Where should I put it?"

"Just over there." He pointed at a clear spot in the snow. "Need to spread them out a bit."

I tried to answer, but it was pointless. How was I so out of breath already? I took a few more staggered steps, doing an awkward half run, half wobble out to where Will had pointed. I dropped the bale onto the ground, my breath coming out in ragged pants that fogged and steamed in the air.

"You all right?" Will asked, appearing beside me.

"It's... Fuck, how the fuck are they that heavy?"

Will patted me on the shoulder. "You'll get used to it." He pulled an old knife out of one pocket and handed it to me. "Just cut the bailer twine and pull it off."

"Bailer twine?"

"The orange twine. Just cut each open, then pull it off and put it in your pocket. Don't leave it lying in the snow or the bloody sheep'll eat it."

"Seriously?"

"Yeah. God love 'em, but they're not the brightest bunch."

"Okay. I can do that," I said. "Do I just leave it here, then? When I've taken the string off."

"If you're not surrounded, take some of the sections and shake them out," Will said. "The bale's made up of a load of compressed slices like a loaf of bread. Get a couple at a time and shake them out so you've got a few piles. Just makes it easier for the sheep, and it'll keep them moving. Mimics grazing a bit more than just getting it off the bale, plus it means more of them can get to the hay at a time. Stops them arguing with each other and means everyone gets some."

"I'd rather not get in the way of any arguments. I am rather squishy."

"You'll be fine. And if you need me, I'll be here." His smile filled me with reassurance, and I watched him walk back towards the main part of the flock, calling one of the dogs over to him.

I turned back to the bale in front of me and bent down to cut the string.

Forty minutes later, I was sweating, sore, and felt like I'd actually achieved something for the first time in my life as silly as that sounded.

I'd put out three bales of hay while Will checked over the flock and moved a few bales of hay in the barn to make sure they weren't all going to come crashing down as soon as we left. I'd tied the bailer twine into a bundle and stuffed it into my pocket alongside the knife, and it felt strange putting my hand in my pocket and feeling them there. It was like having proof that I'd done something.

Afterwards, Will and I climbed back onto the bike, Nellie and Moss hopping on behind us.

"What next?" I asked, wrapping my hands around his waist again. I was surprised by the enthusiasm in my voice because I'd never expected to be excited about the idea of any kind of work, but there I was. I didn't want to go back yet. I wanted to do more. Even if it was just moving hay or helping Will count sheep or whatever other small tasks he could trust me with.

"Don't you want to go back?"

"No, not yet. I want to help."

"Are you sure? I don't mind if you've had enough."

"I'm sure," I said. "I like being out here with you." I tightened my grip on his coat, resting against him as I looked at the sheep and their hay, then out across the moorland. There was something about being there that was making me feel things I'd never experienced before, but I didn't know if it was just the place or the person I was there with.

I already knew there was something about Will that drew me to him, and I wasn't ready to stop exploring that. Not when there was so much left to discover.

CHAPTER SEVENTEEN

Jamie

Having decided that I wanted to stay in Heather Bay until I figured out what I was feeling for Will, my first step was to extend my hotel stay.

Unfortunately, this was where everything went wrong.

"I'm sorry," said the woman behind the desk with a sympathetic smile. "We're all booked up from Sunday night."

"Seriously? You haven't got anything?" I asked, staring at her with disbelief. It was the middle of February in a small town in Yorkshire. How on earth were they full?

"Nothing at all. They're coming in to start filming that period drama at the Castle, and all our rooms are booked for that."

"Okay, thanks for checking," I said, giving her a nod and turning to head back up to my room. I wasn't going to get irate with her because there wasn't anything she could do. I just had to hope I'd be able to find somewhere else to stay.

I spent the next hour on my laptop scrolling through countless websites trying to find somewhere in Heather Bay that both had availability and looked half-decent. But most of the bed and breakfasts were closed for the season, and there were a few places that didn't really appeal. I knew I was desperate, but I still had standards, and a room that looked like it had last been decorated in the seventies was not going to meet them.

Although, if I couldn't find anything else, it might have to do.

I grabbed my phone and opened my message thread with Will, hoping he might have some bright ideas. Since he knew the area well, I was banking on him knowing about some gorgeous secret escape I couldn't find.

JAMIE *I need your help.*
WILL *What with?*
JAMIE *What are your limits? =P*
WILL *For the right person, it goes up to disposing of bodies.*
JAMIE *Good to know, but this time I need a recommendation. I'm looking at staying in town for a bit longer, but the hotel's fully booked, and some of the other options are dire. You don't happen to know of anywhere I can stay? There's not some cute boutique place nestled away somewhere, is there?*

I rolled over on the bed while I waited for his answer, my poor muscles aching as I did. I'd been sore when I'd left the farm earlier in the afternoon, but I hadn't thought it would last this long. At this rate, I wasn't sure I'd be able to get out of bed in the morning.

Rolling myself off the mattress, I landed with a staggered thump on the floor and headed for the bathroom, hoping a long soak in the bath would soothe some of my aches and pains.

The hotel had left me a little jar of locally made lavender bath salts, and soon the room was filled with scented steam. I sighed as I stepped into the hot water, easing myself down and stretching out, resting my neck against the back of the bath. I picked up my phone from where I'd left it and saw Will had messaged me back.

WILL *How long did you want to stay? You could come and stay in one of the shepherd's huts. They're small, but they're cosy and nicely done up. They are self-catering, but if you're that desperate, I'll feed you.*

My heart raced as I stared at his message. While this wasn't quite staying with Will, it was as close as I was going to get, and the idea of being able to see him every day outweighed most of the negatives that came with fending for myself. Especially if Will was offering to help with the catering aspect.

But it did mean I had to work out how long I wanted to stay, and I still didn't have an answer for that. I'd been hoping to book the hotel for another two weeks to give myself a chance to figure things out, and then, if necessary, extend it again. I didn't have a fixed plan, though, because it all depended on how I felt and how whatever this was with Will panned out. And I didn't want to tell him that I was planning to stay indefinitely until I'd made up my mind about what I wanted in life.

JAMIE *If you have one free, that would be great. Thanks! Not sure about how long I'm staying - maybe two weeks? Might be longer, though. My room here is booked until tomorrow morning, so can I come up then?*

WILL *No worries, I'll send you the link to the booking form when I get back from the pub, and you can choose one. Payment is usually half on booking, half on arrival. Just let me know when you're coming up.*

JAMIE *Just bill me for the two weeks now, and I'll happily contribute towards food bills. Also, still want to go out for dinner at some point? Or maybe we could just do another night at yours?*

WILL *Yeah, sounds good.*

There was a pause. The screen told me he was typing, but it seemed to go for a while like he kept rethinking what he was going to say. Since he'd mentioned being in the pub, I wondered if he was with his friends again and whether they were all reading his messages over his shoulder. I hoped at some point I'd get to meet more of them, mostly because I was curious to see if they were all like Spencer.

WILL *What about next Sunday? There's a really nice pub just outside town that does a good Sunday roast if you fancy that. Probably can't get a table for this week but could go next if you're still here. It's not a posh restaurant dinner, but the food is great.*

JAMIE *That sounds amazing! I can't remember the last time I had a roast, and I certainly can't cook one.*
WILL *I'll get us a table, then, and I'll see you tomorrow.*

I relaxed back into the bath and let the hot water wash over me. Then I grinned to myself and lifted my phone higher, opening the camera and snapping a few pictures because I was nothing if not a tease, and I couldn't resist driving Will a little wild.

JAMIE *[sent a picture] Just for you, not for your friends ;)*
WILL *Fuck you, posh boy! I'm in public!*
JAMIE **gasp* were you looking at naughty pictures in the middle of the pub, farm boy?*
WILL *Because you fucking sent me one!*
JAMIE *Do you want more? I took several. Or do you want me to roll over?*

I twisted in the water and pushed my ass into the air. It was a little awkward to take photos over my shoulder, but I managed to get a couple that showed off my perfect peach, highlighted by the water dripping down it. I slid back down into the water again, sent the best of them to Will, and waited.

WILL *I'm not looking at it.*
JAMIE *You're missing out. My ass looks so fucking perfect right now.*
WILL *I'm in the middle of the fucking pub!*
JAMIE *So? Go to the toilets or outside. Or better yet, come find*

me. I miss your dick.

I missed him too, but it would be ridiculous to say that since I'd only seen him a few hours ago. If I focused on the fact that I was tired and horny, I could ignore the aching feeling in my chest that was more than just muscular.

WILL *Are you always this needy?*
JAMIE *Yes, and you love it. Today was a long day. Come here and let me take care of you. I promise to do all the work.*
WILL *Do you? How? I want details.*
JAMIE *But I thought you were in the middle of the pub? I can't possibly send you all those filthy details if someone else could see them =P*
WILL *You're a fucking tease.*
JAMIE *Yes, and?*
WILL *I'll be there in twenty. Just got to find an excuse to leave.*
JAMIE *Make it ten. They'll all know you're coming to fuck me anyway.*

Grinning to myself, I reached down to palm my slowly hardening cock. I should probably wash and maybe prep myself, but I was also enjoying lazing in the water and thinking about all the things I wanted to do to Will when he arrived. I'd been winding him up, so the logical solution would be to draw it out and tease him until he was ready to explode.

But I didn't know if I had the patience for that because teasing him would also involve teasing myself, and now that I'd realised how horny I was, I just wanted to get off as soon as possible.

The hotel had provided the most gorgeous lavender and honey soap to go along with the bath salts, so I quickly washed myself, then climbed out of the bath to start the rest of my prep. As much as I loved making Will eat me out, I just wanted him to be able to slide straight inside me as soon as he arrived.

As I walked out of the bathroom to find my lube, my phone flashed with another message.

WILL *On my way.*

I smirked and climbed onto the bed, kneeling and taking a photo of my front, making sure I got a good shot of my hand wrapped around my erection.

JAMIE *[sent a picture] I'm waiting for you.*

Grabbing the lube, I squirted some onto my fingers and began to open myself up while teasing my cock. I didn't take my time or draw it out; this was all business. There was a clock ticking on Will's arrival, and I wanted to be ready for him.

I was three fingers deep in my ass when there was a knock on the door. With a grunt I slid my fingers free and climbed off the bed, practically sprinting across the room. I did a quick double-check through the peephole to make sure it was Will before I accidentally exposed myself to a member of the hotel staff and got arrested for public indecency. That was not on my bucket list for the evening.

Check done, I pulled the door open to see my gorgeous, rumpled-looking farmer, his expression full of heat and desperation.

"Jamie..." he said, but I didn't let him finish the sentence before I pulled him inside by the front of his jumper and started kissing him. Will moaned, his hands wrapping around me as he pulled me against him. I let out a muffled squeak against his mouth because his hands were colder than a fucking freezer.

"Sorry," he muttered. "I know my hands are cold."

"Get naked and get on the bed," I said, nipping his lip. "You can make it up to me by letting me ride you."

Will moaned, his hands fumbling for the hem of his jumper as he started to undress. I did my best to help as we stumbled across the room, leaving a trail of clothes in our wake. Will fell onto the bed, scooting backwards to prop himself up on the pillows. His cock was already hard, the smooth, red head beading with precum. I crawled towards him, bending down to swipe my tongue across the silky skin.

"Fuck," Will groaned. "I love your mouth."

"I know," I said as I placed a kiss to the tip of his dick. I gave his shaft a few teasing licks, flicking my tongue across his balls before I reached for the discarded bottle of lube.

I straddled his thighs and drizzled lube onto my fingers before I reached down to slick up his cock. Will moaned at my touch, his hands shooting out to grasp my thighs. "Are you ready?" I asked, lifting myself up to kneel above him, guiding his tip towards my waiting hole.

"Are you... Did you..."

"Yes. I had some fun while I waited." I winked at him. "I told you I was going to do all the work."

I gasped as the head of his cock breached my rim, loving how full I felt as I sank down onto him until he was buried deep inside me. I barely gave either of us a moment to breathe before I began to ride him fast and hard, resting my hands on his chest as I bounced up and down on his cock. Need bubbled up inside me, hot and hungry, fuelling my desperation.

"Do you like it when I use you like this?" I asked as I looked down at Will.

"Y-yes," he said, his voice low and breathless. "I want... Fuck, I want you to take what you need."

"Mmm, I will." I slammed down onto him, gasping as his cock hit my prostate before I began to swirl and roll my hips in the most sensual way I could imagine. I wanted to make him see stars, but it felt so fucking good that I knew I wasn't going to be able to last. This was going to be quick, hard, and dirty, and that sent excitement rippling through me.

"Fuck, don't stop," Will said, his fingers digging into my thighs. "It feels so fucking good."

I couldn't stop even if I wanted to. I was so lost in the moment and the way he made me feel that my body was moving of its own accord. "T-touch me," I moaned. "I need you to make me come."

Will groaned and nodded as he wrapped one hand

around my cock, creating the perfect, tight tunnel for me to fuck into as I rode him. My head was spinning as my balls tightened, and as I slammed down on Will's cock again, I knew I was at the point of no return. I cried out as I came, my cum splattering across Will's skin. My hips bucked and rolled as I rode out the last of my orgasm.

I tipped forward, putting my hands on either side of Will's head as I found his lips for a deep kiss. His tongue brushed into my mouth, and I moaned, my body going boneless as I relaxed against him. I felt utterly blissed out, and I wanted Will to feel the same.

I slipped my hand behind his neck as I kissed him again, then I rolled off him, pulling Will with me. It took him a second to get the message, and I groaned softly as his cock slid out of me. But then he was back between my legs and pushing inside me as his mouth claimed me with hungry kisses.

"Fuck me," I said, whispering the words against his lips as I wrapped my legs around him, pulling him deeper until I felt his balls brush against my ass. "It's your turn to take what you need."

Will moaned as he began to rock his hips, his slow thrusts quickly becoming hard, desperate ones as he fucked me with a reckless intensity that stole the breath from my lungs and made my whole body tingle. It was almost too much, but I didn't want it to end.

"I'm… Fuck, I'm close," Will gasped.

"Come for me," I said, my lips ghosting across his ear. "I want you to fill me up."

Will snapped his hips, all finesse disappearing as he

chased his release, but I didn't care. I was just revelling in the endless waves of pleasure washing over me.

With a deep groan and a muttered curse, Will thrust deep and filled me with his release. My hand was still wrapped around his neck as I drew his mouth to mine to trade breathless kisses until the last vestiges of pleasure faded away.

"I could get used to this," I said, letting my fingers trail across the back of his shoulders.

"What?"

"Just… this." I wasn't sure I could put my feelings into words. They were too nebulous and uncertain, but I didn't know if it was because I hadn't figured them out or if my brain just didn't want to acknowledge them. I just knew they were something to do with Will.

"Me too."

We lay there for a while trading soft kisses until I knew the moment had to end.

"Do you have to go back tonight?" I asked.

"Yeah," Will said. "It's easier than getting up at the crack of dawn. Is that okay?"

It was because, although I wanted Will to stay, I wasn't going to put myself first for the sake of a few hours of sleep. Especially when I was going to be seeing him in the morning.

"It's fine. I need to pack anyway. What time should I come up tomorrow? My check-out is at eleven."

"Come up after that. It'll give me and Mum time to get the hut sorted," Will said. "Do you want to pick one? I can show you your options."

"You choose. Pick whichever one you think I'd like. Surprise me."

"Sure?"

"Of course," I said, giving him a final kiss. "I trust you."

Because when it came to me, I didn't think Will could go far wrong.

CHAPTER EIGHTEEN

Will

"HEY NOW, NO ARGUING," I said fondly as I watched Dad's three Highland cows bunt each other as they surrounded the large, metal hay feeder in their paddock, their shaggy, orange coats dusted with frost. My dad was completely devoted to them, and if he could've gotten away with it, the three of them would spend their evenings curled up on the sofa next to him.

"You'll have to be good," I added as I gave Delilah, the oldest and largest of the three, a pat on the neck. "I'm going to put Jamie in the hut in the next paddock, so you can't go waking him up at four every morning when you want attention."

Delilah huffed at me, turning to look at me from under her floppy fringe and giving me a soft nudge with her large, flat nose. We didn't keep a lot of cows because the terrain wasn't really right for them, but the Highlands were more pets than anything else. Dad had always loved them, and when he'd retired, he'd bought the girls from a friend in Scotland. They were full sisters and had happily taken to their new life in Yorkshire, being petted and pampered by an old man who wasn't ready to sit around and do nothing.

"I know, I know. You'd never do anything like that," I said. "You're good girls."

Fiona, the middle one, lowed in agreement, then went back to pulling hay through the feeder bars while Bonnie, the youngest, snuck up behind me in an attempt to use me as an itching post. She was a lot bigger and stronger than she imagined, so I gently pushed her away and instead put my hand on her forehead and dug my fingers into her coat to give her a scratch.

"All right, that's enough," I said. "I'll be here all day otherwise."

"I think they'd like that," Dylan said, and I looked over to see him leaning on the gate. "You can be their butler."

"I'm already their bloody butler," I said as I wandered over to him, leaving the girls to their hay. "Dad keeps messaging me and asking how they are, even though he can look out the window and see them. Higgs is going to help me finish clearing the drive later so he can come down."

Dylan chuckled. "Will that make things easier for you or will your dad just give you updated lists of instructions?"

"The second most likely, but at least he'll be happy." I slipped out of the gate and clicked it shut behind me. "How's the yard?"

"Everyone's fine. Got a few horses starting to get a bit grumpy at the lack of exercise, but they'll live. Higgs told me yesterday he didn't think we'd get any more snow, but once everything melts, it's going to be so wet I think we'll have to limit turnout just to stop everything getting so churned up."

"It'd be best if they didn't turn into mud pits," I said. "But we can roll the fields when they start drying up, and that'll limit any damage. And the grass usually comes through fine afterwards."

"True," Dylan said. "Also, Helen's put her notice in. She and her husband are moving to Wales in March, so she'll be taking her two with her. Looks like we'll have a couple of openings. Are you happy for me to fill them straight away, or do you want to wait until after lambing?"

"You can fill them," I said. "I trust you to find good people. Just let me know if you need anything."

"Will do." Dylan leant on the gate, a frown furrowing his eyebrows.

"Penny for your thoughts?"

"Yeah… I know we have a waiting list for the yard, but I got a call yesterday from a guy looking for spaces. Not sure if it's a hoax or not, but he said his name was Wilder North." The name sounded familiar, but I couldn't place it. Luckily, Dylan seemed to have noticed because he added, "The dressage rider. He was part of the team for the last Olympics. He's the guy who won the double gold medal, then got really angry over all the publicity and pressure."

"I remember," I said with a nod. "I'd have thought he'd have his own yard. Don't most professionals have their own places?"

"They do," Dylan said. "Which is why I thought it was a

hoax, but... I don't know. Why would someone ring up pretending to be Wilder North and ask about livery? It doesn't make any sense."

"We've got two spaces now. Give him a call and invite him down. If it's a hoax, they won't come, and if it's real, then—"

"Then we could have a fucking Olympic medallist here. God, what would Sandra do? She's already convinced she's Britain's next dressage queen, but she can barely do a novice test. She'll be all over him for lessons."

I shot him a wry smile. "You'll figure it out. It's why you're the yard manager."

"Thanks for the sympathy," he said with a roll of his eyes. "I'll need to get a whip or something to keep them all in line."

I chuckled then turned to look over my shoulder at the crunch of a car on the snow, catching sight of Jamie's little hire car as it came slowly through the gate. "By the way," I said to Dylan, "the green hut is booked for the next few weeks, just in case you see a random man walking around."

"Seriously? At this time of year?"

"Yeah, he's a friend of mine."

Dylan gave me a pointed look and grinned, glancing over at Jamie's car. "Ahhh, yes, a *friend*. The same *friend* who was here on Thursday night."

"I have friends," I said. "Lane is my friend. So are you."

"Yeah, but there's friends and then there's *friends*," Dylan said with a smug note in his voice. "Will he actually be staying in the hut, or will he be in the house?"

"God, you're as bad as the rest of them," I muttered.

Last night, when Jamie had asked about accommodation, I'd been in the pub with my friends, and it hadn't taken any of them long to notice I'd been messaging someone. Apparently, privacy was a thing only for other people because it hadn't taken long before Theo, Lane, and Spencer had been reading my messages over my shoulder and dictating responses.

Lane had been the one to suggest taking Jamie for Sunday lunch, seconded by both Oliver and Anders.

I hadn't gotten much of a vote.

Luckily, I'd had my phone back by the time Jamie started sending pictures. They'd come through blurred until I'd downloaded them, but even so, I would have been fucking mortified if anyone else had seen them because I hated the idea of violating Jamie's privacy like that.

I was pretty sure my friends had guessed where I was going when I'd suddenly taken off, though, because Lane had slyly mentioned that I should bring Jamie next Friday if he was still around, and Theo had sweetly promised they'd all be on their best behaviour. Which I didn't believe one bit.

They didn't have best behaviour to begin with.

"That probably means I have a point," Dylan said.

"I'm not answering that," I said as I turned to walk towards Jamie's car. "By the way, you should come to the pub with us some time. It's not good for you to work all the time."

"That's my line!"

I flipped Dylan off and his laughter echoed in my ears as I walked across the yard to where Jamie had parked.

We'd managed to clear a lot of the snow off the main walkways, which had made things a lot easier, and I was hoping if we kept it clear we wouldn't end up with sheet ice either.

"Hey," I called, giving Jamie a half wave. "You made it."

He looked up and smiled at me, the expression catching me off guard in the same way it always did. I'd only known him a week, but that smile had already proved it had the power to turn my whole world upside down.

"It's much easier to find in the daylight," Jamie said. "And it looks like some of the snow is starting to melt."

"A little, but also Higgs and I cleared a ton of it yesterday afternoon."

"You should have said. I'd have stayed to help."

"It's fine," I said. "You'd done enough."

Jamie frowned. "Just make sure you don't do too much and hurt yourself."

"That's very selfless of you," I said with a teasing smile. "What's brought that on?"

"Mostly the fact that if you injure yourself you can't feed or fuck me and then I'll suffer terribly."

"How noble."

"I am nothing if not benevolent," Jamie said, leaning up to kiss me. It was the first time he'd attempted to kiss me in public, and for a split-second, I hesitated. Jamie noticed and pulled back. "Sorry, I—"

"No, it's not you," I said hurriedly. "I'm just... not used to people trying to kiss me. It comes with being a hermit. Don't really get much of a chance to find people interested."

"I'm interested... if you are."

I didn't answer him with words. Instead, I cupped his jaw with one hand and drew him into a kiss. He tasted like coffee and honey lip balm, and I could smell the sharp, warm scent of his cologne. It made me want to bury my face in his neck and run my lips over every inch of his skin.

But I definitely couldn't do that in public.

"Hmm, you have to do that more often," Jamie said. "You're far too good a kisser to only do it when we're fucking."

"Any more demands you'd like to add?" I asked, biting back a laugh.

"What are my other options? How many do I get?"

"None at this rate."

"That's not fair."

"What else do you need? You've already got me feeding you, fucking you, and kissing you."

"True, but most of those benefit you too." He grinned, and I knew I wouldn't be able to say no, no matter what he asked for.

"Come on," I said. "Stop being a menace to society and let me show you where you're going."

"But I like being a menace. It goes nicely with being a hedonist. And a spendthrift wastrel with no concern for reality." I glanced at him in concern, and Jamie shrugged. "Another gem from my father's accountant. It's not completely untrue. Or at least it wasn't."

"Still a bit bloody rude, though." I'd never dare say anything like that to someone's face, even if I was thinking it. I hated that rich people could just say that kind of shit to people's faces and walk away without a care.

"Ah, well, what can you do?" Jamie asked with another casual shrug. "Come on. I want to see which one you've chosen for me. I promise not to attempt any kind of open flame cooking unsupervised. I'd rather not be liable for burning down part of your livelihood."

"How gracious. I'm not sure you can get much worse than your attempt at scrambled eggs, though."

"Ha, how little you know."

"Not sure that's something you should be happy about," I said, waving him towards the house so I could grab the right keys.

"I'm glad you think so highly of me that you can't imagine me doing anything worse than turning eggs into rubber."

"You know that's not an invitation for you to try?"

"It's not?" He grinned. "Your loss."

I chuckled and shook my head, wondering what the fuck I'd gotten myself into.

It didn't take me long to grab the keys and walk Jamie around to the small field where the green shepherd's hut was tucked away. Since he'd let me choose, I doubted he'd gone and looked at any of the pictures, so I wasn't surprised when he gasped.

"Oh my God... Is this..." He'd stopped dead in his tracks, his eyes wide as he stared at the hut in front of him. If he'd been imagining some simple, dated shepherd's hut decked out like the inside of an old caravan, what he saw was quickly proving him wrong, even just from the outside.

The wooden cabin was nestled near the hedge in a small field that was tucked away from everything else. It was raised off the ground and painted deep forest green with steps leading up to it that were stained dark mahogany. It had a little chimney on the roof from where we'd installed a tiny log burner for warmth and double doors with large windowpanes that let in plenty of natural light alongside the other small windows dotted around.

In front of the cabin, partially hidden under the snow, was a small patio area where a covered outdoor dining set sat alongside a small, covered barbecue. To one side, tucked even farther from view to ensure as much privacy as possible, was a raised decking area that held a deep, wooden hot tub that was just big enough for two. It was wood fired and could be used whatever the weather, especially because we'd installed lanterns on the wooden fence that partially surrounded it, creating a cosy, private space for our guests to enjoy.

"This is yours," I said, handing over the key. "Want to go and have a look?"

"Yeah…" Jamie nodded and turned to me, still clearly in shock. "You didn't tell me they were like this."

I shrugged, a smile playing across my lips. "What else would they be like?"

"I don't know. Not this." He practically bounced across the snow to the steps, which I'd cleared earlier in the morning before Mum had come down to make it up. I'd tried to be sneaky and told her we'd had a last-minute booking, but I didn't think she'd believed me.

Jamie unlocked the doors and pulled them open. "Are you fucking kidding me?" He looked over his shoulder and gestured to the interior. "Who the fuck did your decorating? This is just…"

"Is that supposed to be a compliment?"

"Yes," he said. "It's gorgeous. I think it's nicer than some of the hotels I've stayed in."

"Coming from you, I suppose that is a compliment," I said with a dry laugh as I watched him step inside. "And Mum, Dad, Higgs, and I did them. Mum mostly directed while the three of us made and fitted everything."

"You made everything?"

"Well, some of it at least. My best mate Lane helped with some of it because he's a builder, so he and I did all the kitchens."

"Are they all like this, then?"

"Yeah," I said. "They're all slightly different because we didn't want them all to be the same. They're different sizes too. But the layout and equipment in each is similar. We did them about three, maybe four years ago. Figured if we were going to do them, we'd better do them right, then people will come back."

"And you can charge more for them too," Jamie said as he ran his hand across part of the kitchen's wooden counter.

Each hut had a small kitchenette with wooden counters and doors, concealing both storage and an under-the-counter fridge. This hut's kitchen doors continued the green theme with dusty forest-green doors under light brown countertops. It had a small but deep farmhouse sink with art deco tiles behind it and a large window above it with a roll down blind. There were a few open cupboards and shelves on the wall, all made from the same colour wood as the countertops, and the kitchens were well equipped with everything guests might need.

On one side, the counter jutted out slightly and the end had been rounded to create a little table, and there were two padded stools tucked underneath. There was also a basket on top of the little table that Mum had filled with eggs, bread, milk, a bottle of wine, some local beer, homemade jam, local honey, and next to it was a glass cake dome covering a small Victoria sponge cake.

"Mum's cross with me," I said as Jamie examined the basket, his face a picture of delight. "She only had time to make you a Victoria sponge because I sprung your arrival on her at such short notice. I've been told I've got to apologise."

"What could I have had instead?" Jamie asked with a teasing grin. "What have I been deprived of?"

"I don't know. Lemon drizzle or cherry probably. That's what she usually makes."

"I feel like you need to make me one now," he said. "That can be your apology."

"Maybe. If you're lucky."

Jamie snorted and looked around at the rest of the hut. On the other side of the kitchen was a sliding door that led to a small bathroom that had a toilet, sink, and shower, and to Jamie's left, at the other end of the hut, was the bed. It was pushed up against the far wall and stretched across the width of the hut.

We'd built the beds to fit each hut, and the mattresses each rested upon some custom fitted drawers and small cupboards that acted as storage. The beds were covered in crisp white sheets with mountains of pillows, and I noticed Mum had even left a couple of extra blankets in case Jamie got cold.

There was a small TV on the wall opposite the headboard just above a long shelf that had some pretty ornaments spread across it. Both the shelf and the headboard had strings of fairy lights across them as well, and there was a little window in the far wall that you could look out of when you sat on the bed.

The other main feature was on the front wall between the kitchenette and the bed, and that was the small, cast-iron log burner that had a basket of logs next to it, along with another basket of kindling, fire lighters, and matches.

We'd debated whether we should put in actual log burners or just electric fires, and the debate had gone back and forth several times until we'd agreed on the log burners. They weren't used much since we didn't get a lot of guests in the colder months, and those who did come were happy to follow the instructions we gave them to use them safely.

"What do you think?" I asked eventually because the silence was starting to become off-putting. I knew Jamie had said he liked it when he first came in, but I wanted confirmation now that he'd had a chance to actually look at it.

"It's incredible," he said, turning to me and pulling me into his arms. "Thank you."

"Why are you thanking me? You're paying for it."

"Just because." He kissed me softly. "Have you got to get back to work, or can I keep you for a bit?"

I looked over his shoulder and down at my watch. "I can spare about twenty minutes." I grinned at him. "I'm guessing you don't want me to talk you through everything like the Wi-Fi, the local area, the hot tub…"

"You can do that later," he said as he released me to close the door and pull the thick, green curtains across the panes. "But first, I want to properly say thank you for your hospitality."

I groaned as Jamie sank to his knees, his fingers reaching for the button on my jeans.

CHAPTER NINETEEN

Jamie

IT WAS ALMOST funny how quickly Will and I slipped into a routine over the next few days.

It had started when I'd insisted on helping however and wherever I could. Will had come back to see me on Saturday afternoon to check if I was settling in okay and asked what my plans were for the week. I'd told him I didn't have any because I'd realised over the last week that being left alone with my thoughts wasn't conducive to actually achieving anything.

My brain had decided that if I wanted it to figure out what we were supposed to be doing for the rest of our life, it needed me to be doing other things so it could work through the problem quietly on its own without the rest of my thoughts intruding and prodding it to ask how it was getting on.

And since I didn't have anything to do except sit around

and contemplate my own fate, I'd decided that my best bet was to volunteer my services to Will and hope it provided a good enough distraction to allow me to figure my way out of the fucking mess I'd gotten myself into.

Will had taken a bit of convincing, but his concern seemed to stem from taking advantage of me rather than my lack of experience. I supposed we all had to start somewhere, but it was almost sweet how willing he was to teach me.

"Please, Will," I'd said. "I really want to help, and you said you need an extra pair of hands. I might be pretty useless to start with, but I'll try."

"Are you sure? You're supposed to be on holiday… It feels… I don't want to take advantage of you."

"Trust me, the only thing I'm supposed to be doing is working out what the fuck I'm doing with my life and why the fuck I was so bored with everything."

"Okay," he'd said. "But I'm not going to go easy on you. I'm not going to throw you in and expect you to swim or anything, but I can't afford to slow down. And you'll have to be willing to get your hands dirty."

"I can do that," I'd said, even if the prospect didn't totally thrill me. "Although, I will have to order myself some better clothes. Can I just send them to the house?"

"Better clothes?"

"I can't keep wearing your old coat and boots, can I? And I should probably get some better jumpers too since mine aren't the warmest. Do you have any brands you'd recommend? I don't want to throw money at something that's not going to last or is totally wrong for what we'll be doing."

"Er, sure, I can do that."

I'd spent the rest of the afternoon with my laptop, the cake, and the bottle of wine working my way through several websites and ordering everything I thought I'd need with a few extras just in case. I knew the store names would confuse the fuck out of Dad's accountant when he checked my credit card spending, but he could shove it.

My purchases arrived over the next few days, and I was now the proud owner of some gorgeous Ariat work boots, a pair of wellies and thick socks to go under them, several fleeces and woolly jumpers, some waterproof trousers, a couple of thermal base layers, and a thick, tweed shooting coat, which had been an extravagance but was too beautiful to pass up. It was warm, stylish, and came with an abundance of pockets, which Daisy always told me was a good thing. I'd also bought myself a flat cap, a woolly hat, and several pairs of gloves because Will said you could never have too many of them.

I'd also ordered some more of my favourite hand cream and included an extra bottle for Will because his skin was often red and sore. I'd left it on his bedside table one night during the week when I'd stayed in the house because I'd been too lazy to get dressed and go back to the hut in the cold.

And just like that, we'd started to slip into a routine without either of us noticing.

Will would come and fetch me in the morning—if I hadn't stayed in the house the night before—and take me out on his rounds. I'd seen the sun rise more times in the past few days than I had in my entire life, and every time it still took my breath away as it bathed the moors in light. After that, there would be coffee, and we'd start on whatever else needed doing.

I'd helped install a couple of owl boxes in the hay barns across the moors and spent an afternoon with Will fixing a fence, which had been far more exhausting and strenuous than I'd ever imagined. He'd introduced me to Higgs, who showed me the workshop and gave me a crash course in using a belt sander, which verged on the edge of terrifying, but I'd managed not to damage anything or anyone, so that felt like an achievement.

Dylan had taken me round the yard and the fields, talking me through the livery side of the business, and I'd asked an enormous number of questions because I'd never even thought about the complex realities of keeping horses. He'd even introduced me to his two, who'd both nudged my arms to demand treats and attempted to rifle through my pockets until Dylan showed me how to give them mints from the palm of my hand.

Will had started showing me the paperwork for the farm when he sat down to do his weekly accounts, and I realised with horror just how quickly things added up and how little margin for error there was. That was the thing about coming from money; I was incredibly good at spending it, but I wasn't always conscious about where it came from.

Will had mentioned that farming was tough, but every moment I spent with him gave me a new appreciation for his words and for the heavy weight of the legacy he carried.

It was easy to see just how much this place meant to him. It wasn't just words said to make a point; it was a truth that infused everything he did. If I'd doubted what Will had said when he told me he couldn't walk away, one week with him was enough to prove me wrong a hundred times over.

But the one thing that was clear was that Will needed help.

Not more experienced hands like Higgs and Dylan, but someone who could share the mental and emotional load.

I just didn't know if I could be that person, no matter how much I might want to be.

My whole life had been so far removed from Will's reality that it felt like stepping into another world. One week with him might have given me a taster, but I couldn't claim to be an expert by any stretch of the imagination. I had so little idea what half his work involved, and I had no idea whether the fact that I liked Will would be enough.

I was starting to hope it would be, though.

"What're you doing tomorrow night?" Will asked on Thursday evening as we stood in his kitchen and he attempted to teach me how to make dumplings to go on top of the beef stew we'd made at lunchtime. The stew had been happily simmering away in the oven all afternoon, making the whole downstairs smell absolutely delicious.

"Same thing I've done every night this week," I said, attempting to unstick dumpling dough from my fingers. "Nothing."

"Am I nothing, then?"

I snorted. "Technically, I haven't done you every night this week, so that doesn't count."

Our evening routine had varied, but most nights we'd made dinner together and chatted quietly while we watched whatever we could find on Netflix. Then I'd either retreated to the shepherd's hut to snuggle down in bed and continue my secret reading on sheep farming, or we'd ended up in Will's bed.

"I suppose. Do you want to come to the pub with me tomorrow?" He asked it so casually, but when I glanced across at him, I saw a small, nervous twitch at the side of his mouth.

"That sounds fun," I said as I put my not-at-all circular dumpling on the floured chopping board between us. "Will all your friends be there?"

"Yeah. That's the downside."

"Are you really referring to your friends as a downside?"

"No, but…" Will sighed. "I love them to pieces, but they're all really bloody nosy and don't have any form of best behaviour."

"They sound just like my friends." Only Will's were probably nicer and less interested in my money and what club I could get them into. "Tell me about them?"

"Are you asking me to do you a SparkNotes on my friends?"

"It wouldn't hurt. Just so I don't make a total ass of myself in front of them," I said. "Besides, I get the feeling they all have the slight upper hand since they've seen me in person, but I've only caught glimpses of most of them."

"Okay." Will scooped up the last bit of dumping mix and expertly rolled it into a ball. "You've met Spencer already. He runs Novel Tea with his brother Alex, who's a bit of a grumpy bastard, but he's got a good heart. Then there's Noah, he's Spencer's boyfriend and Alex's best mate. He's a pretty chilled lad. Teaches science at the grammar school, so he's got to be fairly unshakeable. Lane is my best mate. He's a builder and can be a bit sarcastic, but he's always there when you need him. His boyfriend is Oliver. Oliver grew up here and moved back last year. He's a bit quieter, but he's fun, and he, Lane, Alex, and Noah all went to school together."

I nodded, trying to hold all the pieces in my mind like they were the cast of one of those *Real Housewives* shows Daisy and I loved to binge. "With you so far. Anyone else?"

"Yeah, a couple more. Laurie's our resident goth, and he runs a funeral home in the middle of town. He lives with Theo, who's probably the more morbid of the two since he collects weird taxidermy."

"Oh, I think I've seen them," I said, thinking back to that first Friday night. "Theo's blond? And more femme? I think I heard him say something about a chess set."

"That's them," Will said. "Don't think Theo's won the chess set battle yet."

"Are they together too?"

"Yes and no."

"How does that work? Are they just casual? Open?"

"No, it's more like none of us know if they're actually together, and at this point, nobody wants to ask. But from the way they act, I'm pretty sure they are, even if they don't realise it."

I smiled to myself. "That's actually kind of sweet. Think they'll figure it out?"

"I hope so," Will said. "I can't imagine them ending up with anyone else." He put the last dumpling on the board, then went to open the oven to retrieve the stew. "Then there's just Anders and Bastian. Anders is an author, and Bastian's a photographer. I don't know them as well since Oliver introduced us to them, but they're a lot of fun. Bastian's a bit dreamy, and Anders is more down to earth. You always want Anders on your pub quiz team. He and Lane are lethal together."

"I don't think I've ever done a pub quiz," I said.

"We'll have to rectify that. They do them in the Sleeping Goose on Wednesday. I don't go very often, but there's usually a couple of my lot there we could go with." He set the large, deep-red casserole dish on top of the oven, lifting the lid to release a wave of steam that made my stomach rumble. I'd been hungrier this week than I had been in ages, and I had to assume it was all the physical labour.

"That sounds fun. We can add it to the list of things I need to do."

I left the *before I leave* unspoken, ignoring the way it hung in the air as Will put the dumplings into the stew. The longer I was in Heather Bay, the less certain I was that I wanted to leave.

I just didn't know if Will would want me to stay.

CHAPTER TWENTY

Will

"ARE YOU READY?" I asked Jamie as we walked towards the front door of the Sleeping Goose.

"Of course," he said. "I'll be fine. Your friends aren't that scary. It's not like they're a pack of ravenous wolves."

Honestly, I thought that might be better. I'd attempted to prime everyone by telling them that Jamie was coming in the hope they could get out all their surprise before we arrived, but I wasn't sure if that might have made things worse because now they'd had time to prepare questions.

Still, it couldn't be as bad as when Lane had shown up with Oliver last year and Spencer had started talking about serial killers and who in town was most likely to have turned their basement into a murder room. Spencer's answer had been Noah, which always made me chuckle now that they were practically living together.

I pushed the door to the pub open and ushered Jamie

inside, turning towards the alcove we usually claimed in the winter months.

"For fuck's sake," I muttered as I surveyed the sea of waiting faces all looking across at us with faux innocence. Even Theo and Laurie had arrived before us, which hardly ever happened because Theo's timekeeping was notoriously bad. It was like a sign that this was about to be an utter shitshow.

They'd left a couple of chairs in the middle free, leaving us no other option than to sit in amongst them all instead of on the end where I'd have preferred. I caught Lane's eyes and raised my eyebrow, and he shrugged, a devious grin crossing his face. Fucker.

"Everyone, this is Jamie," I said as we approached the table, determined not to make a fuss. "Jamie, this is Lane, Oliver, Bastian, Anders, Spencer, Noah, Alex, Laurie, and Theo." I pointed at them all in turn, and they all raised a hand or a glass or gave a little nod as they greeted us. I was tempted to tell them to be nice, but I knew that would just make it worse.

"Grab a seat," Lane said, pointing at the empty chairs, "and we'll get you some drinks."

"You're all here early," I said as I slipped into the seat next to Lane, opposite Anders and Spencer.

"Maybe you're just late for once," Lane said.

"Or this is a fucking set-up," I muttered.

"Why would I do that?" Lane asked, giving me a wry smile as he lifted his glass to finish off his drink.

"A number of reasons." Mostly because he seemed determined to meddle in my life. I knew it came from a good place, but I didn't need Lane hovering over me and trying to fix problems only he saw.

Beside me, Jamie had found himself next to Theo, which was already a mistake, although since Noah, Alex, and Laurie were also down at that end, I hoped he'd behave.

"Do you want a drink?" I asked Jamie, hoping I could steal him away to the bar and buy us a few minutes of breathing space.

"That would be lovely," he said.

"Perfect, I'll—"

"Don't worry," Oliver said cheerfully from the other side of Lane. "We've got this. What does everyone want?"

"Are you sure?" I asked. "Jamie and I can go."

"No, no," Lane said, putting his hand on my shoulder. "Jamie's a guest. We can't ask him to buy us drinks. Not yet anyway."

I couldn't turn him down, no matter how much I wanted to, so I had to watch while he and Oliver took everyone's orders and headed for the bar hand in hand.

"So," Spencer said as he turned to Jamie, adjusting the dark beanie perched on top of his long hair, "how're you finding Heather Bay so far? Have you been out much?"

"It's lovely," Jamie said. "I've enjoyed getting to explore. I've been up to the Castle. They do have some wonderful artwork on display there, and the grounds are lovely. And I found a gorgeous little gallery in the middle of town the other day. Will's been kind enough to take me out onto the moors as well."

There was a stiff note of formality in his voice I hadn't heard before, and I wondered if he was nervous. I had no idea why he would be. Maybe I'd spooked him last night when I'd told him about everyone, but I'd thought that was a better plan than throwing him to the wolves.

Just because I didn't think my friends were scary didn't mean Jamie felt that way. There were a lot of them, and it was intense when they all turned their attention on you at once.

"In the snow?" Theo asked, his eyes wide with shock. "That's very cruel of him."

"Just because you don't like the cold, doesn't mean everyone else does," Laurie said as he shot Theo a pointed look that I was convinced meant behave.

"I'm not a fan of the cold either," Jamie said. "But it's very beautiful out there. I don't think I've ever seen anything like it."

Theo nodded sagely. "It's very different to London. I remember the first time I saw it... It made me think of fairy tales. I mean, I'd seen the countryside on TV, but nothing compares to seeing it in real life."

"No, it doesn't. And it's almost strange to think I've seen more of other countries than I have of England."

"It happens," Theo said with a shrug. "Especially when you're a city boy."

"I didn't know you grew up in London," Alex said from across the table as Oliver and Lane reappeared with drinks and began handing them out before resuming their seats at the table.

"For a bit," Theo said. He'd never really talked a lot about his childhood. I didn't know much about his life before he'd turned up in Heather Bay, with Laurie, nearly four years ago and neatly inserted himself into our friend group by just sitting down with us in the pub one evening. It had been a bold move on his part, but we'd all fallen for the pair of them, and it hadn't taken long for it to feel like they'd always been there.

"Whereabouts?" Jamie asked. "I hope you don't mind me asking. It's just you look awfully familiar, and I'm wondering if we've bumped into each other at a party before."

Bollocks.

Fuck. Shit. Damn. Shit. Bollocks.

I had completely forgotten to tell Jamie that Theo did amateur porn and game streaming. I was pretty sure Jamie wasn't the type to avidly follow streamers. Especially not ones who played the most violent horror games while wearing cat-eared headphones and the tiniest clothing imaginable.

And now the poor man was going to be humiliated, and it was going to be all my fault. It was like watching a car crash in slow motion, but instead of moving, I was frozen in my seat staring in horror.

Theo smiled sweetly at Jamie and laid a hand on his arm, his expression surprisingly soft. "I don't think I'm the sort of person who goes to your parties," he said. "But depending on what sort of fun things you like to watch online, you've probably seen me there. Although I'm usually wearing less clothes."

It took Jamie a second, but instead of turning crimson, he just burst out laughing. "Oh my God! I'm so sorry. You must think I'm such a twat. I should really think before I open my mouth. I doubt you want me bringing that up in front of everyone."

"Why?" Theo asked impishly. "They all know I do porn, and I'm not ashamed of it. We're all adults here. And I love meeting fans in real life, especially when they're cute and sweet like you. Besides, now that I know you know, I can be myself! No more of this best behaviour nonsense."

"I think Jamie might be the only one who's seen any of it, though," Alex muttered under his breath, and I bit my lip.

"What do you mean he's the only one who's seen it? I gave you all free subscriptions!" Theo's shock and horror was clear like he'd never considered the idea that none of us would watch him.

"It's just... It's... Well..." Noah said as he looked uncomfortably down at the table.

"It's fucking weird," Lane said from my other side. "We love you, Theo, we really do, but we all agreed not to watch it. We thought it would be weird as fuck to watch you... well, get fucked."

"Yeah, we didn't want to make it weird," Spencer said, his cheeks tinting. This was turning out to be even more awkward than the first night with Oliver. "There's seeing your friends naked, and then there's..."

"Watching them get gangbanged," Alex said, finishing off his brother's thought with a sarcastic expression.

"But... but... I'm fine with it," Theo said. "I thought you loved me."

"We do," I said. "But there's some lines friends shouldn't cross."

Theo hmphed and folded his arms with a pout. "If you really loved me, you'd watch me get railed. Friends can watch other friends get railed and not have it be weird!"

"Jesus Christ," Lane sighed while Oliver chuckled into his drink.

"You know," I said, giving Lane a pointed look. "If this was supposed to be a fun set-up, it's not going very well."

"I'm so sorry. I didn't think it would end up like this," he said while Theo and Alex began to bicker. Beside me Jamie was watching them with an amused smile as if he couldn't believe what he was seeing.

I saw Laurie at the other end of the table looking equally amused, but his amusement was probably for a different reason. I wondered if he'd ever tried to dissuade Theo from sharing the codes or whether he'd already known that was a battle he'd lose. Despite the fact he was the only one who could exert any kind of control over Theo's behaviour, he seemed to know how to pick his battles. Either that or he quietly enjoyed causing chaos. There was a lot about him I didn't know.

"You've met our friends, right?"

"I know. But this is a new level even for us."

"I think this is more memorable than the murder dungeon conversation," Oliver said with a grin.

"I was just trying to make you feel welcome," Spencer said, feigning a mournful smile from across the table. "Someone could have changed the subject."

"To what?" Lane asked in disbelief.

"I don't know… It was summer. We could have talked about holiday plans or something."

"None of us ever go on holiday," Alex said as he sipped his pint.

"That's because we're all terrible workaholics," Anders said from the other end of the table.

"Wait, is spending three days rearranging the bookshelves in the living room work?" Bastian teased, looking at his boyfriend with a playful smile. "I thought it was just making a mess."

"I was thinking about plot points," Anders said. "Oliver will support me on this."

"I'm not getting involved," Oliver said. "As long as you get your drafts and your edits done, I don't care how many times you rearrange your bookshelves."

"Only because you're just as bad," Lane said. "You've reorganised your library twice since Christmas, and it's only February."

"I'm sorry," I said, lowering my voice and leaning closer to Jamie, trying to ignore the way his scent curled into my senses and made me want to bury my face in his neck. "I should've told you about Theo."

"It's fine," Jamie said. "It's definitely not the first time I've put my foot in my mouth like that."

"It's my fault, though."

"Don't worry about it." He grinned at me, then glanced around the table. "I like your friends. They're fun."

"They're something," I said. "Not sure if it's good or bad."

"It's good," Jamie said quietly, his words nearly getting lost in the sea of voices surrounding us. "They're... genuine. It doesn't feel like they're trying to catch you out."

"Why would they?" That sounded like a really shitty thing to do, and I'd never had time for people like that.

Jamie chuckled hollowly. "Just because, I suppose. For gossip or to hold it over you later."

"That sounds fucking exhausting." I put my hand on his thigh under the table, and Jamie's fingers found mine, squeezing them gently.

"It is. I prefer this. It's chaotic but in the best way."

I looked around at my friends, watching them laugh and bicker and tease each other. They may have been loud and nosy, but they cared about every other man sitting around the tables so deeply that I knew they'd all do anything for any of us.

We weren't just friends; we were a family too. I couldn't imagine any of us trying to manipulate each other—not in a more serious way than Theo's playful pouting—or making each other feel like we couldn't be ourselves or had to watch every word in case it was taken the wrong way.

That didn't sound like friendship to me. It sounded like being trapped.

"You know you're welcome here," I said, trying to make my words sound casual but knowing there was weight behind every syllable. "None of this lot will ever pull that shit with you."

"Thanks," Jamie said, turning his head to look at me with an expression that sent butterflies rippling through my stomach. "I appreciate that."

The world around us faded into the background until it was just the two of us, an island of unspoken words in the middle of a sea of noise.

CHAPTER TWENTY-ONE

Jamie

No MATTER how many times I told myself that Will taking me for lunch at the Green Dragon wasn't a date, I couldn't convince myself otherwise.

I'd changed my outfit at least three times, despite the fact they were all jumper and jean combinations, while wishing I had more options with me because I suddenly hated everything. My stomach wouldn't stop clenching, and I'd never felt so on edge, which was ridiculous because this wasn't a date.

Sure, I'd spent more time with Will than apart from him over the week, and we'd hung out most evenings, but it didn't mean anything, even if we hadn't had sex every night and instead spent half of them curled up on the sofa together just talking quietly and watching Netflix until one or both of us started to doze off.

And yes, he'd introduced me to his friends and invited

me to hang out with them, but he was just being polite because he didn't want me to spend an evening by myself.

And... the more I tried to dismiss everything that had happened between us, the more ludicrous it sounded. Because no casual, sex-only thing included personal cooking lessons, or Netflix binges over bottles of red wine, or the sleepy sharing of secrets and dreams in front of a fire. It certainly didn't include me dragging my ass out of bed at half five every morning to traipse out into the freezing cold to learn the ins and outs of sheep farming. That was something you only did for love or money, and I certainly wasn't being paid.

There was a knock on the door of the shepherd's hut before it swung open, and Will's head appeared through the gap. "Shall we get going?"

"Is this a date?" I asked, the words falling out of my mouth as I turned away from the mess on my bed before I had a chance to stop them.

Will stared at me for a moment. "Do you want it to be?"

"Do you?"

"Yeah... I think so..." he said. "I mean, I guess it was already."

I walked over to him, unable to hide my giddy smile. It was weird because I didn't really do dates or dating, not like this, but the idea of going on a proper date with Will, one that actually had the word attached to it rather than being a date in disguise, made me unbelievably happy.

"I think a lot of what we've been doing would count as dates," I said as I wrapped my arms around his waist and leant up to kiss him.

"Would it now?" Will grinned and raised an eyebrow teasingly. "What would that be? You turning eggs to rubber in my kitchen? You taking up half my bed and stealing the duvet?"

"I was thinking more you drooling onto my shoulder after falling asleep during our first episode of *The Rings of Power* or you snoring in my ear while holding me in a death grip."

"Fuck off. My snoring is not that bad."

"And I don't steal all the duvet."

"I suppose not." Will chuckled and kissed me again. "So... if a lot of what we've been doing counts as dating, do you want to make it an official thing? Or do you want to just keep it casual and not label it?"

I swallowed. I had no idea what the right answer was or even if there was one. It felt like it should be complicated, especially because I wasn't supposed to be in Heather Bay long-term, but in that moment, there was only one thing I could say. "Yes. I want this."

"Okay, then," Will said as casually as if he'd been talking about the weather. The smile on his face and the glint in his eyes were the only evidence of it being different. He slid his hand into mine, the rough skin and calluses familiar against my skin. "Shall we go and get some lunch now?"

The Green Dragon was a higgledy-piggledy pub on the outskirts of Heather Bay just on the edge of the moors. It looked like it had once been a small barn but had had bits added to it over the years with no sense of style or practicality, giving it a rather lopsided and patchwork feel. From the outside, it almost looked charmingly half-abandoned, and I wouldn't have given it a second glance if we'd driven straight past it.

The car park was almost full to bursting when Will and I arrived, but we'd managed to find a spare corner to squeeze the Land Rover into before we headed inside.

As soon as the door swung open, we were greeted with the heavenly scents of Sunday roast and a hum of chatter. There were a few muddy boots by the door, and as we stepped inside, I saw a few old men sitting at the bar in socks with wet dogs at their feet. Will flagged down a passing member of the waitstaff, and soon we were being ushered through the bar, down a corridor and past several busy dining rooms, then into a small, cosy dining room with five tables and a roaring fire.

Our table was near the window, which I realised when I sat down was slightly off-kilter as if it had slipped and shifted over the years. It was an apt visual depiction for everything going on in my head. Once upon a time, everything in my life had been just so, and I'd thought nothing would change. Now my view had shifted, and everything felt off-centre.

"Are you okay?" Will asked once we'd ordered some drinks and been left to our own devices with the menu.

"I think so," I said, tearing my eyes away from the view. "Just thinking about how much things have changed."

"Does it bother you? Do you want to go back? I'd understand if you did."

"I don't know. I think it only bothers me because everything feels so easy now. Not that farming is easy. It's the hardest fucking thing I've ever done, but somehow it still feels easier than being in London." I tapped my finger on the table for a moment. "I'm not sure easy is the right word for it, though."

"Do you think it's just the novelty?" Will asked.

"Maybe? But if that was the case, then I'd have thought it would have worn off by now. I've never stuck at anything for this long before. I've always just been chasing the next high. I think that's the problem with hedonism. It can get very tedious very quickly if you don't keep finding new ways to feed it. New men, new clubs, new ways to spend money. It's just a constant search for dopamine. At least it is for me."

"You were bored," Will said matter-of-factly.

"Yes, I was."

"I don't think it was in the way you think, though."

"Oh?" I was curious to hear what he had to say because Will's insight was rarely wrong. He could read everyone like they were an open book, but he didn't seem to often share what he saw. Perhaps he didn't want to hurt people.

"I think you were bored because nobody ever expected anything of you, so you never expected anything of yourself. My guess is your parents expected you to look and act the part of a good son, but they never really cared what you did with your life as long as you went to the right university, showed up at the right events, and didn't scandalise yourself in a national newspaper. And since nobody expected you to do anything with your life beyond play a part, you've never thought about what you really wanted from life. You told me you thought you were looking for purpose, and I think that's why you're still here. For the first time in your life, you've found a reason to get out of bed in the morning or at least something that interests you enough to make a go of it. And that's an achievement in itself."

I watched him as he spoke. He seemed to consider every word. It was the second time Will had laid the truth out for me like that, and it was strange how just a few words could make me feel so seen. Shining a spotlight on my soul wasn't as scary as I'd expected. At least not anymore.

Because Will had neatly summed up what I'd been trying to figure out for the past two weeks, and it seemed like I'd stumbled onto the answer without even realising it. I just wasn't convinced about the achievement part.

"I think you're right," I said, my heart racing as a new rush of emotion swept through me. "But I think you deserve some credit here."

"Why? I haven't done anything."

"Yes, you have. You were the one who caught me so completely off guard I couldn't think straight. You've called me out on my shit and made me realise just how stuck in my bubble I've been." My lip twitched into a smile as I thought about everything that had happened over the past few weeks. It felt like so much longer than that but also like no time at all. "You didn't push me away either."

"To be fair, at first, I just wanted to get laid," Will said, and I snorted.

"I mean, same. In case I haven't told you, you're really fucking hot."

"I don't know if you have today."

"How outrageous."

"You've said it now, though, so you're forgiven," he said, giving me a wry smile. "But I can't take the credit. You intrigued me, Jamie. The way you just walked into my life like you belonged there."

"Even if I have no fucking clue what I'm doing half the time?"

"Only half? There are some things I'd say you're pretty fucking good at." He winked at me, and I pulled a face at him.

"Don't start," I said, pointing a finger at him while trying not to laugh. "I am not going through lunch with a hard-on, and I'm not fucking you in the toilets."

"I wasn't doing anything. Just giving you a compliment."

"Sure, let's go with that."

A moment later a member of the waiting staff appeared with our drinks, and Will and I had to beg a few more minutes to actually look at the menu. Everything looked so delicious it was difficult to decide, but we eventually settled on sharing a baked Camembert with toasted focaccia soldiers and homemade chutney as a starter, and then I decided on the roast beef while Will ordered the pork. If we had any room after that, we'd decide on pudding, although we did have work to do later, so we had to make sure we weren't so full all we wanted to do was go back to Will's and sleep.

"Okay, I have a question for you," I said as soon as our smiling waiter disappeared with our order.

"Am I going to regret this?"

"No. I just..." I glanced around surreptitiously and lowered my voice before asking the question that I'd been dying to ask all weekend. "Have you seriously never watched any of Theo's porn? Like, I'm not judging, but if my super-hot friend gave me a free porn sub to their work, I would one hundred percent watch them get railed."

Will's cheeks flushed, and he glanced out the window. "I... er... Once. When he first gave us the code. I was curious, and Theo is cute, but I... It wasn't my sort of thing. The one I'd picked had this teacher-student Daddy vibe, and I just... It wasn't for me. But I never had the heart to tell him."

"Aww, you're so sweet," I said, not mentioning that I knew exactly which video he was talking about and had thought it was hot as balls. I'd felt like such a fucking idiot when I hadn't recognised Theo, and I'd almost wanted the group to open and swallow me up when he'd corrected me, but the fact that he'd seemed genuinely pleased that I'd known who he was had made up for it. That and watching all his friends awkwardly try to explain why they'd never watched his work. I'd wanted to ask them all why not, but I didn't know them well enough.

Which was why I was now cornering Will.

"Don't worry, I won't tell," I continued. "But if you do want more suggestions, I can find you some others."

"Nope," Will said. "It'd just be weird."

"Fine. But I can find plenty of other fun things for us to

watch together if you fancy it." I smirked at him. "I think it would be hot."

The flush on Will's face deepened, and I added that to my mental list of things to try with him. "Yeah... that... that sounds fun."

"Perfect," I said. "I'll leave it for a day when you're really stressed."

Will grimaced. "You won't have to wait long. It's lambing soon. It's the most stressful time of the year."

I made a mental note to find those chapters in the books I'd been reading because I knew Will wouldn't have time to deal with my complete lack of knowledge alongside everything else. But I wanted to hear him talk about it as well because listening to Will explain things would never get boring to me. There was just something about his quiet, confident explanations that made me hang on his every word.

"Tell me about it?" I asked as the waiter arrived with an enormous wooden board that seemed to have a Camembert the size of a small tractor tire on it, accompanied by stacks of large, crispy chunks of focaccia and tangy pots of chutney.

I picked up one of the pieces of toast and dunked it into the middle of the cheese, scooping up a mess as I listened to Will start to explain, already knowing that deep down, I wanted this to be my life forever.

CHAPTER TWENTY-TWO

Will

THE CLOSER WE got to the start of lambing season, the more I felt my stress levels rising. No matter how many years passed, I always felt the same because no matter how much preparation I did, it was easy for something to go wrong at a moment's notice. The ewes were notoriously bad at asking for help when they were in trouble, and it meant Higgs and I had to watch every flock like a hawk to spot the signs of a ewe in distress.

It meant long hours of constant vigilance in the freezing cold because, although we lambed in March, the icy grip of winter had only just started to abate.

The earlier snow had finally melted, but I wasn't convinced we weren't going to wake up one morning to another two foot of it on the ground. Sod's law said it would be the day the first ewes went into labour.

We had several flocks of sheep spread out across the

farm, although we'd recently ensured that the flocks of pregnant ewes were all close to each other simply to make it easier for me and Higgs to get between them.

I'd learnt that lesson the hard way the first year I'd taken over from Dad and we'd ended up with one flock several miles away from the others. Higgs and I had endured a nightmarish few weeks trying to keep an eye on everything.

That morning, Higgs, Jamie, and I had finished setting up the lambing barn for any ewes that needed to come in or any orphan lambs that needed to be hand-reared. Sometimes, if the orphans were very small, we often brought them into the farmhouse kitchen for a few days to get them warm and fed.

Usually, Mum would be on hand then, and she'd potter round the kitchen hand-feeding them from bottles, talking to them, and making sure they didn't totally destroy the house once they'd worked out how to climb out of the large cardboard boxes we often kept them in to start with.

"Will? Are you in?" Mum's voice sounded from the kitchen, and I looked up from my laptop in my tiny office off the side of the kitchen, where I'd been poring over an order for lamb colostrum and milk replacer.

"Yeah, in here," I said. I heard her footsteps, and she appeared at the door, looking me up and down with her customary warm, searching expression. She was wearing one of her own knitted jumpers, and her face was flushed from the cold. She'd obviously left her coat in the kitchen, and her short, grey hair was sticking out at odd angles where it had been stuffed under her hat.

"You look tired, love," she said.

"It's nearly lambing season."

"Then you should be making sure you get some sleep."

"I am. It's just stress. I'll be fine when we start."

"Don't lie to me, William," she said, giving me a knowing smile. "You'll be worse."

I just hummed because I wasn't about to deny it to her face. I'd never hear the end of it. Instead, I just asked, "You all right, then?"

"Grand, just grand. I brought you and Jamie another lemon cake. It's just in the kitchen."

"Cheers," I said, casting my eye back to the screen. I'd come back to it later. As long as I got it ordered today, I'd be fine. "Do you fancy a cuppa?"

I followed Mum back into the kitchen, catching sight of the enormous lemon loaf cake sitting on the kitchen counter next to an old, green plastic bag.

"What's in the bag?" I asked as I grabbed the kettle and filled it up, making sure there was enough for Jamie when he got back from his expedition to Tesco. He'd volunteered to go by himself, armed with a detailed list, and so far, I hadn't received any frantic, grumpy phone calls about not being able to find things or asking about substitutions.

"It's a present for Jamie," Mum said as she leant against the counter. "Where is he anyway? I noticed his car's gone."

"Tesco. He offered to go and do the shopping so I could stay here and get a bit of admin done."

"Bless him. That was sweet." Mum smiled approvingly, reaching out to scratch Mog, who'd made a rare appearance in the kitchen. Mum was about the only person Mog would move for in the winter, knowing that she'd get absolutely spoilt rotten for doing so. "Is he staying for lambing?"

"I think so," I said vaguely, wondering if the sole purpose of Mum's visit had been to be nosy. She'd met Jamie in passing a couple weeks ago, and ever since she only seemed to drop by the house when the pair of us were around. It was starting to get suspicious.

I hadn't told her we were dating, but my guess was she already knew and was waiting for me to confess. The present for Jamie was probably a way to try and force my hand, and I didn't know how I felt about that.

Jamie and I were still figuring things out. He'd slipped into my life like he belonged there, but I had this nagging feeling that something was going to go wrong. The past few weeks had been too easy, and nothing in life was like that. I was just waiting for the bubble to burst, and I didn't want to have to deal with everyone's sympathy when it did.

Maybe it was cynical, but I was struggling to believe that someone like Jamie would want to give up his whole life for someone like me.

I was always busy and stressed, and I always put the farm first. I had no money and no prospects. My life wasn't glamorous, and it never would be. I couldn't give Jamie posh holidays or meals out or fancy clothes. All I could give him was me, and I didn't think that would be enough.

It never had been in the past.

"I hope he is," Mum said, rubbing Mog behind the ears. "He's good for you."

"Oh, aye?" I reached into the cupboard to pull out a

couple of mugs, hoping that if I kept my answer vague I could get away without having this conversation.

"He is. I know he's not the farming type, but he seems to be taking to it well, and he keeps you on your toes. He stops you getting so wrapped up in everything."

I grunted because I didn't know what to say to that. Jamie had taken to farming well. Better than I'd ever expected considering he admitted to never having seen a sheep up close until I'd taken him out that first morning he stayed over. I'd expected him to get bored by now, but he hadn't, and that confused me. It had, by his own admission, confused Jamie too, and it felt like the two of us were just wandering around in the dark trying to make sense of our feelings.

"He's a good one," Mum continued. "You'll see."

"Yeah…" I was saved from having to answer any more questions by the sight of Jamie's tiny hire car pulling in next to the Land Rover. "Speak of the devil. Looks like he survived Tesco."

"Go and give him a hand. I'll finish the tea."

"Cheers," I said, walking over to slide my boots on. "Jamie'll want coffee, though. There's some in the cupboard. Two teaspoons of coffee, milk, and two sugars."

Jamie had muttered darkly about going back to London just to get his coffee machine the first time I'd introduced him to instant coffee, and I was surprised he hadn't made good on that threat yet.

"Hey," I said as I stepped out of the house. "How'd you get on?"

"I survived!" Jamie said proudly, his head popping up

from the other side of the car. "I didn't get lost, I found everything on the list, and I didn't go overboard with extras either."

"Congratulations."

"Thanks. I feel like an actual adult, which is absurd to be honest, but I suppose everyone has to go shopping for the first time at some point."

"You've done it before, though," I said as we walked around to the back of the car.

"I know, but this time felt like I'd actually got it right," Jamie said as he popped the boot open. I glanced around. From there we were not quite visible from the kitchen window because the Land Rover was in the way. I wrapped my arm around his waist and pulled him towards me to steal a quick kiss.

"I'm proud of you."

"Why?"

"Because you did it. And you didn't bring back mountains of sweets this time."

He laughed against my lips, the sound filling me with joy. "Fuck you, I like sweets."

"It was like the manifestation of every five-year-old's dream," I said before I kissed him again. "I'll have to take you down to the old sweet shop in town at some point. I'm not sure I'll get you out again, though."

"Not until I've bought some of everything anyway," Jamie said, giving me one last kiss before we broke apart and he went to retrieve some of the bags. "How's your morning been? Did you get the ordering done?"

"Nearly. Mum's here, so I haven't finished yet. She's

brought another lemon cake and a present for you."

"Oooh! I love your mum."

"Am I going to get any cake this time?" I asked as Jamie handed me some of the bags. Jamie shrugged and laughed. "You got exactly the same amount as me last time. You're just used to having it to yourself, which makes it last longer."

"I'm sure your pieces were bigger than mine," I teased.

"Don't worry, I'll make it up to you. I'll find something to bribe you with so I get all the cake. What's my present?"

"I don't know. I didn't ask."

"Hurry up, then," Jamie said as we staggered towards the door, both laden down with shopping. "I want to see."

We carried the bags in and dumped them on the floor. Mum was just pouring milk into one of the mugs, and she beamed at Jamie as soon as she saw him.

"Hello, love. How was Tesco?"

"Not too bad. I managed not to buy half the confectionery aisle this time, and I got everything off the list."

I watched the two of them chat as I started to unpack, fishing Mog out of one of the bags where she'd tried to find the pouches of cat food. It was clear Mum loved Jamie, but it was also clear he liked her too. I didn't know much about his relationship with his parents, and he'd only mentioned his dad offhand or in relation to his accountant. I wasn't going to push the subject, but it was easy to assume they weren't close.

I wondered if Mum had sensed that too because she seemed to have taken Jamie under her wing like a lost duckling, happily bringing him cake, talking him through the basics of the farming year while she showed him how to clean the kitchen, and writing him step-by-step instructions on how to make roast potatoes. And Jamie seemed to have absorbed every word. He'd made her laugh too, regaling her with stories from wild nights in London that sounded too outrageous to be real.

Sometimes when he talked about those nights, it was almost with a note of fond nostalgia, and it made me wonder just how much he missed it. He'd said he didn't want to go back, but I wasn't convinced he wouldn't wake up one morning and realise just how relentless this life was.

Maybe if he stayed for lambing season I'd be convinced. Then again, he might get to the end and realise just how much he hated it.

Either way, I'd have an answer.

"If you grab that bag," Mum said as she handed Jamie a mug of coffee and a plate with an enormous slab of lemon cake, "you'll find a little something just for you."

I stopped what I was doing, a tin of chopped tomatoes still in hand, as I watched Jamie cross the kitchen and swap the coffee and cake for the plastic bag. It was obvious it wasn't heavy, but I still had no clue what it was. Jamie frowned curiously as he reached inside it, then gasped as he pulled out something dark blue and soft looking.

"Is this…" he looked at my mum in shock and awe.

"I hope it fits," she said. "I saw you wearing that one of Will's I made him a couple of years ago and thought you best have one of your own."

Jamie unfolded the knitted jumper and stared, his thumb tracing across the collar. It was the same simple design as mine, but the wool was deep navy with speckles of colour instead of green. "It's... it's perfect. Thank you."

He strode across and pulled Mum into a hug, and it made my heart clench with joy and pain because surely this couldn't last.

"Bless you, love," Mum said. "It's just a jumper."

"No, it's really not," he said softly. "I don't think anyone's ever made anything for me before."

"Well, if you like it, I can make you another. You'll just have to let me know what colour."

"What do you think?" Jamie asked, holding it up to show me and grinning like a kid at Christmas. He was so fucking gorgeous like this, happy and carefree, I wanted to hold on to this moment forever and pretend my worries didn't exist.

"Proper grand," I said. "I can have mine back now."

"But I like it. It's comfortable."

I rolled my eyes, but it didn't stop me from smiling. "First my jumper, then my cake, next you'll be stealing the bloody dogs."

"I mean, Nell licked my hand this morning, so it's only a matter of time."

"That's bloody typical," I said, trying to feign annoyance and failing miserably. Jamie laughed, the sound filling me with the same happiness I felt when I walked the moors in the spring, when the world was beautiful and new and full of life.

Jamie could steal whatever he wanted from me, and it wouldn't matter because he'd already stolen my heart. And I knew I'd never get it back.

CHAPTER TWENTY-THREE

Jamie

THE FIRST LAMB of the season was born at just after midnight on the seventeenth of March, a date I knew I'd never forget for as long as I lived.

We'd gone out to do one last check before bed because Will had been pacing up and down the kitchen with a nagging feeling in the pit of his stomach. So we'd wrapped up warm, loaded Nell up onto the back of the quad bike, and headed out to the fields. The sky was cloudless and studded with a million stars, the moon so close to full it looked like someone had tried to draw an approximation of a circle and flattened it on one side. It was crisp and cold, our breath fogging in the air, and the world felt almost empty.

The first of the flocks we checked were fine, albeit surprised to see us, and the second were the same. It was only when we got to the third, in one of the fields closer to the farm, that Will noticed one of the ewes was in labour.

I couldn't see the signs at first. Over the past few weeks, it had been easy to see the ewes becoming more uncomfortable as they waddled around, their unborn lambs wriggling and kicking, but Will pointed out her pacing, the way she'd taken herself off towards a corner of the field and was restlessly standing up and lying down, pawing her foot into the ground.

"She's trying to make a soft bit of ground for the lamb to be born onto," Will said. He'd parked the bike farther away and switched off the headlights because he didn't want to scare the ewes. Nell sat by his feet, keeping watch over her charges with quiet contemplation. The only source of light was the moon, but it shone brightly as if the universe knew we needed it tonight.

"Does she need help?" I asked, unsure if we needed to intervene. I'd done some reading about the stages of labour for ewes, including one complete with very detailed pictures, but reading about it and seeing it happen were completely different things.

"No. She's fine at the moment. Most of this lot should be because they've all had lambs before, but there's always a risk."

"Will you know?"

"Aye, I will." He pulled his phone out of his pocket. "I'll message Higgs and let him know we're starting. Are you warm enough? We're going to be here a while."

"I'm good," I said, burrowing deeper into my coat, glad

I'd thought to put multiple layers on before we'd left the house.

Will tucked his phone into his pocket and put his arm around my waist, holding me close as we stood in comfortable silence.

"Good girl," Will muttered. "That's it." He turned to me and pointed with a gloved hand. "Can you see the water bag? That's the end of the first stage of labour. We should have a lamb within the next hour."

I tapped the face of my watch to make it glow. "It's just after half eleven."

"Are you sure you want to stay? You can take the bike back."

"I'm not leaving," I said. "I'm not missing it."

Will smiled and nodded, putting his hand down to rub Nell's head.

I'd never felt as strangely anxious as I did watching the ewe in labour. My heart was pounding so loudly I heard it in my ears, and once or twice, I looked around for the source of the noise before I realised it was coming from inside me. Will exuded calm, and that helped, but I also knew he was probably suppressing any emotion he felt because he didn't want me to worry.

"Are you okay?" I asked, sliding my hand into his and squeezing.

"Yeah, I'm fine."

"Are you sure? You can tell me if you're not."

"Just pre-lambing jitters," he said quietly. "I get them every year. I keep thinking about all the things that can go wrong, and sometimes I get stuck there. I know there's a risk of losing some, and sometimes I worry about losing all of them. I just... I want them all to be okay. I want the births to go smoothly and give us happy, healthy lambs. Not just because we need them to if we're going to make it through another year, but—"

"You care about them," I finished. "You want them to be safe because you care. I think you care more deeply than any man I've ever met, and it's incredible."

"Yeah, well... I'm not..."

"Shut up and take the compliment, farm boy," I hissed, jabbing him the ribs and trying not to laugh. Will grinned, but he didn't say anything else.

It was true, though. Will gave so much of himself away, and from the outside, all you could see was selfless generosity. But from where I was standing, it felt like Will was on the verge of giving everything away and keeping nothing for himself. And all I wanted was to fill the void and encourage him, just occasionally, to think about himself.

"There's the feet," Will said a few minutes later. "Not long now."

I watched, almost unable to believe what I was seeing as the ewe panted and strained. I saw the lamb's feet and the round projection of its nose as it began to appear. The second waterbag surrounding the lamb burst, and Will made a pleased sound. Then suddenly, the lamb appeared, its head and shoulders being pushed out, and a few moments later, it fell gently onto the soft ground.

I gasped, my heart clenching at the sight as a raw mixture of emotions rushed over me.

The mother turned and started to clean the lamb up, licking its coat and stimulating its circulation. I heard its babble of tiny bleats, and my heart melted.

"That's it," Will murmured. "Good girl. Clever girl."

"It's so small," I said, watching as the ewe began to nudge the lamb to its feet. It attempted to stand, its new legs wobbling as the muscles were tested for the first time. The first time it tried, it went straight back down again, giving a plaintive little bleat of confusion. "Oh... not quite... come on."

"It can take them a few minutes. They have to figure out how to make everything work for the first time."

"It reminds me of watching people stumble out of clubs at the end of the night," I said as the lamb tucked its feet underneath itself for another attempt. It stood up, then sat straight back down again. "Although, to be fair, that baby has more coordination than I've ever had."

Will chuckled. "I've never been much of a club person, even at university."

"I thought farming students were known for going hard. It's like every university's rugby team. They're always the ones who'll drink you under the table."

"Most of my friends were, and I went out with them a lot during my first year, but I never really enjoyed it. Mostly because a lot of them were straight and ended up dragging me to clubs full of girls because they wanted to get laid. It was always bloody awkward when girls came up to me and wanted to dance and I had to politely tell them they were barking up the wrong tree. After that, most of them just wanted to treat me like some sassy gay bestie, which wasn't really my style either. After a while, I just stopped going out with them."

I nodded. "If you ever fancy reliving your club years, I'll take you out in London one night. Just for fun." I only wanted to do one night, though, any more than that sounded exhausting. "Maybe we could take some of the others too if it's their sort of thing."

"Maybe," Will said, but he didn't sound convinced, and I wondered if I'd stumbled onto something that made him uncomfortable. Maybe I shouldn't have mentioned London at all.

I watched as the lamb staggered to its feet and took its first stumbling steps forward to its mother, who bleated in support and nudged it into place as it searched out its first drink.

"There we go," I said. "Success." I turned to Will and smiled. I was still clutching his hand, and I squeezed it again tightly. "Thank you."

"For what?"

"For letting me stay."

"Of course." His eyes flicked back over to the newborn, who was happily suckling away. "The first one is always special. It's something you never forget."

He was right. I wouldn't forget anything about this night.

"What do we do now?" I asked. "Do we need to wait for the placenta?"

Will gave me a surprised look like he hadn't expected me to know that. "Yeah, I'll wait."

"I guess it's always worth making sure," I said. "The

articles I read talked about some of the issues that can happen post-birth. And during. And before. There were a lot of pictures too. I didn't think I'd ever see what a sheep's vulva looked like up close, but here we are."

Will gave a low laugh. "Just wait. I'm sure you'll have plenty of chances to see more of them."

"Not too many please. I am in no way ready to be a sheep midwife. I'll be the one standing there with towels and iodine."

"We'll make a shepherd of you yet," Will said, giving me a smile that made my whole body light up.

"Maybe. It would certainly be a career change. Although I'm not sure hedonism counts as a career unless you're Oscar Wilde, and sadly, my writing skills are sorely lacking."

We stood in silence for a few more minutes, watching for any more changes and occasionally stamping our feet to keep warm.

"Can I ask you something?" Will said, his eyes still fixed on the ewe in the corner.

"Sure."

"What made you do the reading?"

I shrugged because I didn't know how to answer that without getting into the whole mess that was my feelings. "I don't know. I didn't want to go into this totally uninformed. You have enough work to do without teaching me everything. I thought if I at least read a few blogs and articles and things like that I'd know the basics. I still don't know if I'll be much help, but hopefully, I won't be completely ignorant of what lambing entails."

Will stared at me, his face a mixture of expressions that swirled too fast for me to read. It looked like there were a million things he wanted to say, but in the end, all he said was, "Thank you."

"You're welcome," I said, squeezing his hand again. "I'll probably still ask a lot of questions, though, and some of them might be quite stupid."

"No such thing," Will said. "Especially not if you're learning."

"I'm glad you think so because I'll be holding you to that."

Will hummed and put his arm around my waist, pulling me against him. There were so many things about the future unspoken between us, and I knew we'd have to address them one day, but now was not the time.

It was too perfect a moment to break.

CHAPTER TWENTY-FOUR

Will

"ARE YOU COMFORTABLE DOWN THERE?" I asked with an amused smile as I stuck my head over the fence of one of the pens in the lambing barn to see Jamie sitting on a bale of straw, attempting to bottle feed three lambs at once. They were all trying to climb into his lap, trying to shove each other out of the way to get to the teats on the bottles, even though there was plenty for all of them.

"Not particularly," Jamie said. "But I'll manage." He gave me a bright, beaming smile, then squawked as one of the lambs jumped onto his groin. "Ah! Fuck! Can you fucking not? Please."

I chuckled. "You probably need to stand up. Stops you getting trampled."

"Yes, well, lesson learnt for next time," Jamie said as he nudged one lamb out the way, crossing one arm over the other to shove one of the bottles into a waiting mouth.

Despite my fears, Jamie had taken to lambing like a duck to water and had thrown himself into the season with gusto. He was almost unrecognisable now to the man I'd first met in the pub at the start of February.

His designer clothes had been replaced by a pair of overalls that had stayed clean for about twenty-minutes before they'd been covered in mud, his chin was now dusted with stubble where he'd been too tired to shave, his cheeks were reddened with cold, and his hair stuck out from underneath the beanie he was wearing.

He'd never looked better to me.

"Are you off out on rounds?" he asked, deftly switching one of the empty bottles out for a third one that was full.

"Yeah. I'm going to take Moss out to the far fields to see how they're getting on. I reckon we've only got a few up there left to lamb, but I'm a bit worried about one of them. I might bring her in."

Jamie nodded. "Just let me know if you need a hand. I can get a pen sorted for her."

"Cheers. Are you happy to do the rest of the feeds?"

"Of course," he said. "As long as the triplets here don't suck my fingers off." He smiled affectionately at the smallest of the three lambs who, having had her fill, was now trying to suck Jamie's gloved hand into her mouth.

Triplet births could often be difficult, and theirs had been one of the hardest I'd ever dealt with. The first one had been breech, and things had gone downhill fast from there. We'd lost the ewe, and I'd never forget watching Jamie's face as he cradled the three tiny lambs in his arms, tears streaming down his face as he scrubbed them with towels, trying to keep them warm.

We'd brought them into the house because they were all so small and weak, and Jamie had spent all night sitting on the floor by the fire with them armed with bottles of replacement colostrum.

I'd wanted to tell him it would be okay, but I couldn't lie to him. This was the worst part of lambing, and every loss stayed etched in your heart forever. You never forgot the first time you lost a ewe or a lamb in the same way you never forgot the first time you saw a successful birth. The highs and lows were all part of it, and you could never have one without the other.

All I could do was put a blanket on his shoulders, kiss his forehead, and tell him I was there for him.

I'd wondered if it would be the end of our relationship, if the loss would be too much and burst the pastoral fantasy bubble that so often surrounded farming, and I'd wake up the next morning to nothing but an empty bed and a note saying he couldn't take it.

The bed had been empty the next morning, but all Jamie's stuff had still been there, and when I'd gone downstairs I'd found him in the kitchen with three tiny lambs tottering around his feet as he made up bottles, Moss sitting on the back door mat, wagging her tail in amusement.

Jamie had greeted me with a smile and a kiss and asked how I was doing after all the stress. Then he'd pressed a cup of tea into my hands and told me to sit down at the table while he made me some toast. It was such a small gesture, but it felt so much bigger. It gave me five minutes to just sit and be, and despite the kitchen being full, it felt like it wasn't all on me.

Ever since then, Jamie had dedicated himself to caring for whoever was in the lambing barn—lamb or ewe alike. I loved sneaking in to watch him as he distributed feed and hand fed the lambs, talking to them like they were a bunch of unruly children and sympathising with the ewes like they were mums in a coffee shop.

Moss seemed to have attached herself to him ever since the triplets' birth, and she followed him round like a silent shadow, sitting outside the lambing pens and watching him carefully. I'd seen Jamie talking to her too, asking her questions like they were co-workers and taking her head tilts and tail wags for answers. It made my chest ache every time I saw it because it felt too perfect to be real.

And with every day that passed, my worry grew that everything was going to come crashing down around my ears.

I knew it was ridiculous because he'd been in Heather Bay for nearly two months, and if nothing had put Jamie off so far, then I didn't know what would. But my brain still refused to believe that the beautiful man who'd spent his whole life living in a world of luxury would want to give it all up for early mornings filled with rain, snow, and no small amount of shit and bodily fluids.

"Excuse me," Jamie said, his voice laced with indignant laughter. "Can you not eat my boots, please? I need those." I snapped back to reality and watched as one of the triplets tried to pull at Jamie's laces. He glanced up at me and frowned. "Are you okay? You seemed to drift off there."

"Yeah," I said, blinking several times and forcing my brain back into gear. "Just fucking knackered. Another week or two and it should all be done."

"And then we can sleep until five again." Jamie snorted. "God, I'd never thought I'd consider that a lie-in."

"We might even be able to stretch it to six."

"You spoil me. I'll have to return the favour." He smirked at me, and my stomach bubbled. We hadn't had sex since lambing began, both of us quickly overcome by sheer exhaustion. It was another reason I'd expected Jamie to give up and leave, but instead, it seemed to amuse him.

At some point, I couldn't even remember when, he'd just moved into the house, and every time we crawled into bed for a few snatched hours of sleep, he'd cuddle right up to me and bury his face in my neck. Sometimes he'd drift off before me, and I'd just lie there, listening to him breathe, wondering if there was anything else in the world that would feel like this.

"Okay," Jamie said as he stood, gathering up the empty bottles and extricating himself from the triplets. "Three down. Seven to go. Just let me know if you need to bring any more in, and I'll get things ready."

"Cheers," I said, opening the gate to the pen to let him out quickly. He kissed me softly and smiled.

"Of course. That's what I'm here for."

I was still worrying about everything two days later when I came back to the house to find Lane and Oliver sitting opposite Jamie at the kitchen table, all of them drinking tea and eating thick slices of cake.

"There you are," Lane said. "Glad to see you're still all in one piece."

"Aye, I'm here," I said as I toed off my boots. It was common knowledge amongst the group that at this time of year I'd disappear for a few weeks, and usually, at least one or two of them would pop up at various intervals to make sure I was okay and bring me food since it was all they could do. It was a gesture I appreciated more than they knew.

"How's everything going?" Oliver asked.

"Not too bad. Don't reckon we're too far off being done, but I always say that and then something surprises us."

"Do you want some tea?" Jamie asked, standing up and walking over to the kettle because he already knew the question was more of a formality than anything else. "Lane and Oliver brought us a lasagne, a cheese and herb tear-and-share bread, and a sponge cake."

"The cake's from Mabel," Oliver said. "I mentioned to her yesterday we were coming to see you, and she sent Ivor round with it this morning."

"Tell her thanks from me," I said. I'd only met Lane and Oliver's elderly neighbours a few times, but from what Oliver said, Mabel seemed to spend half her life supplying people she knew with cakes and buns. Usually all delivered by hand by her gruff, grumbling husband, Ivor, who preferred the company of his plants to people.

Jamie handed me a mug of tea and a plate of cake before returning to his seat and pulling out the chair alongside him so I could sit down. "Oliver asked if there's any chance he can see the lambs," he said. "Are you okay if I take him out to the barn in a minute? He can help me feed everyone."

"Of course," I said, looking over at Oliver who was smiling excitedly. He hadn't been around for lambing before since he'd only moved back to Heather Bay last summer. "Be prepared to get mobbed."

"As long as you don't bring one home," Lane said with a wry smile at Oliver.

"I think that's more likely to be you," Oliver said, raising his eyebrow at his boyfriend. "I saw you cooing over those kittens Gary had in the van on Friday."

"But they were so tiny," Lane said. He glanced at me and Jamie and added, "Gary found a cat and a litter of kittens in an old shed of this house we're doing up. The house has been empty for a while, and it doesn't seem like the cats were dumped there, but it's not good for them to be out alone, so Gary decided to take them in. From the sound of it, the mum doesn't have a microchip or anything, so I think she and the babies'll be staying with him."

"Until you take one home," I said.

"I would," Lane said. "I just don't know how Sparrow would feel about it. Then again, we could section off the house easily if we needed to keep them separate. I don't really know a lot about cats, though."

"If you really want one, we can think about," Oliver said, and I knew that was enough permission for Lane to bring one home. "We'll just have to wait until they're older."

"I might talk to Gary on Monday. Y'know, just to see how they're getting on."

We all chatted for a few more minutes, Lane and Oliver catching me and Jamie up on any gossip we'd missed.

Apparently, Noah and Spencer had finally taken the plunge and formally moved in together after dancing around it for months, and Lane thought Alex had been very quiet and secretive for the past few weeks, but Oliver thought it was nothing to be worried about.

"He's just busy," Oliver said. "Especially with all the people coming in for filming. I think quite a few of the production crew pop into Novel Tea regularly, and their orders are never small. I think some of the cast have been in there too. Bastian swore he saw Henry Lu in there last week!"

"Oh, yeah, I'd forgotten the filming had started," I said, sipping my tea. They'd been talking about filming some new period drama series up at the Castle for nearly a year now, but the start of production had been delayed at least once, and with the chaos of lambing, I'd forgotten it was even happening.

They'd contacted me about using some of the land adjoining the Castle estate for filming, and I'd agreed considering they'd offered to pay me. It wasn't a part of the farm I often used for lambing since it was easy for the ewes to be disturbed by people visiting the Castle, but I made a mental note to check my emails and see when they were meant to be going up there. Mostly because I wanted to make sure I knew what it looked like before they started filming so they didn't leave it a total mess that I had to spend time and money fixing.

"Apparently, they'll be here until the end of August," Lane said. "Bits of town keep getting shut down for it."

"Theo managed to get himself and Laurie in as extras, though," Oliver added. "Theo's hoping he might even get a line or two, but I think that might be wishful thinking."

"Does anyone know what the show's actually about?" Jamie asked. "I've heard rumours, and there seems to be some speculation online, but I've not seen anything concrete. It's not an adaptation like *Bridgerton* or *Poldark* is it?"

"I don't think so," Oliver said. "I've not heard anything about a big new adaptation. I think it's an original."

"I'd have thought they'd keep the details close to their chests for as long as possible," I said. "It'll be easier to make a splash that way when they've got a trailer ready to go."

"Maybe we can get Theo to spill the beans," Jamie said as he picked at the last of his slice of cake. "Unless they've all had to sign NDAs."

"Probably," Oliver said. "But maybe if we get him somewhere private, and by that I mean somewhere other than the pub, he'll spill."

Lane sighed. "Does that mean we're going to be hosting another dinner party?" Oliver smiled sweetly at him, and Lane shook his head. "Fine, but we'll wait until lambing's over so these two can come too."

"I love dinner parties," Jamie said. "I can't cook, but I can bring wine."

"Done," Lane said. "Both Laurie and Alex are banned

from bringing drinks to things now. They're both untrustworthy as fuck."

Jamie snorted. "It sounds like there are good stories there."

"There are," Oliver said.

"Come on," Jamie said, draining the last of his tea. "You can tell me while we go and feed everyone. If we leave it much longer, we'll have a full-scale rebellion on our hands, and the triplets will be leading it."

"We'll stay here," Lane said, giving me a pointed look across the table that pinned me to my seat. I had no idea what he wanted to talk to me about, but I got the feeling I was in trouble.

"See you in a bit," Oliver said as he stood up and leant down to give Lane a kiss.

"Do you need anything?" I asked Jamie, catching his hand in mine and giving it a quick squeeze.

"No," he said, stealing a kiss of his own and making my heart skip as he did. "You stay here and sit down for a bit. Then we can do the final rounds when I'm back. Higgs is on duty at the moment, and he'll tell us if he needs anything."

I watched as he led Oliver out the door, the two of them chatting happily together as they went. Then I turned back to look at Lane who had a wry smile across his face.

"So," he said as he sat back in his chair, "when were you planning on telling Jamie you're in love with him?"

CHAPTER TWENTY-FIVE

Jamie

Despite the fact that I'd only spoken to Oliver a couple of times, he turned out to be both a lot of fun and very easy to talk to.

After he'd helped me prep all the bottles, I'd taken him into the lambing barn, and we'd started the afternoon rounds. We currently had eight occupied pens, three with orphaned lambs who we hadn't been able to get another ewe to adopt, so they needed hand-rearing, and the rest with ewes who'd all needed to come in to give birth. Luckily, with some careful help and close supervision, they'd all gone on to have healthy lambs, and several of them were on the verge of being ready to return to their flocks.

We started with the triplets since they were the most demanding, and I showed Oliver how to feed one of them while I sorted the other two.

"That's it," I said, watching Oliver carefully. "Just tilt it up slightly. There you go."

"They're so cute," he said. "How often do they need feeding?"

"It depends on how old they are. When they're first born it's every four hours because the first twenty-four hours are crucial. Then it's four times a day for the first seven days, and after that, we start slowly taking it down to three times, then eventually two before they're weaned. But the bigger they get, the more they need, so it takes longer."

"Wow. So will they stay here until they're weaned?"

"Probably not," I said. "As cute as they are, they're not here to be pets, so as soon as we can, we'll get them out into a flock. We can take bottles out to feed them, and it'll be more fun for them to be with other lambs. But Will wants it to warm up a little more first."

"That makes sense." Oliver nodded, looking down at the lambs with a smile. "They're still cute, though."

"They are. Cute but troublesome." I was very fond of the triplets, but fuck me, raising them by hand had not been easy. Nothing in the world could have prepared me for how exhausting and emotionally draining the experience would be.

If my first few weeks in Heather Bay had been a departure from my normal life, then the last few had been a universe apart from what I'd been used to. But I wouldn't change a moment of it. It felt like I'd finally found a place where I belonged, where more was expected of me than just looking pretty and keeping out of the way.

I just didn't know how to take the next step and make it permanent.

I knew I wanted to. Heather Bay felt like it had been waiting for me all my life, and I'd never felt more at peace before, even if I was physically and emotionally exhausted. It wasn't just the place, though, it was the people. Or more specifically, one person. Will.

Being with Will was like nothing else I'd ever experienced. The closest thing I could compare it to was that feeling I'd only ever heard described in films—a sense of belonging, of coming home.

Will made me feel wanted, welcome, and safe. Like there was a place in his heart that had been there for me all along. I certainly felt that way about mine. It was like there was a Will shaped piece of my soul that had been missing, and I hadn't even known it. Over the years, I'd tried to fill it with other things, but nothing had fit. Then I'd met Will, and with one touch, he'd healed the empty space inside me.

I didn't know how I'd managed without him, and I didn't want to consider the possibility of continuing without him either.

I just had no idea how to tell him.

We'd been so exhausted for the past few weeks that everything outside of lambing had been put on the back burner to be dealt with later. I'd barely even thought of it until two days ago when Daisy had sent me a text asking for proof of life and when the hell I was coming back to London.

I'd sent her a photo of me and the triplets but avoided answering her question.

Mostly because I still didn't know what to say.

I watched Oliver feeding his lamb, giving my two a quick look over as they greedily chugged their bottles. We'd started introducing a little bit of creep feed and roughage into their diet as well, but they still kicked up a stink when they thought it was time for their milk. I didn't know how they knew, but you could set a clock by their internal timers.

"Can I ask you something?" I asked, a random thought sliding into my mind as I looked at Oliver. It was something Will had said ages ago, but it might be the solution I was looking for.

"Sure," Oliver said.

"You moved here from London, right? To be with Lane?"

"Yeah, I did." He smiled fondly like he was remembering something. "I actually grew up here with Lane, Noah, and Alex, but I left when I was eighteen to go to university. Lane and I were dating then, but we broke up when I left, and it hurt so much I didn't want to come back. After uni, I got a job in London, so that kind of gave me an out. Then my nan died at the start of last year and left me her house."

I nodded slowly, wondering where he was going with this. "So you moved back for the house? What made you leave London?"

"Sort of. I came back here to get it fixed up since it was a bit dated and needed sorting before I put it on the market. I was originally intending to sell it and go back to London. Then my mum, who I'm still convinced engineered the whole bloody thing, hired Lane's family to do the work, and Lane was the project manager." He chuckled and shook his head. "It definitely wasn't one of those love-at-first-sight reunions. More like 'oh shit, what the fuck's he doing here?' and then thinking that he'd grown up really fucking hot."

I snorted. "Lust at first sight, then?"

"Pretty much. And then there was some shit with the kitchen, and I ended up going to stay with him... and eventually, I realised I didn't want to sell the house or go back to London. Don't get me wrong, I liked London, but it was so expensive, and I never really had a lot of friends there. Heather Bay felt more like home, and my feelings for Lane just made me realise how much I wanted to stay. It wasn't an easy decision, though, at least not at first. I was worried about my job and whether I was giving up everything I'd worked for to chase a relationship, but I knew I didn't want to lose Lane, so I had to make the leap."

Oliver looked at me with consideration, and I glanced away, realising the bottles were nearly empty. "Are you thinking about moving here?" Oliver asked, his voice gently prompting. It didn't feel like he was fishing for gossip but more like he was enquiring because he was interested. It was a strange feeling.

"Maybe," I said, tilting the bottles up so the lambs could get every last drop. "I think I want to, but..."

"It's complicated?"

"Yes, but it doesn't feel like it should be, so I don't know why I'm so confused." I stood up and walked over to check Oliver's bottle, the two lambs at my feet following me like shadows. It felt easier to talk while I was busy, so I continued. "For a long time, it felt like something was missing in my life. I couldn't figure out what it was, so I just buried it and kept going because it was easier to fuck around and party than to actually do any kind of fucking introspection. But then... I don't know, it just got too hard to ignore. Everything felt so fucking tedious, you know? Like I was just going through the motions."

I beckoned Oliver to follow me, and we quickly exited the triplets' pen, ducking out before the three hooligans could follow me and demand more food. I showed him into the next pen, where we had another four orphans. None of them were related, but they were kept together for warmth and company, and they'd all bonded nicely.

"I get that," Oliver said. "Sometimes you just get stuck, and it's hard to know where else to go or what to do, so you just stay where you are."

"Exactly," I said, handing him another bottle and showing how to feed one of the lambs. I took out another and began to feed a second hungry mouth. "But in my case, I've literally done nothing else with my life, so I had less than zero clue what to do. I did the absolutely logical thing and ran away."

Oliver laughed. "To Yorkshire?"

"I hoped it would dissuade my friends from coming too and turning it into some sort of find yourself wellness retreat where you drink kale smoothies and meditate, then claim inner peace after three days and go out on the lash in the nearest nightclub."

"Yeah, Heather Bay doesn't exactly scream bougie escape from it all," Oliver said with a grin. "It's not exactly crunchy wellness territory. I don't think Gwyneth Paltrow is going to be turning up here any time soon."

"Probably not, although it sounds like this period drama has plenty of star talent attached." I'd seen Henry Lu in a couple of London clubs before, always surrounded by people. I'd never managed to get close to him, but I had bagged a few A-listers over the years. Most of them were never as good in bed as they seemed to think.

"It does. I think they want to make a splash." He tilted the bottle he was holding and looked at me in a way that seemed to suggest he knew we were getting off topic. "So you ran away to Yorkshire, had a one-night stand with a hot farmer, and now you want to stay?"

"Pretty much," I said. "There's something about Will, about here, that just... It changed how I feel about everything, and now I have no fucking clue what to do. I don't think I want to go back to London, but what if I tell Will that and he freaks out and thinks I'm being this weird, clingy guy who won't leave him alone? From the outside, it does sound a bit creepy, the whole track down a one-night stand, end up seeing him more, move onto his farm, learn his job, then never leave. Fuck, I sound like some sort of serial killer. The next thing you know the *Daily Mail* will be printing salacious stories about me murdering Will and burying him in Dylan's perfectly manicured muck heap."

Oliver snorted. "Seriously?"

"What?"

"Can I be completely honest with you? And not in a going-to-be-an-asshole way but as friends. And I know we've literally only hung out a couple of times, but that's the way it works around here. You're one of us now."

"That doesn't sound cultish, honest," I said with a grin, and Oliver rolled his eyes.

"You're the one who talked about being a stalker slash serial killer. Also, if you're going to be friends with us, you should know our conversations always come back to either sex or murder. I don't know how, they just do."

"I can live with that." In fact, I thought I rather liked it. Even though I'd only met Will's friends a couple of times since trips to the pub had been limited due to the start of lambing, I already knew I liked them. They were the sort of people it would be easy to fall in love with, the ones you'd always want at your side, no matter what happened.

It was also clear they'd be the ones calling you out on your bullshit and interfering in your life because they couldn't help but get involved. It seemed to come from a place of love, though, and that made me happy. I had very few friends like that.

It comforted me to know that if things went sideways, Will had a strong network of people around him who'd help pick up the pieces.

"Good," Oliver said. "Now back to Will. You already know you need to talk to him, you admitted that, but if the only thing that's stopping you is that you're worried you've fallen for a man who doesn't want you back, then that's a pretty shit reason to avoid him. You can bury your head in the sand for as long as you want, but we both know it's not going to make things easier. It's probably just going to make them worse because the longer you drag it out, the more time you and Will have to sit and think about it. Plus, the longer you leave it, you'll both start wondering why the other hasn't brought it up, and then you get resentment and anger and all that other shit."

I sighed. Oliver had a point, and I hated it.

"You know I'm right," Oliver continued.

"I know, and I hate it."

Oliver laughed. "Good, it means we're getting somewhere. Seriously, though, I know how hard it is to think about upending your entire life for a relationship. But given what you've told me about your life in London, I don't think you'd be considering it unless Will meant something to you. And just because you're thinking of moving here doesn't mean you have to move in with him or give up your place in London. I get the feeling you can afford to rent somewhere here for a few months and see how things go. If they work out, then perfect, if they don't, then no harm done. Well, you might be heartbroken, but you'll have learnt something about yourself. And I kinda get the feeling you haven't done a lot of that until recently."

"This year has been hideously educational," I said dryly. "But it does mean I can finally do things most people can do by the age of twenty-one like make scrambled eggs and go shopping."

"Trust me, I've met plenty of adults who can't do either of those things. One of my old flatmates was still shit at cooking, and he was, like, twenty-eight, so you're good."

"Don't tell Will. He's still on a mission to get me to learn how to clean the bathroom. I'm still holding out hope he'll let me off if I volunteer to do other things instead."

"I've not tried swapping housework for sexual favours before," Oliver said with another laugh.

"If you can make it work, you'll be more successful than me. Apparently, if I've dealt with afterbirth and lambs covered in shit and bodily fluids, which I have now because lambing season, then I should be able to clean a toilet. If I move in with him, I'm going to offer to pay for a cleaner just so I don't have to do it."

"I guess you'll have to talk to him, then," Oliver said. "It's either that or keep coming up with excuses not to clean the toilet."

CHAPTER TWENTY-SIX

Will

I STARED AT LANE, trying to make my mouth move while the sound of blood rushed through my ears. "I... I'm not... I'm not in love with him."

Lane raised an eyebrow and gave me a knowing look. "Yeah, and pigs can fucking fly. You love him, Will, and that's not a bad thing."

"I'm not saying it would be," I said, not sure why I was arguing. I didn't know why the idea of being in love with Jamie terrified me, only that it did. "I'm just not."

"Will," Lane said softly as he reached out over the table to grab my hand that was resting on it, still cradling my cup of tea. "Look at me. It's okay to fall in love with him, and it's okay to be fucking terrified about it."

I didn't say anything because I couldn't find any words. I just let him squeeze my hand and stared at the table wondering why I felt so scared when all I'd ever wanted was to find someone to love. Maybe it was because I didn't believe this could be real.

"For as long as I've known you, you've always put everyone and everything else first," Lane continued. "Even when we've tried to talk you out of it. And maybe, at times, we haven't been the best at dissuading you, but I don't think you'd have listened to us anyway. You've always been the one shouldering everything, and I'm pretty sure you've never opened yourself up to the idea of sharing the burden with anyone because you don't think anyone will want it."

"They don't, though," I said. "When I've tried in the past... it's always been too much. There's too much work. It takes up too much time and too much of my money. Nobody's ever really understood what it means to be a shepherd."

"No, they haven't. But I think Jamie might, or at least I think he might be willing to learn. I mean, look at what he's done since he arrived. I barely even know the man, but even I know you don't throw yourself into dating a farmer just before lambing season if you're not willing to get involved."

Lane had a point, but it still felt like there was a wall between my head and my heart.

"I'm just... I keep thinking, what if he gets bored? What if he realises how rough this life can be and discovers he's made a mistake being with me? Jamie has a whole life back in London. I can't ask him to give that up just for me."

"You're not forcing him," Lane said. "He's already been

here since February. If he wants to be here, that's his choice. The question is, do you want him here?"

"Yes," I said, the answer coming before I could even think it through.

"There you go, then. It's not rocket science, Will. If he wants to be here and you want him here, then that should be enough. And if you're worried he doesn't know what he's getting into, then I think you're doing him a disservice because the man I saw today isn't the pretty tourist you took home that first night. I don't think he's even the same man you first brought to the pub. I think there's more fire and determination in him than you've given him credit for, and I think there's a farming heart in there too. You want to know why?"

"Why?"

"Because this is the first year you haven't called me when you lost a ewe."

I stared at him, trying to process what he'd just said. Lane smiled softly, then added, "Every year since we've been friends, the first time something went wrong, you called me afterwards. And this year, you didn't. I thought at first it was because nothing had gone wrong, then you sent those photos in the chat of the lambs in the barn, and I realised things had, but this time, you didn't need me. Because you had someone else to lean on."

"Shit," I said, suddenly worried I'd massively fucked up. "I'm so sorry."

"No, that's not what I meant," Lane said, giving me a fond but exasperated expression. Apparently, I'd missed his point by a mile. "You've found someone else you can share those experiences with, and that's a good thing. I know you, Will. You take everything on by yourself, and you're not good at being open when you're struggling, so the fact that you felt comfortable showing Jamie that part of you is a sign that he's special. He means something to you, even if you don't want to admit it."

"It's not that I don't want to admit it. It's just that if I do, it makes it real, and then it'll be so much worse when it falls apart."

Lane frowned and flicked my fingers. "No. We're not having that."

"Not having what?"

"None of this fucking pessimistic bollocks. Yeah, it could all go wrong, the same as every relationship. Or it could all go right, and you'll never know that if you fucking clam up and push him away. You have a good thing here. Don't you dare throw it away before it's even gotten off the ground because you're so convinced it's going to go wrong you won't even try. I love you, Will, but this is just bollocks."

"What happened to being supportive?" I asked, trying not to smile because I knew Lane was right.

"I've been supportive, and now I'm calling you out on your bullshit before you shoot yourself in the foot with your nonsense." He grinned at me. "You know you'd say the same to me."

"I'm pretty sure I did when you started hooking up with Oliver last year."

"Exactly. This is just me returning the favour."

"I suppose I should be grateful, then."

"Yes. And you should be grateful I'm the one sitting here instead of Spencer. Or Theo."

"I could just distract Theo with the lambs," I said. "Probably could do the same with Spencer too."

Lane laughed. "True. I know you too well to get distracted by you throwing cute shit at me."

I nodded. "It's good, though. As much as I don't want to admit it, I think I needed to hear it." Lane's brutal pep talk hadn't eased all my fears, but hearing his perspective had helped. It had reminded me of the little things I'd just brushed off because they'd seemed so incidental at the time but were so much bigger than I'd realised.

Jamie and I had never really talked about what our future would look like, and that had been a mistake, but we'd still managed to muddle through and build something together. It felt like our lives had become so intertwined over the past two months that it would take forever to untangle the threads if we broke up, but I didn't want that. I wanted to keep building a life with him, no matter how messy and muddled and busy it was.

"I think you're right," I said quietly, a small smile twisting the corner of my lips.

"About what?" Lane asked with a shit-eating grin that told me he knew exactly what I was talking about. He just wanted to hear me say it.

"I think I love Jamie."

"Ha! I knew it!" Lane did a ridiculous fist pump, and I chuckled.

"Yeah, yeah, you win," I said. "Fuck, when did this happen?"

Like I Needed

"I don't know. It's love. You don't exactly plan for it. It's not something you stick in your calendar or order on Amazon," Lane said. "It just happens. Whether you want it to or not."

"I suppose I'll have to talk to him now."

"Yes, but you knew that anyway," Lane said. "I'm happy for you, though. Jamie's good for you."

"He is. I don't know how to describe it, but when he's here, I just feel... balanced. Like everything isn't so heavy. He makes everything a little brighter just by being here." I smiled to myself and looked down at the table. It felt like my heart was glowing in my chest as I thought about Jamie and everything he meant to me. "He's not perfect, but he's perfect for me. And that's all that matters."

"I—"

But whatever Lane was going to say was cut off as the back door swung open and Oliver and Jamie clattered inside. The pair of them were chatting happily, and Lane's expression softened as he looked at his boyfriend. I'd never seen him look as happy as he did when he looked at Oliver, and I wondered if I looked at Jamie the same way.

"Did you have fun?" Lane asked.

"I did! They're all so cute, but they're so cheeky too. They kind of remind me of puppies, just bigger," Oliver said, unzipping his coat and toeing off his boots. "Don't worry, I didn't put one in the car. I don't think I could cope with all the energy."

"How're the triplets?" I asked Jamie, who was stripping off his overalls by the back door.

"Honestly? They're hooligans. I'm surprised they

haven't all ganged up on me and forced me to hand over more food."

I chuckled. "I think we can look at putting them out next week. They're big enough to play with the others, and Higgs said it's meant to warm up on Monday."

"That would work. I think it would be good for them to have others to play with. And we can just stick the bottles on the bike and take them out twice a day. It shouldn't be too hard," Jamie said. "Also, I just saw Higgs. He said that everyone looks peaceful, but he wouldn't be surprised if that last ewe in the far fields went into labour later. Apparently, she looked more uncomfortable than normal but wasn't showing any visible signs of distress. He's just going back to his to grab some tea and then he'll go back out there."

I nodded. "Okay. We can go and do an early set of rounds in a minute, see if we can see anything."

The ewe in question was the only one we were waiting for, and all of us were holding our breaths. When we'd had the vet out a few days ago, he'd said he couldn't feel anything wrong, and the lamb was still happy and healthy but just taking its time. The ewe had had three previous successful pregnancies, but the longer this went on, the more anxious I was becoming. But the fact that Higgs thought something was starting to happen was a good sign.

"That sounds like our cue," Lane said, standing up from the table. "We'll leave you to it. Let us know how everything goes."

"I'll send you a message later," I said. I stood up and

walked around the table to give Lane a hug, and he gave me a fierce one in return.

"Don't let him go," Lane whispered. "If you love him, tell him. Don't make the mistake of thinking he already knows. You'll never forgive yourself otherwise."

"I won't."

"Good." Lane clapped me on the shoulder and released me, walking over to Oliver and stealing a quick kiss before he put his coat on. Lane knew more than most what it was like to watch the love of your life walk away, and I knew he wouldn't have laid it on so thick unless he thought I needed to hear it.

Jamie slipped past Lane and Oliver and appeared by my side. I put my arm around his waist without thinking, pressing a kiss to his temple. "Are you okay?" I asked.

"Yeah, just a bit nervous. I really want everything to be okay."

I nodded, pleased that Jamie and I seemed to be on the same page. "Do you want to go out and keep an eye on her? We can take some food out with us. There's a barn in the field too if we need to camp out for a bit."

"That sounds perfect. We can take a couple of flasks of soup out and some of the bread Lane and Oliver brought. That should do us for a while," he said, and I saw him thinking everything through.

My heart swelled, and I wondered how I could have ever doubted Lane. It seemed so obvious to me now.

Jamie was the love and light of my life.

CHAPTER TWENTY-SEVEN

Jamie

IT DIDN'T TAKE LONG to heat some soup and pour it into a couple of thermoses, wrap some of Oliver's delicious smelling tear-and-share bread in some foil, put my boots and overalls back on again, and load up the quad bike with everything we might need. Nell and Moss perched on the back as I slid on behind Will, clutching him tightly.

If I was going to stay, we were going to have to talk about getting another bike.

Maybe I could actually use my sizeable trust fund to be productive for once and get a few things the farm desperately needed. If Will protested, I'd gently argue my point, and if that failed, I'd resort to bribery in the form of blow jobs. It wouldn't be the most ethical way to get what I wanted, but I wasn't above it. Especially if it would get us some extra equipment and stop Will muttering about repairs.

The sun was starting to sink beyond the horizon as we approached the gate, and I saw Higgs leaning against it.

I'd grown very fond of the quiet, insightful man over the past few months and enjoyed his company. He was a good teacher and hadn't seemed to think anything of showing a city boy with no experience how to mend fences, change the bike's oil, feed lambs, get stones out of sheep's feet, and everything in between. He'd squeezed my shoulder when I'd cried over our first death and hadn't given me some spiel about sucking it up like I'd expected. He'd just told me it never got easier.

Higgs had even introduced me to the knackerman when he'd come to collect the bodies in his truck. He was a tiny old man named Frank with kind eyes and a kinder smile, who'd patted my hand and asked me about myself. In return, Frank had answered my questions, and I'd walked away from the whole encounter with a strange feeling of peace and community.

Out here, everyone shared in the joy and tragedy of the season. It was something I'd never experienced before.

"How's she doing?" Will asked as he stopped the ATV just short of the gate and climbed down. I followed him.

"Well," Higgs said, pointing at a spot in the corner of the field, not far from the gate, where the ewe had hunkered down away from prying eyes and the nippy wind that had blown up as the sun set. "Things are finally on the move."

"She's taken her time about it," Will said, leaning on the gate next to him.

"She did last year and all. Nowt in the world that'll rush her."

"Did Forest think there's more than one in there?" I asked, referring to the vet who'd come out at the start of the week.

"He thinks there's just one," Will said. "But it's always hard to tell without a scan."

I nodded and slipped my hand into Will's. "However many there are, let's just hope for a safe arrival."

Will smiled at me and squeezed my fingers before turning back to the ewe. She kept pawing the ground, digging up the soft earth, then walking away and coming back. She looked up, noticing us for the first time, and I wondered if she'd want to move away. But she didn't seem upset by our presence, and a moment later, she was back to digging again.

This continued for a while, and like the rest of her pregnancy, the ewe seemed in no hurry to get things over with.

"If you want to go home, you can," Will said to Higgs. "We can manage."

"Are you sure?"

"Yeah. Go and get some sleep. I'll give you a call if we get into serious trouble."

Higgs looked at the ewe for a moment, then across the rest of the field at the flock all huddled together, the lambs all tucked in alongside their mothers in the growing dark. "All right. I'll have my phone on." He nodded at Will. "I'll see you tomorrow."

"See you tomorrow."

Higgs turned and walked back down the track. This flock was the closest to the farm, so it wouldn't take him long to get back. The only reason Will and I had used the

ATV was because of the amount of stuff we'd needed to bring, although most of it would only be needed in an emergency.

Soon, Will and I were alone, leaning on the gate together while the dogs snoozed on the back of the bike. I knew now probably wasn't the best moment to bring up everything I'd talked about with Oliver, but I couldn't get it out of my mind. And if we were going to be here for a while, we might as well fill the time.

The only problem was I had no idea where to start.

"So," Will said eventually and my heart skipped. "Oliver liked the lambs, then?"

"Yeah," I said, smiling to myself. We'd had this conversation at least twice now, and I wondered if he was trying to use it as a segue into something else. "He was good with them too. And we had a good chat while we were out there. He's really nice."

"He is. I didn't know him before, but I got to know him last year, and I like him. He's very down to earth in some ways and creative in others. I think he and Lane balance each other out."

"I got that feeling." I looked up at the blanket of stars beginning to twinkle above us, wondering if I should just go for it. The ewe was lying down now, seemingly very unbothered by everything, so maybe this was my window. "Oliver told me a bit about moving here. About how he worked things out with Lane."

Will hummed but didn't say anything, and I didn't dare look at him in case I lost my nerve.

"It made me realise something," I added. "Something

I've sort of known for a while, but now I'm completely certain."

"What's that?"

"I don't want to go back to London. Ever." I gripped the top bar of the gate in my gloved hands and ploughed on, determined to get everything out before Will cut me off. "These past few months have been incredible. I've learnt so much about, well, everything, and it's made me realise what I really want in life. And I'm not going to find it in a London nightclub."

"What... what do you want?" Will asked softly. I finally turned my head and saw him gazing back at me, hope and longing shining in his eyes.

"You. This. All of it. I know it's a world away from everything I had before, and I know you're worried I'll get bored and want to leave. But I'm not. I know that. And I'm not going to get bored of you either, Will. I lo—" There was a plaintive bleat from behind me as I spoke, and I whirled around to see our ewe on her feet, visibly distressed and straining despite the dimming light.

"What's wrong?" I asked. Will was already opening the gate and darting through, ordering the dogs to stay put.

"I don't know. The lamb might be stuck." He pulled a head torch out of his pocket, slipping the band around his beanie and flicking it on. I did the same as I followed him. At first, I'd thought the head torches were ridiculous, but they definitely had their uses.

"It's all right," Will said softly as we approached. "Steady, girl, steady. That's it. We're not going to hurt you."

The ewe bleated again, and I saw her body shake as she

strained, her body following its instincts and starting to push. Will made quiet hushing sounds as we got closer, and I kept behind him until he could get a hand on her, carefully swinging his leg over her to hold her carefully in place.

I walked around to the back, trying to think through all the various articles and PDFs I'd read through about abnormal deliveries and lamb presentation. The golden rule was making sure that intervention was actually needed, and there was a chance we'd jumped the gun a little, but I knew Will was on edge because it was the last one.

Also, seeing her suddenly so upset after being so calm wasn't the best sign.

One quick look told us the first waterbag had burst, and I saw two small hooves and the smooth curve of the lamb's nose, covered by the membrane of the second waterbag, which hadn't quite burst. It was immediately obvious what the problem might be as the ewe strained again, trying to push the lamb free.

The lamb was enormous.

"Shit," I said. "That's a chunky baby you've got there, mama."

"No wonder," Will said. "You've been cooking him for a while."

The ewe bleated again as she panted and pushed, but the lamb barely moved. She was going to need some help to ease it free.

"Okay," I said, looking up at Will. "I'm going to get some gloves and some disinfectant. I'll be right back."

Will nodded and gently soothed the ewe as I hurried

back to the ATV. Nell and Moss were waiting but were happy to stay put as I grabbed some new plastic gloves that would cover my arms, some lubrication, and some diluted disinfectant in a bottle. The one thing we needed to avoid was the ewe getting an infection, so I needed to be as clean as I could be in the middle of a muddy field.

I'd barely been away for two minutes by the time I returned, but the lamb still hadn't moved. I quickly ripped open the pack of gloves and rolled them on, looking up at Will. I'd only had to do this once before, when the triplets were born, and that had been completely different.

With another shuddering contraction, the lamb was expelled a tiny bit farther forward and the waterbag surrounding it burst. We had to make sure the membrane didn't get stuck over its nose, or it would suffocate before it was even born. But a quick glance showed no immediate danger.

"Okay," Will said. "Grasp its forelegs gently, and when she pushes, you pull. You might need to add some lubrication." His eyes met mine and he gave me a little smile. "You've got this."

His words made a layer of calm settle over me, and I let out a long breath as I added lube around the lamb to ease its passage, then gently wrapped my hands around it's front legs. "All right, mum," I said. "Time to push."

I watched as the ewe began to strain again, and as she pushed, I began to pull back, slowly and carefully easing the lamb's shoulders through the ewe's pelvis.

"That's it, good girl," Will said. "Couple more times and you'll have a baby."

"A beautiful, big baby," I said as the ewe started to push again.

The lamb began to slide free, and suddenly, there was a sticky, messy, and heavy baby sheep dropping into my lap and covering my overalls with all the fluids that accompanied birth.

"Shit. There we go!" I carefully lowered the lamb to the floor as Will released the ewe. Her instincts kicked in and she turned, immediately starting to clean her baby who started squeaking and bleating, the bond between them forming before our eyes.

I looked across at Will who was grinning, his eyes taking in the state of me. "You know, you were going to say something before that happened," he said.

"I was," I said, walking over to him and leaning in to press a kiss to his cold lips, trying to avoid letting my body brush against his. "Maybe I should clean up before we have this conversation, though?"

"Maybe. Or I can just say it. I love you, Jamie Stone, and I don't ever want you to leave. I want you to stay here, with me, for as long as you'll have me."

I smiled, my heart feeling so big I thought it might burst. "I love you too. And I don't ever plan on leaving. You're stuck with me now."

"Good," Will chuckled. "Then I can tell you, you really need a bath. Especially because you have birthing fluids on your face."

"What? Fuck! Ew, how?" I looked at the ewe and her safely delivered baby, who was just starting to stand. "It's a good thing I love all of you. Because that is absolutely fucking disgusting."

Will grinned and drew me in for a carefully placed kiss. "Good thing indeed."

CHAPTER TWENTY-EIGHT

Will

CONFESSING my love to Jamie while he was covered in blood and bodily fluids hadn't been part of my plan, but that was farming. Sometimes you just had to roll with it.

We stayed out in the field until the ewe had passed the afterbirth, and once I was satisfied mother and baby were safe and healthy, we packed up and headed back to the house. I knew Jamie and I had a lot to talk about because one declaration of love didn't solve everything, but it was a start, and it meant a few things could wait.

Jamie stripped off as soon as we set foot in the house, dumping his overalls on the kitchen floor so they could go into the separate washing machine I kept for work clothes. I unpacked the little bit of food we'd taken but never eaten and watched as he started pulling off his jeans and jumper until he stood there in a t-shirt and his underwear.

Desire ignited in my chest, fuelled by happiness and

relief. Jamie wanted to stay, and the worst of lambing season was over. He loved me too, and that was still something I couldn't quite believe. But if I wanted to make this work, I had to. Lane had said I needed to stop being so pessimistic, and that was the first step.

"Don't think too hard," Jamie said. "You'll hurt yourself."

"What if I'm thinking about you?"

"Then by all means, think away." He grinned, scooping up the armful of clothes and carrying them through into the utility room. "Where do you want me to put these?"

"Just on the floor. I'll sort them tomorrow."

"Are you sure?"

"Yeah," I said. I had much better things to do right then than sort washing, and it wasn't as if Jamie was short of clothes. "Come here."

Jamie strolled back into the kitchen, smirking at me. "You do realise I'm smelly and kinda gross right now?"

I shrugged. "I can still kiss you."

"Can I at least grab a quick shower before we fuck?" Jamie asked as he slid into my arms and wrapped his hands around my neck. "Because I *really* need you to fuck me right now, but I also don't want to smell like birthing fluid."

"Go have a bath," I said, drawing him in for a soft kiss. "We can fuck later."

"Hmm, a bath does sound tempting. But you promise you'll fuck me? And give me exactly what I want?"

"Yes. I always do. I like it when you tell me what you want."

"Good, because I like bossing you around. It suits you,"

he said teasingly. He kissed me again, nipping my lip and drawing a moan from my throat. "I'm going to bathe. You can come and sit with me if you want. Just give me a few minutes to clean up."

"No worries. I'll tidy up down here."

Jamie stole another kiss before he slipped out of my arms and towards the stairs, and I watched him go with an appreciative eye, my cock thickening at the thought of being inside him again. The exhaustion of lambing had overtaken any new relationship honeymoon phase we'd been having, and as a result, we hadn't fucked properly in weeks. The closest we'd come were some very sleepy hand jobs one night when Higgs had been on the night shift and Jamie and I had actually managed to get to bed before eleven.

I heard Jamie moving around upstairs and the rush of water filling the bath as I pottered around the kitchen packing things away. We hadn't eaten anything since the cake with Lane and Oliver, but I could easily reheat us something later. Food was the last thing on my mind.

When the kitchen was clean and the fire had been stoked, I headed upstairs. The bathroom door was slightly ajar, but I still knocked before I went in.

Jamie was sprawled out in the bath, which was full of bubbles, looking more relaxed than he had in days. I wondered if he'd been worrying about talking to me as much as I'd been worrying about talking to him.

"You know," Jamie said, watching me with a hungry smile. "I think you're wearing too many clothes."

"I'm not going to fit in that bath with you," I said. "We'd need a fucking swimming pool for that."

Jamie sighed but conceded. "Fine, but you can at least take off a layer or two." I pulled off my jumper and my t-shirt, leaving me shirtless, but left my jeans on so I could sit on the floor, which was wooden and not warm. "Very nice," Jamie said. "I've missed getting naked with you. And I don't mean just like the five minutes every morning when we're trying to get dressed."

I sat down on the floor opposite the bath, leaning against the wall next to the radiator. The wall was cold but bearable. "Do you regret it?"

"What? Not having sex? I'll be honest, I've been too fucking exhausted to even think about it." He chuckled and flicked some bubbles into the air. "Which is a fucking novelty for me. When I first arrived, I thought not having sex for, like, three days, was the worst thing that could've happened to me. But no, I don't regret it. Because if I regretted it, then I'd be regretting everything that's happened with you. I do miss it, though, which is why you're going to absolutely rail me when I get out. I want to get utterly dicked down until I can't move."

I chuckled. "I think I can manage that."

"Good." He flicked a couple of bubbles towards me and grinned. "So you love me, then? And you want me to stay?"

"Yes, and yes," I said. "I always wanted you to stay. I just didn't think you'd want to. I'm not like any of the other men you've been with. I can't give you anything like your life in London. And I... I've never been good enough for anyone before, so I didn't think this time would be any different."

"Would it help if I told you I had some of the same fears?" Jamie asked, twisting onto his side and folding his arms on the edge of the bath, resting his head on them.

"You did?" I stared at him. It had somehow never crossed my mind that Jamie might have fears too. I didn't know why. Maybe it was because he'd always seemed so carefree, but that had been so selfish of me to assume.

"Yeah. I didn't think you'd want me to stay. I mean, I'm basically the cute equivalent of one of those men you see on those true crime TV shows. I basically just inserted myself into your life, moved into your house, and started working for you. I know you said you were okay with it, but I couldn't help thinking I might have crossed a line. Besides, just because I wanted to be here didn't mean you actually wanted me to stay."

"Never think that," I said, getting up and walking across to the bath, dropping to my knees in front of him and pulling him into a fierce kiss, not caring that he was wet and covered in bubbles. "I need you Jamie, more than I've ever needed anything in my life. You make me feel like I matter."

"You do matter," he said, pulling me closer until we were pressed together over the edge of the bath. "To me, to your friends, to this place. You changed my life, Will, so don't you dare tell me you don't matter because to me you are everything. And you don't need me half as much as I need you."

I took his head in my hands and looked at him, drinking

in every detail of his face. "Let's call it even. We both need each other."

"Done," Jamie said. "Now take me to bed."

I smirked, getting my feet under me before reaching into the bath and lifting Jamie out, not caring that he was soaked and I was half-dressed. Jamie yelped, wrapping his hands around my neck and clinging to me as I carried him, bridal style, towards our room.

"That wasn't what I meant," he said, breaking into laughter as I deposited him on top of the duvet.

"You said to take you to bed."

"But I'm still wet."

"You'll dry," I pointed out as I undid my jeans and pushed them off along with my underwear. Then I grabbed the lube off my bedside table and tossed it over to him so we wouldn't have to try to find it later.

I climbed onto the bed, blanketing him with my body, and claimed his mouth with a deep kiss. Jamie groaned, his hands tangling in my hair and sliding down to my shoulders, his nails trailing over my skin in a way that made me shiver with anticipation. His tongue slipped into my mouth, and I moaned, my hips grinding down against his. I felt Jamie's cock thicken against mine, the friction sending a bolt of pleasure rushing up my spine.

Jamie opened his legs, and I fell between them, groaning as he wrapped his ankles around my waist to pull me closer against him. I rolled my hips again, revelling in the feeling of my cock against his.

"Don't come," Jamie growled in my ear, his voice low and commanding, and I moaned. "I mean it, Will. I know it's been a while, and you're desperate, but you are not allowed to come until you're buried inside me and you've given me everything I want, and that includes making me come."

I stilled, my body trembling as desperation flooded me, but I loved it when Jamie took control, and all I wanted was to make him happy.

"Good," Jamie said, running his nails down my spine. "Now I want you to suck my dick and play with my hole. Get me ready to take your perfect cock so you can slide right in and fuck me."

I kissed down his body, filling every touch with devotion as my lips etched adoration into his skin. Jamie's whimpers and moans flooded my ears as his fingers twisted in my hair, guiding me exactly where he wanted. I pressed a soft kiss to the silky head of his cock before wrapping my lips around his shaft and taking him into my mouth.

Jamie gasped, his hands tightening in my hair as I started to suck him. I tightened my lips as I pumped his cock, occasionally slowing to flick my tongue across his slit, teasing him as I licked up the beads of precum collecting there. My fingers slid down to tease his balls, using the saliva that dripped from my lips to slick the skin as I rolled them between my fingers.

"Mmm, yes... You can, fuck, you can go harder," Jamie groaned, lifting his hips to push his cock deeper into my mouth. "Fuck, I... I want it a little rough. Use your nails. I'll tell you if it's too much."

I hummed around his cock, slowly sliding my nails across the sensitive skin of his balls, pressing just a little

harder than I'd ever normally consider. Jamie moaned
loudly, a shiver of delight running through him. I did it
again, then tugged them, using my other hand in combina-
tion with my mouth to jack and tease his dick until Jamie
was writhing in pleasure underneath me.

"More," he said. "Will, I need more."

"Tell me what you want," I said, letting his cock slide
out of my mouth.

"Eat my ass and get me ready for you. I fucking need
you inside me."

"As you wish," I said with a wink as I lowered my head
to run my tongue down his taint. From somewhere above
me, Jamie chuckled affectionately. Then he gasped and
swore as I flicked my tongue across the puckered skin of his
hole, teasing and sucking it until it relaxed enough for me
to press the tip of my tongue inside.

Reaching out, I fumbled for the bottle of lube, trying to
remember where I'd put it. My fingers met Jamie's, and he
caressed my hand, sending a little burst of heat across my
skin before pushing the bottle into my searching fingers.

I clicked it open, pouring some out. I was sure it went
half onto my fingers and half onto the bed, but I didn't care.
I was too busy showing the man in front of me how much I
adored him to worry about spilt lube. Especially when the
sheets were going to need changing anyway.

"Oh fuck, yes!" Jamie moaned as I carefully pressed a
slick finger into him alongside my tongue, trying to avoid
getting too much lube in my mouth since I hated the taste.
"Don't go slow. Please, Will, just give me more."

I looked up at him and grinned as I started to pump the

single digit in and out of his tight ass. "Does the please mean I get an option?" I asked teasingly.

"No," Jamie said. "I'm just being polite."

"That's not like you. Usually, you're just a bossy brat."

"And you find it hot as fuck, so do as you're told and give me another." Jamie groaned happily as I did as I was told and pushed another finger into him, starting to stretch him open. I added my tongue, sliding it between my fingers to tease the sensitive skin and pressing kisses wherever I could.

I pumped my fingers in and out, working them faster and harder and curling the tips to rub them over his prostate, making him gasp and moan and thrust back onto me. My cock was achingly hard between my legs, but I didn't want to touch myself. I didn't trust myself not to try to get myself off, and I wanted to save all my desperation for Jamie.

"Fuck me," Jamie said. His hands were still on my head, and he tugged my hair to pull me towards him. I went willingly, letting my fingers slide out of him as I moved up his body. I rested my hands on either side of his head, kissing him slowly so he could taste himself on my tongue.

"How do you want me?"

"Like this." He lifted his hips again, wrapping his legs around my waist like he'd done when we'd first been making out. "I want you right here, where I can see you. I want to watch your face and kiss you as you give yourself to me. I want to watch you fall apart."

I groaned and nodded, unable to think of a response before he was kissing me again. Getting a hand between us was awkward, but I managed to grasp my shaft and press the swollen head of my cock to his hole. Jamie groaned into my mouth as I slid slowly into him, the pleasure threatening to overwhelm me. He nipped my bottom lip, each of his kisses a raging inferno of need.

"God, fuck! Your cock feels so fucking perfect inside me," Jamie said.

"Love being inside you," I said, my lips pressed against his as I began to rock my hips. He was so fucking tight and hot, and I'd forgotten just how perfect he felt around me.

I fucked him slowly at first, giving both of us a chance to adjust, but with every thrust, I felt my patience stretching out like a rubber band.

And eventually it snapped.

"Yes! Fuck yes, Will. Give it to me!" Jamie cried out as I snapped my hips forward, power and control in perfect balance as I gave him everything I had. My muscles started to tremble as I fucked him deep and hard, pouring all my love and lust into every move.

All I wanted was to make Jamie happy. To give him the pleasure he craved and deserved.

I reached down with one hand to adjust his hip, lifting his legs around my waist so I could fuck deeper into him. It meant I could adjust the angle of my thrusts, and Jamie cried out as I began to hammer his prostate, the sound of his pleasure filling the room and driving me wild.

His words melted into moans as he clutched at me, burying his face in my neck as I sent him higher, his cock trapped between our bodies. Wild desire coursed through me, overtaking all my senses. Heat flooded my muscles, and I felt my balls starting to tighten. I was so close, but I needed to make Jamie come. That was what I'd been told to do, and that was all I wanted.

"Touch yourself," I said. "I want to feel you come."

"Just, fuck, just keep doing that," Jamie said, his voice messy and breathless. "I... fuck, Will... Just there. Oh fuck, don't you dare fucking stop."

I wasn't planning on it. My whole body was burning, but I held on with everything I had left, thrusting deep into Jamie and giving him everything he wanted.

Jamie cried out, his fingers scrabbling at the back of my neck and digging into the skin. His body tensed underneath me, and I felt his release coat my skin as his channel tightened around me, milking my cock and making it impossible to hold back.

"Jamie," I growled, losing all sense of pace and rhythm as I chased my release.

"Come for me, Will," Jamie said, sounding utterly wrecked as he peppered my neck with kisses.

Those words were all it took to send me hurtling over the edge, still wrapped in his arms.

CHAPTER TWENTY-NINE

Jamie

"WHAT ARE you going to do about the flat in London?" Will asked me. We sat on the sofa the following evening, eating Oliver's lasagne and tear-and-share bread while an old episode of some sitcom played in the background. Neither of us were really watching it.

I thought for a second while I chewed. The whole day had been a blissfully normal one filled with work and the warm serenity of knowing the farm was my home now. But of course, Will had to go and lovingly ruin that with his practicality, which I appreciated.

Sort of.

I didn't see why I couldn't just mysteriously vanish from London and leave everyone wondering what had happened to me.

Except Will had pointed out I was still posting on Instagram, and if I didn't at least tell Daisy what my plans were,

I'd be betraying our very long friendship. Because even if I'd changed and didn't want the same things, I at least owed her an explanation so she didn't think I'd been abducted and brainwashed by a cult. And Will had also told me it would be polite to at least inform my parents, even if it was just so my father's accountant knew why my spending habits had changed.

Not that I intended to spend the money in my trust fund nearly as liberally, but I hadn't yet told Will of my plans. I wanted to run them past someone financially minded before I told him so I had evidence and spreadsheets to back me up when Will inevitably worried.

Although I did intend to use some of my money to take him on holiday at some point. I'd have to speak to Higgs, Dylan, and Will's parents to make sure they'd be able to cope without us for a few weeks, but I was going to make him take a break by hook or by crook.

"Maybe sell it," I said. "Although I need to check whether it's actually in my name or my father's. If it's in his, then it's not really my responsibility. I'll just go down and pack up what I want and bring it here. Maybe we can go down for the weekend and you can see if there's anything there you'd like me to bring. I'm definitely bringing my coffee maker, though, because I refuse to keep drinking that ditch water you call coffee."

"You're just picky, posh boy," Will teased.

"Absolutely. I need my occasional luxuries, and coffee is one of them." I leant over to kiss him. "Your dick is another. And your ass."

"Are you hinting?"

"Absolutely," I said. "Can I fuck you later?"

Will pretended to think for a moment, but I couldn't help noticing the way he shuffled in his seat, his hand reaching out to absent-mindedly palm his crotch. "Yeah, I want that."

"Good. I'm going to make it fun, though."

"Isn't it always?"

"Extra fun," I said. "You'll like it, I promise. And if you don't, then we'll stop."

"But we're still going to fuck?"

"Obviously. I need to own your ass again. It's been too long, and I've missed it."

I kissed him once more, still holding my plate of food. I was so tempted to just climb into his lap and leave the rest of the conversation for later, but there were things I needed to know before I started talking to people.

"Do you want me to find a place locally?" I asked, sitting back on the sofa and twisting my fork in my hand as I tried to ignore how hard I was already.

"Why?" Will asked. "Didn't you want to move in here?"

"Would that be okay? I mean, we haven't been dating that long, and it's not like we know each other that well. If something goes wrong, I don't want you to feel obligated to let me stay."

"I won't." He shuffled closer and put his arm around me, pressing a kiss to the side of my head. "I know it hasn't been that long, but I think the fact that we lived together through lambing and didn't come to blows is a good sign. We just spent the last six weeks going through the most exhausting and stressful period of the year, and we still want to be together. If that isn't the ultimate test of a new relationship, I don't know what is. So move in here. There's plenty of space, and I don't want you anywhere else."

I smiled, my heart feeling like it was almost too big for my chest. "Would you get lonely without me?"

"I would, but I'd also get the bed to myself again so swings and roundabouts," Will said with that wry smile I loved. "Besides if you don't move in here, then I'll have to face judge and jury in the form of my mum and the nosy bunch of bastards I call friends, who'd all want to know what I did to make you move out."

I snorted. "Technically, the whole finding a separate place suggestion was Oliver's, so we could blame him."

"We could, but I'm not one to start an argument. Not when I don't need to. I want you here."

"Good, because I want to be here," I said. "Plus, I can't imagine trying to go through the hassle of trying to find somewhere to rent. Ugh, it would be a nightmare."

"Mostly because you'll never find somewhere to live up to your standards."

"Exactly, and that's because I have taste."

I hadn't told Will that I'd love to potentially redecorate some of the rooms here, especially our bedroom. That could come later when we were all settled. I didn't want him to think I was taking over, and I could live with the simplicity for a while longer.

We continued eating, chatting here and there about what needed to be done tomorrow, the plans for the lambs, and Dylan's shock at the fact that Wilder North had actually accepted the livery terms and would be bringing his horses up next week. Dylan still hadn't worked out how to tell the yard, but I'd made him promise to let me know when he was doing it so I could come and watch because it was bound to cause drama, and I still loved a tiny bit of mess. Especially because Dylan seemed to get ever so flustered whenever Wilder's name was mentioned.

I felt so at peace as I sat there, cuddled up with the man I loved, in a place that felt more like home than anywhere else, and I couldn't wait to make it permanent.

"I'm sorry, you're doing what?" Daisy sounded so shocked it was almost comical, and I bit my lip so I wouldn't laugh. I stood in the kitchen at lunchtime the next day, leaning against the counter and looking out the window to where Nell and Moss were dozing in a small patch of April sunshine.

"I'm not coming back to London," I said. "I'm moving here, to Heather Bay."

"But why?"

"Because I love it here. It's beautiful, Daisy. And I've found something that I want to do with my life and a man I want to spend it with."

"Seriously? But what about your parties? And the trip to Ibiza this summer? Are you seriously going to give it all up for someone you just met?"

"Pretty much," I said, knowing that I was bordering on blunt. I just wanted her to try to understand what I was feeling. "Look, I don't expect you to get it, but I was so fucking bored with everything in London. I needed to do something with my life, give it some meaning, and farming has. Yeah, the hours are long, the weather can be absolutely shit, and it's the hardest thing I've ever done, but I can't imagine doing anything different. London sounds so boring in comparison."

Daisy laughed softly, but it was the sweet, affectionate laugh she only ever used when she was happy. "Only you, Jamie Stone, could do something like this, and I'd think it was genuine. And only you could ever think London was boring."

"You must think I've lost it."

"No, actually, I don't." She paused for a second. "I think you sound happy. The happiest I've heard you in years. And I'm sorry for not taking you seriously. It was just such a one-eighty, and I was worried, but... I don't think I've ever heard you sound this excited about something. Or someone."

I smiled and felt myself relax, no longer worried that I was going to need to justify myself. "Thanks, I really am happy here. I'm fucking exhausted but happy. And Will... he's fucking amazing."

"Is this the guy you wanted to make breakfast for?"

"Yes, and it was completely shit. I burnt scrambled eggs, Daisy!"

"How? I didn't think making them was that hard."

"It's not, but I managed it anyway."

"You'll have to, I don't know, take some classes or something. I'm sure Milly's sister did one of those Cordon Bleu courses. You could look at those."

"I'm pretty sure Milly's sister could already make more

than scrambled eggs," I said with a snort. "I need, like, Cooking for Dummies, not Cordon Bleu. Although Will has been teaching me, so I'm not complete and utter shit any more. Just a little bit."

"You must really like him then if you're willing to learn to cook," Daisy said teasingly. "I remember you telling me you hated cooking and thought it was pointless if someone else could do it."

"I was, like, eighteen when I said that! I've learnt to clean as well, although I absolutely hate that. It's so boring, and there is no playlist in the world that'll make it better."

"Wait, you're cleaning too? Oh my God, you must, like, love him or something!"

"I do," I said quietly, feeling the familiar warm glow in my chest. "I really do. He's amazing, Daisy. I can't imagine my life without him."

Daisy made a happy sound, and I grinned. "Okay, you have to tell me everything. I need all the details."

We spent the next two hours catching up as I told her all about Will, the farm, and everything I'd been doing. Daisy was a good listener and excitedly asked me questions before declaring that she'd have to come and meet him at some point. I knew she was taking our relationship seriously because visiting a farm in Yorkshire was something I'd never have imagined Daisy doing.

In return, she caught me up on her life and everything in London I'd missed. She'd dumped whatever terrible boyfriend she'd been dating, thank God, and found someone new—an art gallery owner, who not only treated her like a princess but had also been encouraging her to try new things. Apparently, they were going to take a private pottery-making class together next week, something Daisy expected to be utterly terrible at, but she was looking forward to it because the pair of them could be terrible at it together.

According to her, Kai had found a new man to latch onto, and I made a mental note to send him a message and explain everything. We'd had a lot of fun together, and I owed him that.

Eventually, we came to the end of the conversation, and I promised Daisy I'd catch up with her soon and let her know when I was coming down to London to collect my stuff so we could meet for lunch.

"How'd it go?" Will asked, sticking his head around the office door once he'd heard me say goodbye. He'd come in about forty minutes ago and gestured to the office, so I assumed he had paperwork to do.

"Good," I said. "I thought she'd give me a hard time, but she didn't, and it was really nice to catch up. She's thinking of coming to visit at some point."

"Oh, aye?"

"Yeah, but I think it'll just be her or maybe her and her new boyfriend if he sticks around. I get the feeling she's mellowed a little, maybe because I'm not there to encourage her. I love Daisy to bits, but I think we might've needed space from each other. We're the kind of friends where you encourage each other to do things for the fun of it and never really think it through. I still want her in my life, though. I think we might even get on better now."

"Good," Will said, coming out of the office and walking

over to give me a kiss. "I'm glad. I wouldn't want you to lose your friends just because you're here."

"I'll definitely lose some, but I don't think they were my friends in the first place, just hangers-on." I wrapped my arms around him and leant against his chest. "I'll just replace them with your friends if that's okay?"

"I don't think you have a choice. You're one of us now."

"Excellent. We can all get matching jumpers or something."

Will chuckled. "Did you ring your dad yet?"

"No, that's my next job. I'm going to need a drink after. Do we still have some wine?"

"We do."

"Good." I sighed and let myself stay in his arms just for a little bit longer. One more phone call and everything would be settled.

Then with one trip to London, my move would be complete, and there would be nothing stopping me from building the life I wanted with Will.

CHAPTER THIRTY

Will

"YOU SURVIVED LONDON, THEN?" Lane said as he put a pint down in front of me before sliding onto the bench I was sitting on.

As usual for a Friday evening, the Sleeping Goose was standing room only, although that might have been more to do with the weather. Although it was the end of April and nearly warm enough for us to sit in the pub's garden, it had pissed it down for the last two weeks, so everyone was still crammed inside. I'd been glad of the rain at first, but now I was sick of it. My fields looked more like a bog, and everyone was cold, wet, and miserable.

"I did," I said, glancing over at Jamie, who sat on my other side and was deep in conversation with Oliver. "We got everything, and that's all that mattered."

"How was the lunch with Jamie's parents?"

"Not as bad as I expected. They both seemed a bit

surprised and confused by the whole farming thing, but at least they realised Jamie was telling the truth about everything. I expected them to accuse me of brainwashing him for his money." When Jamie had first told his dad about his plans, the reaction had apparently been stunned silence followed by some sly questions about my intentions since it seemed his dad didn't believe Jamie had any interest in farming whatsoever. His dad's accountant had had even more questions, and Jamie had spent a lot of time grumbling about the fact they seemed to care more about him getting his life in order than they'd ever done about him partying it away.

We'd offered to have lunch with them to smooth things over when we went down to London, and I'd been dreading it. Jamie had insisted on buying me new clothes since his parents were snobs, but once we'd all sat down and they'd realised I wasn't going to be intimidated, things had evened out. Jamie had done a lot of the talking and shown them pictures before following up with the fact they were very welcome to visit any time.

Apparently, that offer had been enough to convince them, although they politely declined under the guise of being very busy.

The only thing we'd heard from them since was through two letters in the post, one telling Jamie that he wasn't going to be cut off from his trust fund but his spending would still be monitored, and the other confirming that his name was the only one on the deed to the London flat, as it had been a gift.

Jamie was still debating what to do with it. We'd moved

everything he wanted out and brought it all home two weeks ago, and Jamie kept flicking back and forth between selling it and renting it out. I'd offered my advice on both, but the final decision would be his.

"You mean you're not starting a cult?" Lane asked with a wry chuckle. "Damn."

"Why? Were you hoping to join?"

"Not really, but it would be fun to say I knew someone who started a cult." He picked up his pint and took a long sip. "Did you see that message from Alex earlier? Something about bringing a friend with him, but we weren't allowed to say anything."

"Yeah, I did."

"Did it feel a bit weird to you too?"

I nodded and reached for my own drink. "Yeah. Do you think he's hiding something?"

"Oh, he's definitely hiding something," Spencer said. He sat on the other side of the table, a little farther down, but he'd clearly been listening. "We were just saying the same thing. Plus, he's been, like, super mardy at work lately. Like even more than normal. I'm a bit worried."

"This is Alex," Noah said from Spencer's other side. "If there's a problem, he'll tell us. And if not, we know where he lives. We can figure it out."

"It has to be a secret boyfriend, right?" Jamie said. "I'm not the only one who thinks that, am I?"

"It's what my money's on too," Oliver said.

"That's so boring, though," Theo said. "Why would Alex keep a boyfriend from us?"

"Probably because we have a habit of making their first

encounters with us nothing short of nightmarish," Laurie said, giving Theo a raised eyebrow and ignoring the kiss that was blown his way in return.

"I don't think mine was that bad," Jamie said with a grin. "I enjoyed watching all of you try to explain to Theo why you weren't interested in his fabulous body of work."

"And none of you have still given me a good answer," Theo said. "I'm cute! And I look even cuter naked."

I shot Jamie a look, and he smirked. He reached out under the table and put his hand on my thigh, squeezing not far from my crotch. "What are you doing?" I asked, lowering my voice and leaning closer just in case anyone was listening, even though the conversation had moved on.

"Having fun," Jamie said. "I can't wait until we get home later. Do you think we can get away with leaving early?"

"Depends. Don't you want to see what's going on with Alex?"

Jamie hummed. "I do, but I'm also really horny, so…"

I snorted and picked up my drink, trying to pretend we were having a totally normal conversation. "So you're going to tease me?"

"Yes, it's fun," he said. "I'll stop if you want. I don't want you to be uncomfortable."

"You can leave your hand where it is," I murmured. "Just keep the dirty talk to a minimum."

"Done." Jamie kissed me quickly, then went back to talking to Oliver, his hand still pressed to my thigh.

I'd been worried when we went down to London that Jamie would realise how much he missed it despite his insistence that he didn't want to go back. I needn't have worried, though. Jamie had been tense the whole time like a wild animal in a cage, and whenever we'd met someone he knew, it had felt like he'd been putting on a performance. The only time he'd relaxed was when we'd gone out for dinner, just the two of us, to a tiny Italian restaurant that was one of his favourites. Afterwards, he'd taken me back to his empty flat, overlooking the city, and fucked me slowly, whispering in my ear how much he loved me.

We'd packed up his stuff faster than I'd anticipated because I could tell Jamie wanted to be back on the road, and as soon as we'd hit the M1 heading north, he'd visibly relaxed in the passenger seat of the van we'd hired. We'd gotten home late that night, and he'd slept curled up next to me, his arm around my waist like he didn't want to let me go.

The next morning, I'd woken to find the bed empty but still warm, and I'd been able to hear the strains of music from downstairs. When I'd gone down, I'd found Jamie dancing around the kitchen, singing along to the radio and unpacking his things, slotting them in alongside mine. It made it truly feel like our home.

"Fucking hell," Lane muttered from next to me, and I followed his gaze across the room towards the door, where Alex had just come in. He was closely followed by a dark-haired man who was instantly recognisable.

"Are you seeing what I'm seeing?" Noah asked.

"I think so," Spencer said. "Is that…"

"Yeah, I think it is," I said, still unable to take my eyes off the three men.

Alex stopped in front of us, his expression fixed in a scowl. "All right, listen up, assholes. This is Henry Lu. You might recognise him from a few things. He'll be... joining us this evening."

We all stared, every single one of us shocked speechless for the first time in our collective lives.

"Aww, you don't need to be so grumpy about it," Henry said to Alex, then gave all of us a charming smile as he slipped his hand into Alex's. "Hey, everyone. I'm Henry, Alex's boyfriend. It's so lovely to finally meet you."

There was a beat of silence, then the whole table erupted.

"Well, that could have gone better," Jamie said as we opened the door to the kitchen and stepped inside.

"I'm not sure how it could have gone much worse," I said, kicking off my shoes and shaking my head. We'd ended up staying a lot later than we'd originally intended, but it was hard not to when Alex had shown up with a bloody Hollywood superstar on his arm. And a very charming one at that.

"One day, Alex will look back on tonight and laugh."

"Yeah, but not for a long time," I said. "He's the sort to hold a grudge. Mind you, I'm not sure what he bloody expected. It would have been better if he'd given us some notice."

"I don't think that would've helped, though. It would've given us time to think of questions," Jamie said with a sly smile. "Although, I still think Theo gets the prize for the best on the spot question."

"That's just normal Theo, though."

Jamie chuckled. "True, and I love him for it. I love all your friends actually. They're so much fun."

"They love you too," I said, walking up behind him and putting my arms around his waist before trailing kisses down his neck. Jamie sighed happily.

"Can I tell you something?" he said as he leant against me, tilting his head so I could keep kissing his neck.

"Of course."

"It's going to sound silly. Or maybe just horrifically sappy."

"I don't care either way."

"You might."

"I won't," I said, tightening my arms around him. "Tell me."

"I didn't think it was possible to be this happy," Jamie said quietly. "I thought I was happy before, and maybe I was but in a different way. I feel more complete now. Like I have everything I ever needed, even though I didn't know it until I got here. Does that make sense?"

"It does." I squeezed him gently, my heart so full of love for this man I didn't know how I'd ever be able to contain it. We were building something special together, and I knew that no matter what happened, we'd always have each other to lean on. "I feel the same."

"Yeah?"

"Yeah. I thought I was fine. I guess I'd kind of resigned

myself to life as it was, but then you came along and turned everything upside down."

"I'm good at that," Jamie said with a chuckle.

"You are, and I'm glad you did. You're everything to me, Jamie, and I don't want you to ever forget that."

Jamie turned in my arms, and his eyes met mine. "Never, as long as you promise to do the same. We need each other, Will. And I know I'll never stop needing you as long as I live."

I smiled. "That's a bold promise."

"Go big or go home," he said. "I don't do things by halves."

"Neither do I."

He leant in and kissed me softly. His lips were soft and sweet and tasted like a lifetime of promises. I knew things weren't going to be easy because nothing in life ever was, but I also knew I would never stop loving him.

Jamie was right. We needed each other just as much as we needed the farm, and it needed us.

"Take me to bed," Jamie whispered against my lips.

I grinned, wrapping my arms around him and scooping him up. Jamie yelped, wrapping his legs around my waist and his arms around my neck as he clung on like a startled koala.

And our laughter filled the house as I carried him upstairs.

EPILOGUE

TWO YEARS LATER

Jamie

"You know, if you stop getting under my feet, I'd actually be able to make you some breakfast without nearly breaking my ankle. Or is that too much to ask?" I glanced down at the two tiny lambs tottering around my legs. They'd been born yesterday evening, but despite the fact it was a healthy birth, the ewe had rejected both of them immediately, so Will and I had needed to step in.

The pair of them had already realised I was the one with the food, but that was probably because I'd stayed up all night with them. I'd been up every four hours to sleepily make bottles and try not to fall asleep while sitting on the kitchen floor, feeding them. I was sure one of them had peed on my jeans at some point, but luckily, they were an old pair of Will's that I'd borrowed during my first lambing season and had never given back.

One of the lambs bleated plaintively and looked up at

me with large eyes that melted my heart. From her place by the back door, Bonnie, my sixteen-month-old sheepdog in training looked up and tilted her head, clearly wondering if she needed to be doing something about the lambs standing in the middle of the kitchen.

"It's okay, Bon," I said. "They'll be fine."

Bonnie huffed and raised her eyebrow, giving a perfect imitation of the disapproving expression her mother, Moss, often gave me. I chuckled.

A couple of months after I'd permanently moved to Heather Bay, Will had floated the idea of breeding Moss past me, not just so we'd have very well-bred puppies to sell but so I could have a dog of my own. Moss had a good reputation, and she'd had a litter in the past, so she was the ideal mother.

I'd been totally on board with the plan. I just hadn't realised how nervous Will would be.

If I thought he'd been anxious during lambing season, his worrying during Moss's pregnancy had reached new levels, and when she'd finally gone into labour, I'd been convinced he was going to pass out. Everything had gone smoothly, though, and she'd had six beautiful puppies.

Will had let me choose one to keep, and Bonnie had been the obvious choice. I'd fallen in love with her as soon as she was born, and then she'd pooped on my hand when she was six hours old, so that was it.

She was the best dog I could ever have hoped for, even if she did have an uncanny knack for giving me the most critical looks ever known to man.

Like I Needed

The lambs bleated again, louder this time. I shook my head and smiled. "I'm going. I'm going."

I finished making the bottles and lowered myself down to start feeding the pair of them, who hungrily latched onto the bottle teats and began sucking loudly.

"Honestly, you'd think they'd get better staff in this hotel," Will said, leaning over the counter and grinning tiredly at me. "The service is terrible."

"I know. They need to fire the chef," I said. "And the beds are definitely not up to par. Two stars."

"Worst review we've had in years."

I chuckled sleepily. "How was the rest of the night? Everything going okay?"

"Looking good. We had another three births in the early hours—all your triplets within about an hour of each other. Two of them had one each, and one had twins, but everyone looks happy and healthy."

"Good," I said with a sigh. "They're good mums those three. And I'm not surprised they were all close together. The same thing happened last year."

Will nodded and walked around the counter, bending down to take one of the bottles from me and continuing to feed the larger of the two lambs. "Higgs is going to take the morning shift, and Dad said he'd come down for a bit to give him some company."

"Are you going to bed, then?"

"Yeah, I was going to. Just to grab a few hours kip. Want to join me?"

I glanced down at the two lambs. They'd soon be ready to go out into the lambing barn, which was warm and cosy,

293

especially because we had a couple of heat lamps strung over a few of the pens. "Shall we feed these two and take them outside? Then we can crash for two or three hours before they need feeding again."

I yawned as I spoke. Lambing season never got any easier, and I was already absolutely exhausted after only two weeks.

"That sounds good. I can always ask Mum to come down and feed 'em," Will said.

"If she doesn't mind." Despite the fact they were supposed to be retired, Will's parents insisted on giving us a hand throughout lambing every year and refused the idea of us hiring an extra pair of hands to take their place. We were both grateful for their willingness to be involved, even though we both privately agreed we didn't have a choice.

Last year, Will had tactfully tried to suggest we'd be okay without them, and it had gone over like a lead balloon.

There was almost rioting.

"She won't. I've already seen her this morning and gotten an earful about not sleeping properly."

"Your mum does realise you're thirty-five, right?" I asked with a wry smile.

"Apparently not."

We finished feeding the lambs, then wrapped them in towels to carry them out to the barn. There was a small, cosy pen at the far end that was perfect for them, and it didn't take us long to get them settled. My chest ached as I watched the pair of them curl up together in the straw.

Despite the exhaustion, I wouldn't change anything about my life for the world.

I wrote down their details, including the time they were last fed, on the little whiteboard hanging from the pen gate before Will and I traipsed back into the house.

Both of us were virtually dropping by that point, and I was surprised we managed to make it up the stairs without falling over.

Once we were in our room, we shed our clothes at speed, dropping them into a heap on the floor before we crawled into bed. Will set an alarm on his phone for three hours later, and I wrapped my arms around him, loving the way his bare skin felt against mine.

It had been just over two years since I'd fled to Heather Bay on a whim and found the home I'd never imagined having.

Things hadn't always been easy, and Will and I had argued more than once, but we'd always come out of our disagreements stronger. The first year had been eye-opening in more ways than one, and every time I thought I was starting to understand farm life, something new came along and yanked the rug out from under me. But Will had always been there to catch me, and I was so grateful for that.

I'd been there for him through all the ups and downs and late nights worrying about making things work. One of our biggest disagreements had been when I'd wanted to inject some of the money from the sale of the London flat into the farm, and Will had point blank refused to take it at first. I'd won eventually, but it had taken a lot of long talks to convince him.

Despite his insistence that we were a team, Will had struggled with some of the aspects of that, the financial part being the biggest one. He'd been so self-reliant for so long that he wasn't used to sharing his struggles with someone else. And even though he'd wanted to, it still took time to unlearn his need to keep things to himself and figure it out alone.

We'd gotten there, as we had with the things I'd struggled with, because we loved each other, and we wanted to be together more than anything.

"What're you thinking?" Will muttered sleepily, pulling me closer until I was virtually lying on top of him.

"Not much. Just how much I love you. And that I can't believe this is my third lambing season already. I'm not sure where the time went."

"Me either." He pressed a kiss to the top of my head. "I love you too. I couldn't do this without you."

I sighed and buried my face in his chest, letting out a deep sigh of contentment.

"I've been thinking," Will said.

"What about?" I asked, trying to keep myself awake so I could listen.

"This. Us."

"Aye? What about us?"

"Do you fancy getting married?" Will asked.

It took a moment for the question to sink in, and when it did, I sat bolt upright, looking down at him with wide eyes. "What?"

"Do you want to get married?" He grinned, running his hand over my thigh. "I've got a ring downstairs. I probably should have picked a better time, but I just… I'm too tired to think of a plan right now."

I laughed, throwing myself into his arms and kissing him. "Yes! Yes, farm boy, I'll marry you."

"Good," he said, cupping my jaw with his other hand and drawing me back into a kiss. "Guess that makes you a farm boy now too?"

"Mmm, probably." I wanted to keep kissing him, but my whole body felt heavy.

"We can celebrate later," Will said like he could read my mind. Although, I guessed he was feeling the same since he'd been up all night. "Let's get some sleep."

"I like that plan," I said, snuggling down into his arms again and pressing a kiss to his chest. "Love you."

"Love you too."

Will's arm tightened around me, holding me close as sleep began to pull me under, a smile curling my lips.

I really couldn't be any happier.

I had everything I'd ever needed.

The End

ACKNOWLEDGMENTS

I've had Will's story in my head since I first came up with the concept for Heather Bay. His blurb was the first one I wrote and it's one I've been looking to since the beginning. As a life-long country girl, it was one of my writing dreams to bring a bit of the English countryside to life in both a romantic and realistic way.

As with everything I do, I would be nothing without the amazing team of people who lend me their love, strength, help and support.

Firstly, I want to say a massive thank you to Louise for all her help with the farming details, for sending me a ton of fabulous information, and for letting me bounce ideas around about Will's business. I am incredibly grateful.

To Charity, my friend, confidante, and the world's most incredible PA. Thank you for everything, always.

To Carly, Toby, Noah, Rosie, and Jodi for being the best group of friends a writer-goblin such as myself could ever wish for. I love you all so much.

To Susie, for helping me bring Heather Bay to life with the most wonderful editorial guidance.

To Natasha for creating my truly beautiful covers.

To Lori, for fixing all the mistakes I missed.

To Dan, who is a freaking rock star and brings these men to life in ways I'd never have imagined.

To my husband for never minding when I disappear to write, for letting me bounce plot points off you, and for just generally being awesome. And to Biscuit and Pippin for keeping me on my toes.

And last, but never least, to you, my fabulous readers. Whether I'm new to you or you've been here since the start, I am grateful for you love and support.

If you enjoyed *Like I Needed*, please consider leaving a review. Reviews are invaluable for indie authors, and may help other readers find this book.

Until next time.

Love,
Charlie x

ALSO BY CHARLIE NOVAK

HEATHER BAY

Like I Pictured

Like I Promised

Like I Wished

Like I Needed

Like I Pretended *(July 2023)*

ROLL FOR LOVE

Natural Twenty

Charisma Check

Proficiency Bonus

FOREVER LOVE

Always Eli

Finding Finn

Oh So Oscar

KISS ME

Strawberry Kisses

Summer Kisses

Spiced Kisses

OFF THE PITCH

Breakaway

Extra Time

Final Score

The Off the Pitch Short Collection

Off the Pitch: The Complete Collection (Boxset)

STANDALONES

Screens Apart

Couture Crush

Up To Snow Good

SHORT STORIES

One More Night

Twenty-Two Years (Newsletter Exclusive)

Snow Way In Hell

AUDIOBOOKS

Like I Promised

Like I Wished

Natural Twenty

Charisma Check

Proficiency Bonus

Always Eli

Finding Finn

Oh So Oscar

Strawberry Kisses

Summer Kisses

Spiced Kisses

Up To Snow Good

For a regularly updated list, please visit:

charlienovak.com/books

charlienovak.com/audiobooks

CHARLIE NOVAK

Charlie lives in England with her husband and two cheeky dogs. She spends most of her days wrangling other people's words in her day job and then trying to force her own onto the page in the evening.

She loves cute stories with a healthy dollop of fluff, plenty of delicious sex, and happily ever afters — because the world needs more of them.

Charlie has very little spare time, but what she does have she fills with baking, Dungeons and Dragons, reading and many other nerdy pursuits. She also thinks that everyone should have at least one favourite dinosaur...

Website charlienovak.com
Facebook Group Charlie's Angels
For day-to-day-musings, giveaways and teasers.

Plus sign up for her newsletter for bonus scenes, new releases and extras.

facebook.com/charlienovakauthor
twitter.com/charlienwrites
instagram.com/charlienwrites
bookbub.com/profile/charlie-novak
amazon.com/author/charlienovak

Printed in Great Britain
by Amazon

23085736R00179